THE LIES AND CRIMES
OF SWEET CAROLINE

THE LIES AND CRIMES OF SWEET CAROLINE

DARREN WILLS

Matador
9 Priory Business Park,
Wistow Road, Kibworth Beauchamp,
Leicestershire. LE8 0RX
Tel: 0116 279 2299
Email: books@troubador.co.uk
Web: www.troubador.co.uk/matador
Twitter: @matadorbooks

ISBN 978 1800462 168

British Library Cataloguing in Publication Data.
A catalogue record for this book is available from the British Library.

Typeset in 11pt Adobe Garamond Pro by Troubador Publishing Ltd, Leicester, UK

Matador is an imprint of Troubador Publishing Ltd

Dedicated to Shirley Ann Fellows and Charles Wills.

TRAGEDY

"What's going on?"

"It's a bad business. A very bad business."

"How bad?"

"Can't say more than that at this stage."

Everything was orderly. The quietness of the reception area suggested that things weren't all that bad around here. The lack of activity suggested that crime was on holiday, sunning itself on the Algarve or the Costa del Sol. It was a typical Wednesday night.

There was still a negative feel in the air, however. Suspense was looming, like the gloom of an oncoming dark grey cloud. The police station hadn't quite been abandoned. There were a few people scattered around, yet no one was saying anything, and the odd uniformed officer entered and left the area with only the fewest of words being spoken.

"What's it about, then?" The man was clean-shaven, in his twenties, sporting a dark grey raincoat with a notepad clutched in the depths of his right coat pocket, and he had a determined and enthusiastic look on his face. Something big was going down in this very station – right here, right now. Freelance was pretty tough at times. So much hanging around waiting for something that would invigorate a struggling career, an opportunity. For him, an event in this town today might bring such an opportunity, the chance of an exclusive. His big break.

The desk sergeant was as firm as a dry stone wall, and even drier, with his bowed head unshifting. "I'm not at liberty to divulge that, but I'm sure you'll hear all about it in the morning."

"Come on, mate. It's my livelihood. Just give me a sniff, something I can work from. Is it a murder?"

"I've already said that I can't say. You'll have to wait."

"Just tell me if it's a murder. You don't even have to say the word. Just nod your head."

The sergeant finally raised his head and his steely eyes seemed forceful enough to be seeing right through to the back of the younger man's skull. "Sir, I think you'd better leave."

"Oh, come on."

The sergeant dropped the pen he was holding. In a child it would have been petulance. "If you don't leave, if you don't go out of that door right now, I'll have you arrested for making a nuisance of yourself. And I warn you, our cells aren't all that nice."

The younger man, with a deep frown, loosened his grip on his notepad and shrugged his shoulders. "OK. You win. I'm off." He took a couple of steps than turned back. "Where's the nearest phone box?"

The officer merely pointed to some imaginary location in a distant place to the right, beyond the station perimeter. He uttered no words.

For Joe Tibbs the wall of silence would not do. One day he would have the exclusive he sought, writing about a vicious attack and near-murder by two prostitutes, but he could hardly know that today. On this occasion, things weren't quite so fruitful. He consequently scurried out into the dark, where the tension seemed to extend, a spreading virus of doubt intruding on the mood of the night. Invisible it might have been, but it had taken an unpleasantly firm hold this evening in this part of the town. People walking past the building were having frank and tense conversations. This was coincidental, since such problems and revelations were standard features of life in any city and bore no relation to the things going on inside this office of law and order.

Similarly, but not quite so coincidentally, officials going into the building in their stark dark uniforms also appeared to sense something unpalatable, aware of something serious and problematic that might have some kind of impact on their working lives. Much was thought-inspired rather than evidence-based. A little knowledge was fuelling speculation of the grimmest kind.

Something notable had occurred.

Back inside the cluster of rooms and offices inside the police station, the uniformed personnel not out patrolling were moving around with an unusual sensitivity and stealth. Everyone was trying hard not to disturb others who were operating similarly, as if common crime had suddenly become a gentle pursuit, almost obscure, in what had become a heavy environment. There were whisperings going on around corners. Banter was absent today, while speculation raged. Several were content just to shuffle papers and scribble notes, whilst always keeping their ears on red alert, since knowledge meant power, not to mention a free pint or two in the Old Crown later.

The desk sergeant, the greying Tom Hooper, was an officer with an abundance of experience. Having necessarily and willingly rebuffed the intrusive journalist, he was distracting himself from tonight's awful reality by looking through his copy of the training manual, and making the occasional notation, whilst the only others around, three men of varying ages, sat silently on the long seat on the facing wall, nursing their own concerns. Two of them had been burgled and one had been on the wrong end of a mugging, all waiting for crime numbers and meetings with officers that were likely to be somewhat delayed this evening, even if they weren't yet aware of it. Not that things were solved so much these days. It was obtaining the crime number that was the crucial thing. Each of those sitting there had to be patient, since this was the only way. None of them realised just where on the spectrum between triviality and outrage their grievance actually was.

Tom Hooper knew one thing. Whatever happened in the next hour or so, at some point in the lightening and tightening earliness of morning, things would change.

It would be more than a change. The station was going to be thronged with reporters from local and national newspapers, all desperate and enthusiastic, and he would be hard pushed in the final hours of his shift. They would want to know every sordid detail and would probably make up more of those for good measure. They called that journalism. Tom despaired. Tom often despaired.

For now, there was an ominous calm about the place. It would have been comforting if it hadn't indicated that something disturbing was further down the line.

There was a door to the right of the front desk, a black door with the gleam of a recent paint job and large silver letters declaring 'Restricted Access'. When opened, it exposed a long bare corridor that ran to the rear of the building. There, activity of a different nature was taking place. Deep in the recesses of this building, probably its bowel, if the front desk was taken to be its face, there was a small room amongst several small rooms, where a voice inside could be heard protesting loudly. "I don't see why we had to be brought down here. She's seven years old.

It's not like she did anything. Look at her." It was a feminine voice, but without much femininity.

Inside this interview room, two grim-faced police officers were trying to handle a truth that had claws that would tear hearts and carve out holes in careers. They were seated opposite a mother and her daughter, a pale child who seemed to be utterly clawless in both possibility and intent. The girl was rubbing her finger along the edge of the table in front of her. She had never been in a police station before. This was not the case for the mother, who sat back with her arms folded and who maintained a scowl that seemed to have been etched into her face by an aggressive sculptor.

The officers, professional to a fault, were trying to play down the confrontational aspects of the proceedings with calm utterances and open hands. It was often best to be positive. Sometimes good cop, good cop was more effective than good cop, bad cop. Today that was not easy.

Across from them, the mother's posture and demeanour were intense. She was straining at an invisible leash, keen to show both strength and resilience. She seemed to be gripped by a sense of outrage and was making the most of hand gestures and eye-rolling. Her eyes flashed, darted and lunged. Her body language made it clear that for her, all the seconds spent here added up to unwanted minutes. Here was where she'd been brought, transported in a marked vehicle that would have got the tongues wagging, but here was not where she was going to stay any longer than she had to. She was half-seated in the chair, looking as though she would get up and leave at any time, at the slightest provocation.

At her side, the little girl looked as vulnerable as a fox looking up at red jackets on horseback. She was a pitiful little creature, pale and fragile, with overly-dry long hair that partially eclipsed her face, a face that gave the impression that she was one good meal a day and several vegetables a week short of decent nutrition. She was like several of the kids on her street in that respect, as both officers in the room knew.

The detective sergeant, in his early fifties, the older of the two officers, with closely-cropped grey hair and a defiantly dark moustache, managed a reassuring smile. He tried to look comfortable in a way that masked the bubbling frustration and curiosity inside, as well as the prevailing sense that he was investigating the worst tragedy of his career. "We're not saying she's done anything. Of course we're not. We just need answers."

"How's she going to give you them? She wasn't there."

"OK. We accept that. We just want Caroline to give us her version of events."

The mother unfolded her arms momentarily to point a finger at the male officer. "Oh, for crying out loud. Who the hell do you think you are? She's already said she didn't see anything. What was she supposed to have seen anyway? Don't you think you should tell us?"

"Try to stay calm. I'm well aware of what she's said. Sometimes this happens, Miss Lawrence." The officer, whose name was Hawkins, looked into the innocent eyes of the child, before abruptly switching back to the mother. "It's hard to remember things sometimes. I do know that. I just want to know the full details of what happened." He switched his attention back to the child and lowered his head with a softening of his voice, just like they had told him to do in his training so many years ago. "We just want you to try to recollect, Caroline. Tell me again. How did you, Edward and Sally Cassell come to be near the railway line this afternoon?"

The child's lips parted, as if she didn't understand why such a question was being asked.

In a quiet, hesitant voice, she tried to answer. "We just were. We just went up there."

"Were you playing some kind of game up there?"

Blinking and half-smiling, the girl nodded.

"What were you playing?"

"Nothing much."

"And what was that? We need to know a bit more."

"Walking round. Exploring…" Something appeared to snap, a jerk in the child's attention. "What happened to them? To Eddie and Sally?"

Her eyes had suddenly widened.

The officer's eyes narrowed. His mouth showed suppressed impatience. "And what happened when you stopped playing?" His words had lost their gentleness.

The girl, dwarfed by these adults, who were all so much bigger than her and who had much louder voices than she had, stared at the clock on the wall behind the officers. Was she trying to remember, or was she managing to forget?

"Caroline, I need you to answer this question. Do you know what happened to Eddie and Sally?"

The mother tutted and raised her eyes to the ceiling. "She doesn't know. She would have told you if she did. Obviously."

He looked at her. "Obviously. Maybe. Possibly. The thing is, I have two hysterical parents in another room on this corridor who are in the worst state of their lives. We all need answers. You must understand that."

The mother half-nodded.

The senior of the two police officers turned his attention to the child. "You do understand that we all need to know what happened to Eddie and Sally, don't you?'

She nodded, with more commitment than her mother.

The other officer, a woman, interrupted, addressing the mother. "Do you often allow Caroline to wander about on her own?"

7

The mother stiffened. "Of course not. I was ill today. She just took advantage. You know what kids are like."

The officer shook her head. "I have two children, Miss Lawrence. Two children I love like any other mother. I have to tell you that no way would I allow either of mine anywhere like Etherton Hill. And just as importantly, I know that there's no way either of them would have been up there without me knowing."

"Why didn't you know?" echoed the senior officer, wanting to prod and poke.

The mother sat back and exhaled significantly. "Oh, come on. It's hardly against the law. So what if I don't know where she is all the time."

"But you should know," he said.

"I should? Christ, you'll be arresting half the parents in this town if that's a crime."

"It's neglect. You're meant to be responsible for your child. Especially when she's as young as Caroline."

"Three children went up that hill. Not one."

"Yes. And only one came back down."

"Like I said, I was ill. Do you not listen? Do you ever listen to people like me? No wonder people slag off the police."

"Ill in what way?" asked Hawkins. "In what way were you ill today?" He knew about Judy's past. He had read through her records. Drunk and disorderly on numerous occasions, shoplifting, several assaults and one city centre arrest for abusive behaviour towards a police officer. There had even been the part she had played in the robbery of a supermarket as a teenager. In recent years, only the fact that she had official responsibility for this vulnerable little girl had kept her out of prison, which was the best place for her, and which would undoubtedly have been best for the daughter as far as this policeman was concerned.

He knew little about Caroline, though. He was already

feeling bitterly sorry for this little waif. After all, she couldn't have had it easy with a mother of this calibre. He actually half-wondered, but no more than that, how much better off this little girl would have been if she could spend the next few years of her life staying at his house with his family. What kind of a future might that give her? He would have another fifteen years in the job, maybe twenty. Who knew what would happen with this unfortunate young child and her reckless mother in that time? He silently predicted that their paths would cross again, perhaps some time after the dust had settled on this.

"It's my stomach. Always gives me trouble. Always has done," Judy said.

Richardson, the female officer, turned towards Caroline. "Just tell me this. Why did you go up that hill near your house?"

Caroline remained blank-faced. Her face was a moon of simplicity.

"Why did you want to venture up there? It's a good walk from your house."

Caroline opened her mouth then paused. She looked into the eyes of the woman as if she was confessing something serious, something that would carry the deepest of consequences. Her voice was gentle and again hesitant, almost a stutter. "We went up there to see the rabbits."

Hawkins didn't know whether to sympathise or be suspicious. Professionally, he had to choose an approach that wasn't so instinctive but which was deemed to be appropriate when dealing with innocence like this. "Are there rabbits up there?"

"We heard there was."

"I never knew. Did you know?" he asked his colleague, who just shrugged her shoulders.

"Can you remember what happened? What happened to Eddie and Sally?"

Caroline shook her head. "I left them in the crags at the top. I didn't see them. I came home."

"Why did you come home?"

"Because the rabbits weren't there." The little girl looked despondent, reliving the disappointment.

"What were they doing when you left them?"

"Messing about. Throwing stones and stuff. I told them it was dangerous to throw stones."

"What did they say to that?"

"They didn't say anything. What's happened to them?"

Hawkins became more intense. "Were they near the railway line throwing stones?"

The child didn't answer straight away. Eventually she felt able to shake her head. "I don't know."

"Could you hear them as you walked down the hill?"

"No."

"Can we go now?" asked Judy. "We've been here ages."

He felt himself reddening. "Listen. Two children have died. We can't end this until we know all that Caroline knows." He pointed in the direction of somewhere further along the corridor. "Their mum and dad need to know."

After about half a minute of silence, Judy unfolded her arms again and made a conciliatory gesture with her open palms. "Of course I'm sorry. I'm sorry if something's happened to those two kids, absolutely gutted. But it's nothing to do with Caroline. As if it could be. Just look at her."

Butter wouldn't melt.

Hawkins, irritated, said, "She can go home soon, but we do need to know more. Two children are dead, Mrs Lawrence. We need to figure out why."

Caroline had found a place away from the questions. She was watching a memory play out in her mind.

That sunny afternoon had had the lightest of breezes. The gentle gusts of wind had caressed her face and made her almost smile. Eddie and Sally had agreed to go exploring with her. This had been a surprise. She had thought they would refuse. They had called her names too many times over the previous two weeks, nasty names. They had said she smelled. They had said she was stupid. Sally had said she was as stupid as dog muck and Eddie had laughed loudly at that. She had felt hurt. The pain had grown. She had thought about that pain in bed. Something had needed to be done about it. She hadn't been sure how she would do it, but had hoped that exploring would help something to happen.

It had helped.

They had said more bad things. Eddie had been angry with her. "You said there were rabbits up here, but it was a lie. You always tell lies."

Sally had been an echo. "And she steals."

Caroline had hated that echo. She had felt her face tighten and her right hand had become a fist.

Then that fist had loosened and her eye had sharpened.

Click click click. Something had landed in her head. "It doesn't matter about the rabbits. This might be more fun," she had said. "Here's a dare," she had said. "A train is coming," she had said. "We walk alongside the train as it passes us. We walk like heroes. We'll be soldiers like in Ancient Greece. Anybody who gets scared or who moves away has to walk home with no clothes on." She had said.

Sally had protested. "That's silly. That won't prove anything. I'm not walking home without my clothes on." She had turned to her brother. "I told you she was an idiot. I don't know why we came up here with her."

Caroline had felt the pain being rekindled at being called an idiot again. She had stood still and tried to appear unaffected, but the hate returned. It was a feeling that burned.

Eddie had wanted to prove himself. He liked Caroline, this girl from the next road who was only a year younger than he was. "No.

We can do it. There's no way I'm going to have to walk home with no clothes on. It's easy to walk at the side of a train." Caroline had nearly smiled at that. Well, almost nearly.

She had made sure they were walking in front of her. When the train roared past, one push was all it had taken. With the desperate grabbing of a hand, Sally had taken Eddie with her into the wheels of the metallic monster, which had chewed them up. There was lots of blood. Caroline had never seen so much. It had been like a big red wave. It was good that none of the red stuff had gone on her clothes.

Hawkins closed the book in front of him and gave a telling look to his colleague. "Thanks for trying to answer our questions, Caroline. We may want to talk to you again if that's OK. So we may be seeing you again soon."

Caroline came out from her memory but said nothing.

"No way," said Judy. "We'll go to the funerals, but that's the end of this. It's just a horrible accident and she's not suffering for it. Nothing to do with her. Anybody can see that."

The mother and daughter were escorted from the interview room. Caroline had a half-smile on her face as she left the police station with her mother firmly clasping her hand. She made sure that her mother didn't notice.

ANOTHER DAWN

The coming of daylight has its own natural fanfare. The singing of the birds isn't particularly loud, but it's enough to provide a clear signal for the emerging day. Is it music? Perhaps not, perhaps too lacking in tunefulness, although some think differently and some may seek solace in the natural sound.

The time is important. The mood inside the room seems to be steadily and unceremoniously leaving behind the dark shades of grey as daylight begins to make its presence felt. Uncomfortably, she allows more of the coming brightness to enter, raising herself gently from the pillow and craning her neck to peer through a crack she forms between the edge of brown curtain and the magnolia wall. Connecting with the outside world, her eyes scan the various branches and clusters of branches within her eyeline, as she tries to locate where the birds actually are. There are a number of trees outside, all deliberately and obviously planted at intervals in an orderly way that shows intention rather than accidents of nature. She wonders if the little creatures she admires so much occupy every one of those vertical creations or just one or two.

She always wants to know where the birds are, always has. She never seems to be able to see them properly. She never has, yet she knows they are there and likes their music. Just like always, she feels supported and encouraged by their tuneless meaningful warble, their song of morning. She half-smiles. It's such a shame that she can never understand what the birds actually mean. Why do they exist?

The musing gives way to a reality check. There is an accompanying sound that is less welcome, and which irritates, shattering the early morning mood, and she finds herself disturbed by a buzz-saw within the room that cuts through any harmony. This unpleasant sound comes from the hill of slumbering humanity next to her. This masculine lump has in the past twelve hours displayed a wide repertoire of unwelcome sounds, including absurd ridiculous sentences, sexist jokes and farting while in a state of oblivion. It was some night, last night. This is some morning.

She puts her hand over her mouth to prevent herself sighing. Last night's Moet is now making its presence felt. It always does, even a mere one and a half glasses of the stuff. From underneath the lump formed under the fabric, further communication of an unwelcome kind comes from the unhealthily bloated body that pressures the surrendering mattress. Should such a creature continue to breathe? she asks herself. In the wild, animals like this die, far more tragically.

It's five o'clock and it is time to move. She purposefully but gently raises herself from under the pale blue duvet and frees herself from the bed so that she can quickly put on her dress and shoes. There is an urgency about this, since speed is an important part of the game she is playing this morning. Underwear and stockings are quickly pushed into a small black handbag. She does this just like she has done it before. This is a game she once again plays adeptly, one that she has played many times, one in which she has expertise, one in which she demands and expects success and gain.

This woman, a slender twenty-six-year-old brunette, surveys the room, ensuring that she has missed nothing, all the time preserving the silence. She doesn't quite manage contentment or appreciation, but why should she? She has been under no illusion regarding this room, both for what it was last night and for what it remains this morning. Admittedly, to call it a hovel would be harsh. She has stayed in worse, and at least it's clean, with a new-looking little white plastic kettle and two untouched undersized mugs with twin glass tumblers that attempt to be crystal. All in all, the room probably justifies the amount he has paid for this night.

It has been no night of restful slumber. She hasn't resorted to sleep. She never does.

Sometimes a bad bed is a good thing. This bed has helped her to stay alert. Overly hard and unyielding for her light frame, definitely a bad bed, it has far too little give for her tastes, so staying awake was inevitable. Being conscious through the night is fine and necessary, since she has to be awake to win. Even so, she thinks, if she had been on her own after a long and difficult day, in a more relaxed situation, perhaps grabbing some private solace away from a world of distractions, sleep would still have been a challenge on this mattress.

She daydreams at this point. Life won't always be like this. One day, it will be a five-star first-class lifestyle, with a four-poster bed and twenty-four-hour room service. By then, whenever that time is, she will be living a much more luxurious life, like the one she experienced in the dream she had last week, the one where she was swimming in a river of fifty-pound notes. Or maybe it will be like the one she had a couple of weeks ago, where she owned a plush hotel next to a beach. She has not had her recurring dream for several weeks, however, the one where she is surrounded by paintings, as though she is living in some kind of art gallery. That dream disturbs her, although she's always liked painting and drawing.

One day, at the very least, she tells herself, the bottom line will be something special. She will be reliant on no one and will envy no one, because she will have everything she needs. She hangs on to that belief with determination and firmness. She is set on making it more of a certainty than a speculation. With the ideas she is forming, fact will at some point replace fantasy and what happens after that is a mystery she looks forward to dealing with.

Having dressed, well almost, she walks around the room, never losing the stealth, never discarding alertness, taking in every bland detail of the room as if there might be something of significance. Business-like, she picks up the black suit trousers on the other side of the bed. She takes from the back pocket the thick shiny leather wallet that resides in the left-hand pocket with the golden initials DVN in the corner. Classy stuff, but on the other hand, is it just ego-led garishness? She opens it up and the half-smile returns as she enjoys the true meaning of the evening. Everything has led to this. Whilst intermittently monitoring the snoring lump, she takes from the folded leather the wad of notes, as well as the bank card, before dropping the wallet back onto the floor. The notes, folded tidily around the card, are all deposited alongside her underwear in the small leather handbag that she now clings to like a trophy.

The buzz-saw continues, oblivious, and he makes an unintelligible utterance. Perhaps he's dreaming about her. Whatever is going on inside his head, she despises the sound he's making and would willingly silence him forever, but this morning she will settle for just robbing him. Taking a life creates risk. Anyway, that awful snoring means security, as it affirms his lack of consciousness. However, she is not one to surrender caution. As she puts on her jacket, she is icily prepared for confrontation, as always, but believes that the temazepam she added to his drink several hours ago has done the trick. He probably won't wake up before noon. They don't, usually.

She sneaks out of the room, gently closing the door behind her. This is always one of the best bits of the whole process. She strolls briskly down the lightly-carpeted corridor to the stairs and descends. There is nobody around and she makes a point of turning her head away from the reception desk as she exits. Within just over a minute and a half from leaving the room, she is on the pavement a couple of hundred yards away from the hotel. She could feel vulnerable. She doesn't.

She never does.

With daylight shining on the windows, windscreens and car bonnets that she passes, there is the sound of some kind of street cleaning vehicle moving along the next road, whilst the sun is beginning to make its mark on the day. She hopes it will be a nice sunny day, even if she will end up sleeping through most of it. It is always good to wake up to sunshine.

She looks down the road, seeing nothing of note, so she turns her head the opposite way. The headlights of a car about a hundred yards away blink on and off. The enterprising young woman, this pretty brunette in a black dress, Caroline Lawrence, to the few people who know her, JoJo to some who are more often than not less fortunate, feels a sense of reassurance. The half-smile returns. Moving into a jog, she makes her way confidently towards the vehicle.

When she reaches the car, a dull red Nissan Micra, with a dent in the wheel arch on the passenger side, yet with an engine that purrs resiliently and optimistically, she drops herself into the passenger seat and smiles at the driver. This one is all ears and expectation, underneath a mass of blonde curly hair.

With hands gripping the steering wheel, she is a similar age to Caroline. Unlike Caroline, she is all smiles and anticipation.

Instantly the engine of the car roars into life and straight away they make their getaway, driving along a deserted road in the town centre.

"How much?"

Caroline takes the wad of notes from her bag and quickly counts them, with all the speed and confidence of a bank teller. "A hundred and eighty quid."

Leoni nods her head without taking her eyes off the road. "Not bad."

Caroline points a finger ahead of her into an imagined distance. "There's more. A lot more." She puts the money away. "Cashpoint. You got those numbers?"

"Yes. Think he's using his son's birthday. First digit was a five and his son's born on the 5th of June. Reckon it'll be zero-five-zero-six or zero-five-zero-two. Only just got it though. He was a big bloke."

"A heavyweight geezer, the Londoners would say." Caroline is studying the shops they pass, thinking that she may never pass this way again, and sees nothing to suggest to her that it is something to feel sorry about. She turns from the dullness and looks ahead.

"Yep. A real sun blocker, so I only just caught it. Do you think he'll be good for it?"

"Not half. Top of the range Porsche. You don't drive one of those and have an overdraft."

"Plenty in there then?"

"I reckon so. We'll soon know."

"I hope you're right."

"Lu, it's a two-hundred grand car. Loaded. Trust me."

"OK. Cashpoint one on the left. The one on the right's not working." They park up bang next to the machines. They both look around, turning to survey their surroundings in all directions and their eyes meet in approval. There's no one around. From the glove compartment, Caroline grabs two Mickey Mouse masks. She passes one to Leoni and secures the other to her face. With the card in her hand, she goes up to the cash dispenser and inserts it. She presses the buttons and requests two hundred pounds. Some clicking and whirring, then a metal door opens, signalling success. Zero-five-zero-two works and brings forth smiles all around. She takes out the crisp twenty-pound notes. They feel nice. Tonight has done some good.

"Remember, the CCTV is to the right, next to the exit." The work isn't complete yet.

First stop is the nearest Asda, open twenty-four hours thankfully, where they use that same card to do some shopping, this time with baseball caps and sunglasses as meaningful disguises. The supermarket is deserted thankfully, with just three cars in the far corner of the car park, and they make their way to the spirits aisle. They select some expensive bottles, mainly Moet et Chandon and specialist gins, put them in a basket, then head for the only checkout that is operating at this time of day.

Leoni does the little talking that is necessary, and Caroline almost smiles. She has never become used to her partner's feigned London accent. They are buying six bottles of champagne and five bottles of gin, which they both know they can trade when it suits, or even drink if they feel like a crazy night. While Leoni makes the purchases, Caroline is constantly scanning the area around her, positioning herself so she faces away from that camera near the exit.

After that, they head quickly to the car and put the bottles in the back. The journey now resumes, and they work their way through the outskirts of the town and find the blue signs they now need. Soon, they are on a slip road. "Well, here we are again. The multi-lane experience."

Caroline sighs.

"One day we can do a local job perhaps, and just fall into bed. What about somebody on the next road? Sharp Street is good for me."

"We did plenty of local jobs, didn't we? Too many. That's why we're doing this now."

"Yeah, I know. The travelling makes the work harder, though."

Caroline keeps her lips firmly together. She knows they are both very tired.

"What was he like, then?" Leoni doesn't take her eyes off the road, although she strokes Caroline's leg.

Caroline responds by touching her friend's hand with her fingertips. "He was like most of them. Just wanted my knickers off and a ten-second shag. Wanker."

"Was he rough with you?" Leoni takes her eyes off the road briefly and scans Caroline's arm for bruising.

"Not really. Enthusiastic though."

"Yuck."

Caroline remains matter of fact. "He just shot his load then became unconscious. Thank God for the Tammy. Did the trick."

"Was he interesting?

"Was he fuck! He just talked about himself. On and fucking on. Kept telling me all about travelling business class to the Caribbean and these famous people he knew."

"Famous? Who?"

"Exactly. That's just it. I'd never heard of them. Z-list celebrities probably. Sports people, some of them. Dead obscure. Like I was remotely interested."

"An arsehole."

"Yep. So now he pays. Another high and mighty knobhead who needs a lesson. And now he learns."

"Well, we're teaching. That's for sure."

"Aren't we? You and I should have been teachers."

"You didn't like him then?" Leoni is smiling now, teasingly.

Caroline looks at her friend in disbelief. "I hated him."

"What? Really hated him?" Leoni's eyes and mouth widen at the same time.

"That's right. Really hated him."

"Violently hated him?"

"Yep. How far are we going with this? I'll tell you. This should satisfy your bloodthirsty soul. He annoyed me enough to put himself at serious risk. Just as well for him he was Mister Sleepy Head. Saved his life," that did.

Leoni laughs out loud. "Good old Temazepam. Where would we be without her?"

"Yeah, she kicked in eventually. But I did have to do some waiting."

"What? Nothing straight away?"

"No. A bit bad, that."

"Why the delay?"

"No idea. Took a while. He must have been on some medication or something."

"Or it's because he was a big bloke. And was he fucking big. I wouldn't have wanted him on top of me."

"He was that." She moves her body around in the seat as if to reassure herself. "I think I survived him."

"How did you see to him?"

"On top. Quick finish. Then I waited for Tammy to put him away. Just wanted his bullshit to come to an end."

"How long did he stay awake?"

"Too long. About half an hour. Droning on about some shit."

"Still, we've made some."

"Yes, we've not done too bad." Caroline pauses, knowing that the words 'too bad' carry their own connotations. "We need a new plan now, though." Caroline's eyes are in sharp focus.

"What do you mean?"

"Well, it's all very well us hitting these towns, but all we're doing is avoiding shit. I don't want to just avoid shit. I'm not doing this stuff just to pay sodding bills. We have to do better than that. And there's another thing. At some point our luck is going to run out doing these crap jobs and we'll be rumbled. Do you fancy being up in court? I don't."

"I'm not doing prison. You won't see me again if I have to do time."

"Exactly. Making a couple of hundred quid and some booze isn't enough for the risk we're taking. We need to make some serious money so we don't have to do as many of these jobs. The more jobs we do, the greater the risk."

"I've been thinking about that too. I have these big ideas then I just think, oh well, we're doing OK."

"But doing OK's not doing OK at all," Caroline says. "Doing OK is just so much nothing. We need to be earning bigger amounts, life changing ones."

Leoni is struggling to concentrate on the driving. "So what are you thinking?"

"I'm thinking that we need a cash cow or two!"

"Minted punters?"

"Of course. A really big pay day or two."

Leoni smiles and Caroline's expression creates symmetry in the front of the car. Two women on the same page on their way home after a profitable night.

Caroline, her mind in overdrive, continues. "We need to gain access to blokes with serious money and take the lot, much more than we've ever taken. We need to spend some time with one or two loaded bastards and stir it up a bit. Make some real money."

Leoni looks across. "Sounds interesting. How?"

Caroline smiles. "I've got some ideas."

"Tell me."

"Tomorrow."

"No, Caz. We're going to be on the road for a while. Tell me now."

'We do it carefully and with purpose."

"Don't be vague. What does that mean? We do everything now carefully and with purpose."

"Well, basically, loads of planning and preparation. We do things with even greater care, and bigger things."

"How are we going to manage that?"

"With the right amount of thinking about the details. It's all about details. The who we do it to is just one of those key details. Once that's sorted, we have to be in the right place at the right time, with the right attitude."

"What do you mean? You're talking in riddles."

"We need to target big money. Businessmen. A factory owner, perhaps. A farmer with loads of land might be good. Seriously minted fuckers. This guy tonight was OK, and we need to hit knobheads like him, but a lot richer, and hit them a lot harder. It's not just shag money. Much more than that."

"More? How?'

"We use leverage."

"How do we do that?"

"By using this, Lu." Caroline points her finger at her temple and her eyes widen. "We're going to be aspirational. Get ourselves in the nicest places. If I'm going to go to work with these twats, let it be in a posh hotel, not some budget shithole. That was one tacky hole."

"Five star next time, then?" Leoni grins.

"Why not? And we sting for thousands, not hundreds."

"Sounds good." She emphasises the second of the two words. Leoni's smile is becoming broader by the minute.

"Exactly. We have to do the research and head upmarket. From here on in, I'm only opening my legs for year-changing money, if not life-changing. Shagging for the supermarket shop is a joke, a sick joke. My sense of humour doesn't stretch that far. Not anymore."

"Can we do that, though, what you're suggesting?"

"Course we can." She moves her index finger in an arc in front of herself. "Why else did they give me this face and body?"

"Shall we hit another cashpoint now, see if that fat fucker was good for it?"

"Why not."

OPPORTUNITY KNOCKS

"Are you sure this is the one?"

Caroline is pressing the laptop keys almost rhythmically, as she navigates through a maze of questions, whilst simultaneously taking sips from a large glass of gin and tonic. She turns to Leoni. "I'll tell you again, since you weren't listening just now. This is the one."

This is the fifth dating site they have considered, and Leoni's patience is not everlasting. "But it's just like the others."

"Hardly. It's made for us, this one."

Leoni has a look of comfortable bewilderment on her face. "They all look the same to me."

"One word makes the difference."

"What word?"

"Elite. It's got Elite in the title. You know what that means."

"Top people, I guess. But it's bullshit. They call themselves that to make them seem superior in some way."

"Yeah, but the word attracts the people it describes. Snob value. I can see that already." She makes a hand gesture in the direction of the screen.

"So there are quality clientele using the site?"

"Exactly. Men with money. So much money that I can even smell it online. Flash houses, big credit limits and fuck off cars." She turns her head in an attempt at uncertainty that is clearly feigned. "Are we a woman seeing a man, Lu?"

"Are you daft? Definitely."

Caroline's attention returns to the laptop. "Too right. We need their stupidity."

"And we can rely on that. That brain inside their underwear thing's the key to our everything."

She again gestures for Leoni to look at the screen. "I'm basing us in Nottingham."

"Good idea. Everybody knows us in this shithole. Too risky."

"What are we looking for then?"

"What do you mean?"

"What kind of relationship?

She looks across. "What are those options I can see?"

"Long term, friendship, casual?"

"Mmmm. Casual?"

"Don't know. None of them work for me." Caroline looks to the ceiling for guidance.

"Put friendship."

"Why friendship?"

Leoni leans over to her friend. "It'll make you seem hard to get. Unavailability's key. Especially when they see how sweet-looking you are."

"Oh. You say the nicest things." She reaches out to touch Leoni's cheek.

"Might be more attractive to the big fish if you put friendship. These arseholes don't usually want a relationship, and neither do we."

Caroline shakes her head doubtfully. "Possibly, although any man we land won't be somebody looking for friendship. Like I need a friend."

"I know. More than likely, he'll just be another dirty bastard with money anyway."

"Think business, Lu. We're gonna milk them big time."

"Well, we can try it whichever way you want. If it doesn't work, we can always change it. What picture are you going to put up?"

"Two. Two pictures. Maybe three if I can find a decent third one. Got to pull them in."

"Of course. Which ones?"

Caroline has her photographs in front of her on the screen. "The full-length picture of me in Marbella, the bikini shot."

"Yeah. Use that one. Totally hot."

"I'm going to add that selfie from last week. My make-up was really good on that one." Smiling broadly, Caroline presses more keys before turning the laptop in Leoni's direction to reveal the two photos mentioned, now side by side in the allotted window.

"They'll work, babe. You look fab in both of them."

Caroline frowns. "You make it sounds like that's a rare occurrence."

"No, of course not. You always look good, babe. But that selfie makes you look like butter wouldn't melt. Pretty lethal combination if you ask me."

"Well, I always like the butter wouldn't melt look. Always have."

"What about a classy one?"

"Good idea, but we'll need to add that later. We're going out, remember. We'll dress up and do a restaurant tonight and take a few shots there." Caroline manages a half-smile.

"Which restaurant?"

"Dunno. Some place with a tablecloth and smart crockery. We'll need that for a posh photo or two."

"Sounds good. Think I'll go on that site now and see what quality punters there are."

A few minutes later and things have become more intense. They are both in the midst of a manhunt, each scrolling, reading and pausing, then scrolling reading and pausing some more. Every now and again one of them lands on an advertisement and laughs out loud.

"What about this one? Company director."

"That sounds like decent status. What's the company?"

"Doesn't say. Why would it? Likes riding and sport."

"Well, they're pretty good hobbies, I reckon, especially if it's show jumping and motorsport."

"I always did like Formula One. Don't rich blokes like cricket and rugby? Avoid football, though. All the chavs like football."

Both young women are in pyjamas, holding mugs of hot chocolate in their hands as they do their serious planning. "Sounds promising. This one likes sport too, but looking at him, it'll be football."

Caroline almost loses her grip on her mug as she makes a declaration and considers a possibility. "What if the sport is darts? I meet up with a fat sod with a massive beer belly and a sparse bank account. Wonder what this knobhead's company is. No good if he's going bankrupt. There'll be some liars on here. I don't think I'd be nice to a liar."

"Bound to be. Internet's full of liars." Leoni nods. "Arseholes just can't stop lying. Never have and never will."

"Hey, this one here's a consultant surgeon. That's some job. I'd check out his specialism. Interesting. He's looking for someone for some good times and nothing serious."

Leoni scowls. "Dirty bastard." She points a finger at Caroline's screen. "Let's take him. He'll be good for it."

"Maybe. Consultants are seriously minted. He'll certainly have the kind of money we're talking about."

"Are you going to make contact?"

28

"Too right. Watch and learn, Lu. Getting my profile completed first. Want to make it irresistible."

"Then what?"

"After that, I'm going to send him a message to die for."

"Bet he's married."

"Hope so. Easier to make big money if he's got a wife." Caroline's voice has lowered in pitch, and Leoni turns towards her.

"You thinking what I think you're thinking?"

"Too right I am. Leverage. That old friend of the helpless."

Leoni looks puzzled. "When the fuck have we been helpless?"

* * *

Times are going to change. Times are going to be better. Times are going to bring life-enhancing rewards. They have to. As they walk from the car park of the Four Seasons Shopping Centre, heading into the complex, Caroline is reminded just how much she hates shopping malls. Wrong and demeaning on every level. She wants her time in this horrendous concrete box, with all those uninspiring, unsatisfying units, to be as brief as possible. She hopes the sacrifice she is making by coming here will be worth it.

As she approaches the concrete, she is thinking about how they can do everything more satisfactorily and she is visualizing what things they need to acquire for it all to happen. They are moving up a league now. They are ascending into greater difficulty and risk, but she knows, like Leoni, walking beside her, that this is utterly right. It is necessary for their development, for their lives to be better. Scratching around for small change will get them as far as small change will get anyone, but no further.

They pass several businesses that offer them nothing. They

pass a card shop nonchalantly, since neither of them has sent a card in years. Caroline scoffs as they pass Gregg's and Leoni grins, acknowledging how her partner feels about pastry and bread. They speed up slightly past a shop selling sportswear, with shorts, trainers and leotards dominating the window display, and pass with relief, since running up the stairs of their house is the nearest either comes to strenuous activity.

First Stop is *Precious*. A silver-framed window displays femininity and class, pink and white being the main colour combination on show, with an elegant logo overhead that suggests something special and exclusive.

Both women enter energetically. This is a moment. The duo have had so many over the past few years, but this marks a transition. They have talked about this experience several times over the past few days. Caroline has called it power-shopping. They separate enthusiastically to search for special things, and for a while neither pays any attention to the other while they seek out appropriate garments for the jobs in hand. Caroline has offered a suggestion as they part. She says, "Remember. To make a hundred thousand quid, we each need to look like a million."

"I thought you were going to have the luxury gear?"

"I am. But not just me. We're going to both have the right gear."

Leoni stops and steps back. "You should."

"No. Not just me. I want you to look the part too."

"Why? I'll be in the background or in the car. I probably won't even be seen."

Caroline looks at her. "Maybe so. But if we're both looking classy you can do much more than if you're wearing shit clothes. Good gear for both of us means no limits."

"Do more? Aren't I the back up? Haven't we decided that you are going to be the hands-on part of this?"

"I am, but you're not going to be a silent partner, babe. I want you active in what we do."

"How?"

Caroline reaches out and gently grips Leoni's upper arm. "You can come up close if needed. An extra pair of eyes and ears. Could be helpful too if there's some kind of tangle. That's why."

"How do you mean? Isn't that risky?"

"I don't think so. You within eyeshot helps in every way. At the very least, you can say what you see. Anyway..." She relaxes her hold on Leoni and breaks off. "Let's just get on with the buying. Whatever we buy, the key words are elegant, classy and sexy."

Separately, they move amongst the racks and along the walls purposefully, scrutinizing, enjoying and reluctantly rejecting most, but for different reasons. Leoni picks up a black and white polka dot blouse, but Caroline shakes her head. She moves across to Leoni, takes the blouse from her and replaces it on the rack. "Remember. Don't worry about the prices. This is investment."

Both women now move around the shop with serious expressions on their faces.

Caroline sees something. It's ideal. The killer garment for a killer lady, she thinks. A short black dress, an elaborately displayed creation, placed to be conspicuous, featuring striking seams and sophisticated stitching. This dress now has her total attention. Male or female, young or old would appreciate it like she does now. She holds it up for Leoni to see. Leoni nods, mouth open. As she approaches, an assistant is to the side of her attending to a display, so Caroline coughs to get her attention.

"Hi, there. Can I help you?" The woman, in her forties, with a round pale face and black headband with scraped back hair to accompany her light application of mascara and a simple black dress, has the smile of corporate convenience on her face, the face of implied sincerity and the suggestion that this woman will go to great lengths to help the customer.

Caroline points at the bewitching dress with its stitching she would kill for. "I like that dress, the one on the mannequin." She points casually to the far wall. "Do you have it in a size ten?"

"That one is a size ten." The woman's voice betrays her, as the employee makes little effort to hide the element of doubt. She forces a smile, wanting to be helpful, but her look towards Caroline gives her away.

Caroline is aware of how she appears to what to her is a glorified shop assistant. This woman thinks she isn't good enough, that somehow being here is not totally appropriate. Caroline begins to simmer. How many times has she encountered this? All her life, it seems. Here is yet another human looking down at her. She is showing the same disdain that she had to contend with at school and it makes her temperature rise.

However, today is not going to be a day for conflict. Caroline smiles sweetly.

"How much is it?" She retains a business-like composure and knows that the order of the day is for coldly calculating thoughts to prevail.

The judgemental woman with the simple headband looks across at one of a line of exquisitely dressed mannequins that line the far wall then back at her prospective customer. "Eight hundred and fifty-five pounds." Caroline knows exactly what the woman is thinking. She will have decided that this isn't her usual type of customer, that this is probably someone who has drifted in here from some council estate somewhere or a dodgy two-up-two-down terraced house. She will have written her off as an irritation, probably hoping that the price of this and other dresses will see her off. Behind that smug smile will be the belief that she will be sent packing by the costs of shopping here and will probably leave the shop to head for Top Shop or Marks and Spencer, more appropriate places for Caroline's type.

Caroline is here on business. She simply stares through her as if she is made of glass. "I'd like to try it on."

The woman's eyes widen slightly. "Certainly." She calls for another assistant.

She emerges a few minutes later wearing the dress. She waves at the other end of the shop, and Leoni comes over, beaming.

"Very nice." She moves around her partner in crime, looking at Caroline from different angles. "Hey, it really suits you."

"Not bad for a work outfit, I suppose." Caroline feels pretty satisfied.

At that point, Leoni holds up something she's found. "I've got mine. I'll look pretty good in this, I think." She holds up a black and cream arrangement.

Caroline half-smiles. "Hey I noticed that one. Try it on, Lu. That will definitely suit you."

In. another couple of minutes, both their minds are made up. They can now invest in the future. Together, they approach the counter. Caroline declares, "We'll take both of these." She holds out her bank card.

The assistant glances between the two customers. This is only for a split-second though, before she reaches behind her for a bag.

Caroline looks straight at the woman as she talks to Leoni. "We'll go to London tomorrow. Get our main garments."

"What?"

"This is just a practice run. Back up gear." As the woman looks down, she winks at Leoni, who retains a puzzled demeanour.

The dresses are neatly bagged up and paid for. They leave the shop, with the assistant looking on as they make their way out.

Outside, Leoni is taken aback as they walk back down the mall. "I don't get it. These things are stunning."

"Think outside the box, honey." She gently but firmly pulls Leoni away from the counter. She has her index finger pointed at her head. "Who are we after?"

"Punters."

"Exactly, but more. The men we are after, sweet girl, buy dresses for their women. They know the cost of these things. They buy them to cover up their guilt after all the shagging around. We either dress like we're in the top league or we're not in the top league."

"OK. If you say so."

"I do. Second rate dresses will get us a second rate return."

"But these aren't second rate. I've never spent this much on a dress."

"I know. These will be our base camp dresses, if you like. We're going to go higher up in London."

Leoni stops. "But the blokes will be drinking, probably. Maybe thinking about sex. Will they notice?"

"They'll notice. We can't take the chance, Lu. And why should we? No unnecessary risks. I don't want to be seen as just some bar-room prossie who's tarted herself up a bit. We're past that stage. We've done it all."

"OK. I get that."

"Good. One of us, probably me, but with you doing what you need to be doing, is going to hook a really big fish. Let's provide the best bait we can."

"So where are we going next? London?"

"That's right."

"It's a long drive."

"We'll get a train. More serious shopping. Can have a nice meal, see a few sights."

"It's a lot of our money being used up on this."

"It's investment, Lu."

"When are we going?"

"Tomorrow morning."

Leoni has a wide smile on her face. "It's a bit like Christmas, this. This has a real Christmas Eve feel about it now you're saying that. "

"Yours maybe. Nothing like mine."

"What do you mean?"

Caroline puts her hand on Leoni's arm. "Put it this way. You must have had better Christmases than me, if you think that this is like Christmas."

Leoni looks at her and shakes her head. "No. That's not true."

"I didn't think so."

"I had rubbish Christmases. Chicken for dinner, the odd present, but pretty rubbish apart from that. Other people had magical ones, though."

"Yeah, didn't they? I always noticed that. Had it rubbed in my face. Big presents, new clothes and family parties. Stuff like that."

"Those are the Christmases I'm on about. That's what this feels like."

"Yeah, pretty perfect, but we deserve times like that too." Still in the Four Seasons Centre, not far from the exit, Caroline holds her arm out to the side to stop Leoni walking any further. She gesticulates towards the bottom of the window of a jeweller's they're passing. "And that is just what I want."

"What?"

"That bracelet."

"What?"

In a display area at the bottom of the main window, there is a range of items labelled 'Jagged Rocks', a group of dramatic-looking features on display, jewellery that seems to be lines of scowling gemstones, each a linked series of sharp blue and glassy jewels that nobody has dared to smooth.

"You like that? But the jewels haven't been finished. They're all rough and stuff."

"Exactly. Perfect. Especially that bottom one. Leoni, meet Alice."

"Alice? Hate to quote a pop song, but who the fuck is Alice?"

"You're going to give a piece of jewellery a daft name?"

"Let's see," Caroline says. "Could be an important part of the operation."

They're immediately inside the shop, with Leoni at Caroline's heels. A middle-aged balding guy in a brown suit with matching tie is behind the counter.

"Can I help you, miss?"

"I think you can. I like those bracelets in your window, the Jagged Rock ones. I want to look at the one at the bottom of the display."

"Aren't they fab? Really exciting designs. Came in a month ago." He walks to where they're displayed and unlocks the rear of the cabinet.

"I just want to see the one at the bottom."

"Of course. I'll get it out for you and you can try it on."

Caroline is happy. With the bracelet on, she raises her arm and puts her finger inside to test the fit. It has large spiky sapphires and transparent crystals alongside some small rugged gems. Close to perfect. As she rubs the jewels with her fingers, she feels the sharp ridges cutting in to the upper layers of her skin and that brings a satisfied smile to her face. "Welcome to Mummy, Alice. I'll take her."

The jeweller raises an eyebrow, but not much, since he has been a jeweller for fifteen years. This is far from the most dramatic reaction to jewellery he has seen in his time.

Leoni, standing beside her, is bemused, but not quite getting it. She herself scrutinizes a diamond necklace in the cabinet at the front of the counter. It's pricy, eye-catching, yet a couple of hundred pounds cheaper than the bracelet. "Can I have this? It'll go a treat with that dress."

"Of course. It'll suit you."

"I'm not giving it a name, though." She laughs.

As she retrieves her credit card from her handbag, Caroline turns her attention back to the man behind the counter. "Can the bracelet be strengthened?"

"What do you mean?"

"So it can't be pulled apart in any way."

"Oh, it's pretty strong. They make them that way."

"It needs to be very strong. Unbelievably strong. I'm very clumsy. I've had bracelets break on me before. I catch them on door handles and things."

"I see. Well that's not a problem. We can increase the thickness of the chain and put a more resilient clasp in place. It will cost more, though."

"How much more?

"Well, with the thicker chain and the new clasp, it'll be twelve hundred pounds."

Whilst Leoni raises her eyebrows, Caroline doesn't even flinch. "That's fine. And the fitting."

"The fitting?"

"It's a bit loose for my tastes."

"Well, it is meant to be loose fitting. It's that kind of bracelet."

There is a demanding firmness in her voice now that arouses Leoni's curiosity even more. "I don't want it loose fitting. I need it tight-fitting."

The jeweller's eyebrows furrow. "How tight?"

"Close to the skin. As tight as it can be without causing a circulation problem."

"I suppose so. If that's what you want. I'll need to measure your wrist." He takes a tape measure from a shelf behind him whilst Caroline holds out her wrist.

Caroline leaves the jeweller with a piece of paper in her hand, a receipt that doubles as a reminder to her to collect it after it has been tweaked for her taste. That will be a week from now, which suits perfectly.

As they leave and head towards the car, Leoni stops and looks at Caroline. "What the fuck was that about?"

"What do you mean?"

"You've spent over a grand on a bracelet. Did we really need to do that?"

"And almost as much as that on a necklace for you." Caroline is totally sure of herself. "Yes, we do. We're playing to win. Makes things perfect. Besides, we'll get all the money back."

"Well, how is a bracelet going to make a difference?"

"Don't know. Just a weird thought I've had."

BIRTHWRONG – THE ORIGIN OF SWEET CAROLINE (1983)

Well, life was pretty dingy before and things were now looking a whole lot worse.

Around twenty-seven years before the bracelet and dresses were purchased, a woman called Judy just pushed. There was no one around now to tell her to push, no one to instruct her. This was a house, not a hospital, and midwives were in very short supply. Having taken what she wanted, that cow had gone, whilst the labour continued. There was more pain this time.

She consoled herself with the realisation that she was still alive. Judy reminded herself that she was resilient, if nothing else. She had managed to stave off the unconsciousness that for a spell had seemed to threaten. Above all, she didn't want the constant pain to encompass her, to envelope her, so she pushed. She only half knew what was happening. Everything had become blurred.

It should have been all over after the first one, yet here it was continuing.

To avoid the intense stabbing pain that had been relentless for the past ten minutes, she carried on forcing the thing within her outwards. Within some electrifying seconds, the head of a second infant born that hour began to appear and Judy could only study the area between her legs with horror. This was far beyond what she had anticipated. This was now a living nightmare that no amount of sleep was going to rescue her from. A new life was coming forward to stake its claim on her. With a sensitive violence, she forced the new life outside herself. She groaned out loud as her body parted with this thing she had housed for three-quarters of a year. Suddenly, she had in front of her a lifeform she had not expected, had not wanted. It was a creation that offered nothing, a being that would not free her from any of the things that pained her or restricted her. It would bring no benefit. How would a baby help her to cope with the demands and expectations she had in her life? Judy felt tears roll down her cheeks, tears that reflected a combination of frustration, anger and misery.

"Oh, fuck."

Judy felt very weak now, so her movements were slow and clumsy. She reached out into the top drawer of her bedside cabinet. She blindly felt for the scissors that she knew were in there, the same scissors she had used to shorten her nails a few nights ago. A world ago. She gripped them tightly and fell back onto the bed. She sought the fleshy cord that she knew had to be cut, for her sake more than for any other reason. Uncertainly, charged by only a vague idea, she did the necessary cutting, then strained and spluttered as she lifted the baby into her arms. She wasn't exactly sure about any of it, just an instinct that came from God knows where. For some inexplicable reason, she had to make sure that this baby was alive and that it would remain so.

The baby itself was a purple lump, and she could see that it was a purple female lump. She needed something to inject life and destroy the stillness. When Judy held her up by the legs and slapped, just like that Stewart woman had done with the other one twenty-five minutes ago, part of her was hoping that either the slapping would fail to bring the baby to life and her new problems would end before they started, whilst the rest of her wanted her slap at the very least to change the colour of this unanticipated arrival to something easier on the eye.

It achieved the latter. The baby girl let out a small piercing cry that announced her entry into the uncertain unwelcoming world that was Judy's life.

The ambulance arrived, and a man and a woman wearing NHS uniforms and reassuring smiles were soon upstairs and at the side of her bed. They were young, and they had not yet seen anything like this before, the difficult situation where a mother delivers her infant on her own. They began to make themselves busy, checking out Judy and checking out the baby. "It's a lovely girl," a red-faced woman in a pale blue uniform said. "Have you done it yourself? You've done really well."

At this point, Judy couldn't reply, but was staring at the curtains, creased and faded, closed to block off the harsh sunlight as further teardrops ran down the new mother's face.

She was exhausted but fended off the sleep that now wanted to engulf her. There was thinking to be done. Her life had always been problematic and how it now threatened to be more so. She wanted to work out some kind of exit strategy. She was wondering how she could get out of this with no consequences. Being on her own had been tough, even before the pregnancy. She'd barely coped with the lack of money and the everyday problems of living alone. She was now looking ahead through a fog that had become dirtier and greyer. Having this baby, a pathetic dependent creature, in her life was not what she had envisaged for her future. The main challenge she had foreseen facing her prior to now had been a simple one. Judy had just wanted to enjoy the basic pleasures of life, legal and otherwise, and not be held back by having responsibility for anyone other than herself.

That had always been the plan. A baby would get in the way. In her mind, Judy wanted to recapture those lost days of the Seventies when everything had been so free and easy. Back then there had been the concerts, the films and the parties. Back then she had had friends. Carole Harper, her best friend, whom she had known since infant school, now married and living somewhere in the West Midlands. Lost, Judy hadn't heard anything from her in three years. Judy herself had never married. Loads of sex. Loads of men. Plenty of alcohol. Some drugs. No marriage. Some wild times, but never boring.

Now life was going to go beyond boring. Misery had arrived.

She was just too exhausted. Sensing the fading of her resistance, she sank into unconsciousness.

While she was out if it, the reality remained. This was a woman who had made no arrangements to prepare her for this baby. Having a baby was only something she would do to make some money, like from that rich Stewart couple. There was no other possible benefit. She was hardly a cosy couple creating a room awash with primary colours, with a pretty mobile hanging from the ceiling and a fluffy carpet. Judy Lawrence had nothing planned like that. Worse still, she knew nothing about being a mother, nor had she ever wanted to know anything. It had not even been on the horizon. The pregnancy had been initially an unwanted gift from Ray, an American from Montana, with a big smile and an even bigger wallet. He had visited these shores for a series of conferences in the Midlands and had been partial to the occasional one-night stand. Pregnancy had been a consequence of too much gin and no condom. For over a month Judy had been deeply disturbed, sitting around thinking about an abortion. An offer had come out of nowhere so there was going to be no termination. That appreciative couple, with their high-end bank balance, had been glad to take on the challenge that was now in front of Judy herself, who nevertheless slept soundly now, after all the exertion.

On the dining table was a list. With the money she had earned herself for giving birth, she had written down all the possibilities. There was the odd holiday abroad and the odd trip to acquire some quality clothes, as well as some new electrical gadgets, such as a state-of-the art television set. She had seen herself taking a month in Tenerife and drinking Tequila Sunrises and Pina Coladas, having restaurant meals every night, hopefully meeting some beau out there who would add other qualities to the adventure. It would have been an adventure too, since Judy had never had a holiday abroad.

In actual fact, in normal times, when she wasn't receiving thousands of pounds for going into labour, she'd become used to life's severity. Buying a cot and a pram would have been about as much an anticipated and achievable reality for her as a starship to take her at warp speed beyond the confines of the solar system. Money issues were perpetual. Her benefit payments barely covered her costs, and a child would be crippling. All in all, looking at her life up to today, she knew the sum total of the circumstances she had endured, and the decisions was a life of guaranteed desperation. And here she was again, burdened in a new way and soon to be looking for some kind of solution so that she could re-join the miserable world she was used to.

After a mere five minutes of slumber, Judy's eyes opened. The woman in the uniform was still there, standing over her. "It won't be long. We're just preparing for your journey. Is there anything you need to bring with you?"

Judy, twenty-two a month ago and experienced in the wrong things, shook her head. She looked down at the now silent creature. If she was expected to feel something, some burst of maternal electricity like in the movies and soaps, then it wasn't happening. The beat of her heart would not quicken. However, the presence of the infant was triggering plenty of thoughts. This pink lump had her eyes currently closed to the world, a pink lump that would one day be a woman like Judy, but one who would be leading who knew what kind of life.

She said nothing in the ambulance and replied to questions monosyllabically. But her mind carried on. At least it was a girl, she thought. Boys were more troublesome. After considering that, she rejected the idea. She became irritated with herself. She needed to avoid looking through rose-tinted glass. A female might grow to be more needy than a male would have been. A boy might have a greater sense of independence and perhaps not require quite so much of Judy. Judy needed to be Judy after all.

"We'll soon be there. Just relax. Everything is going to be fine." The mother and the new baby were soon being transported through a series of double doors. The Mother and Baby Unit was an intimidating place for her, all those bright colours, and, once settled into a ward containing four other women, she ended up sleeping through most of it, facing the plain pale blue wall close to her bed with the baby behind her. She woke up tense, still in the middle of that dirty grey cloud. What was she going to do? A baby needed reliability on her part, responsibility, and these were things she wasn't very good at. She found it hard to accept a role in the life of a wretched little mite like this, a throbbing lump that slept with no knowledge of the world into which she had emerged.

At least I'll get my figure back now, she thought.

She sank into unconsciousness again. It was probably for the best.

When Judy awoke, amidst a load of white and pale blue, with NHS equipment and furnishings all around her, she was disappointed that she hadn't dreamed all this. The problems hadn't gone away. She couldn't help sighing heavily.

A day later found Judy still in the same room, still continually musing miserably over her new set of problems. The confinement didn't suit her. She felt frustrated. The deal with the Stewarts had left her with a substantial wad of notes in her upstairs drawer, but now some of that money would have to be squandered on stupid stuff for this wretched baby.

"How are you, love?" A woman in a nearby bed had stopped to talk to her on the way back from the toilet.

"I'm OK." Judy spoke half-heartedly. The woman, with the same swollen belly that they all had in here, looked down at Judy's baby and sighed. "What a lovely baby. Is it a girl?"

Judy nodded.

"I'm having mine in the next couple of days. Just wish it could happen soon. Has her father seen her yet?"

"No. Not yet. He's in America."

"He'll be over the moon when he sees her. She's beautiful. Babies are priceless." In Judy's mind, her last sentence was like the throwing of a barbed spear as the woman continued back to her bed. If only there had been somebody to hand over money for this one. She'd never anticipated twins. As far as she knew, there had never been twins in her family.

The money. That crisp wad of notes that had been given to her was everything. The ambulance man had locked the door properly, hadn't he? He better had. She needed that money, needed it to be in that drawer of her bedroom when she got out of this hell hole and was back home. She prayed that there wouldn't be a burglary. There had been some thefts in the past three months on the street, so she hoped nobody had targeted her for that.

She hadn't had too much experience of being a victim of crime, but once was enough. Eighteen months ago, some desperado had entered her house while she had been out and had stolen the television. She had opened the front door, taken one step inside, then, "Oh fuck." There had just been a massive gap in her living space. Some bastard had invaded her home and had managed to damage her life.

OK, thanks to a male friend she had been able to replace the set, and the thief, well known in the area, had received a beating for his trouble, courtesy of her mate Big Dan. However, she was unable to count on the same kind of happy ending this time, since she was between male friends, and Big Dan couldn't help this time. He was inside doing six months for aggravated assault.

She attempted to calm herself down. This was only going to be one more night away. Surely somebody like that wouldn't choose this night above all nights to take a covetous interest in her property. The odds on anything that bad happening that night must have been pretty long, very much on her side, and it wasn't as if anybody knew that she had money in the house. Judy believed that her sanity, perhaps even her survival depended on that money being there still when she returned home. It was a pity she had nobody she could trust, and regrettable that she lacked a true friend.

More realism was here and now. Hard truths now took the form of little noises, barely audible, at her bedside. She looked down at the cause of her current woes, and surprisingly had to admit that she actually looked quite sweet for a baby. There were the expected wrinkles and narrow eyes, but with something pretty going on as well. This infant was not so much a female Winston Churchill, as so many babies were, but more like a tender, peaceful-looking little soul with the skin of an angel. So pale and delicate.

Judy responded, even if unwillingly. There was the surprising skipping of a heartbeat. "I guess I have to try," she told herself,

"Make the best of things. No choice." These attempts to reassure herself were not entirely convincing since she would be losing so much. Somehow, she had to get through this.

Then a powerful image took shape in her mind. It came out of nowhere. It was an image that had always had an impact on her, and had done when she had first seen it back in the Seventies. It was the picture of a man with an unbuttoned shirt singing live to a highly receptive audience. In her mind, she was thinking of 'Hot August Night', the live album. She sought comfort in her hero, the American singer Neil Diamond, a man whose pictures, in frames bought from Woolworth's at three for £7.99 to add that touch of class, adorned Judy's living room.

Now, if the baby had been Neil's, that would have been another story. That would have been sheer bliss. This might have been a much more tolerable episode, with she and Neil setting up home together in his Hollywood mansion. On the other hand, knowing the way things usually went for her, the situation was more likely to be one in which she was forced into blackmailing her idol, if only so that she could live in comfort for the rest of her life. She did come from a rough part of town, after all, so street survival was never far away from her consciousness. Being her idol would only go so far.

As if hearing a reply, she decided on a name there and then. The baby was sweet, with a little round face, and maybe one day she would be contented and funny. This baby would be called Caroline, like her favourite Neil song. Could she actually call her Sweet Caroline? That sounded fab. She thought for a whole minute. No, she decided. That would probably be too much. Besides, kids would bully her mercilessly if her first name was Sweet. That was too American for these parts. There had been a bloke at school whose surname had been Kindly, and he had had a terrible time at the hands of the tough kids there.

Twenty-four hours later, the police were quizzing her. A well-meaning and knowledgeable gynaecologist had examined Judy and had made an unsettling discovery. He asked Judy about the birth, paused after her response before emphatically suggesting that baby Caroline had not been the first, that she had certainly been the second-born baby that day. This suggested something sinister and, more than that, illegal. There was the strong scent of something illicit, the suggestion that the situation was not as innocent and natural as it had seemed.

Hence, the doctors wanted to know what had happened to the other baby, Caroline's twin. Of course, she denied it emphatically. "You're mistaken." It wasn't enough, however, and within two hours of a phone call being made, two police officers were at her bedside, wanting a more serious conversation, with implied threat.

Judy knew what she had to do. She was well aware that playing dumb and staying dumb was a necessity, the only thing that would guarantee that she didn't pay a huge price financially and personally. She'd assured the Stewarts of that. Saying anything now would stop her getting the second payment they would be making to her as the closing part of the deal. She might have been weak, post-natally tired, but she wasn't weak enough or tired enough to make an error at this point. "The thing is, I just don't remember anything."

The police were pushy, one of whom had just been made godmother to her sister's new arrival, a fact that made her particularly involved in the discussion. "Oh, come on, Judy. This is a baby. What did you do?"

"I did nothing with no baby. I don't know why you're saying these things to me."

"Was it a boy or a girl?"

Judy felt desperate and pressured. She tried to make herself seem more so. "I just don't know. I don't remember having another baby, apart from this one. Somebody has got it wrong."

"So, basically, the truth is, Judy, you had a baby and it's disappeared."

"Not that I know. And I do think I would know."

"But is that what you're trying to tell us?"

"I think I would know if I had another baby. Come on."

Both officers had deadly serious expressions on their faces. It was obvious that a crime had been committed. They just weren't sure what the offence was. Therefore, they went in search of the specifics of the matter. "What's happened to it, then?"

She opted for emotion. It had worked for her so many times in the past. She decided to be loud and irate. "Nothing's happened to it. I had no other baby."

"Oh yes, you did. You had twins. The medical examination was pretty clear."

"For crying out loud, there was only this one." Indicating the crib alongside her bed, she raised her head and stared at her inquisitors. "One is going to be hard enough. For fuck's sake, don't wish another one on me."

The senior of the two policemen was unmoved. His face showed firmness. "You're maintaining a charade, if you don't mind me saying so. The fact is, a baby is missing. It's some kind of mysterious disappearance but I stopped believing in magic a long time ago. What have you done with it? I ask you again. Just tell me this. Was it a boy, or another girl?"

"I've done nothing. From where I'm lying, I just have one baby, this one. I just want to care for this little cherub, if you'll allow me to do that.'

"Just answer the question. A boy or a girl? C'mon Judy. It's the least you can do."

Judy stayed silent, turning her head away from the interrogation. She had been through the legal process a few times. Always say nothing. Definitely say nothing today.

The female officer, opting for a different tack, moved closer to the new mother. "Listen, Judy. We understand how things happen sometimes. Really, we do. We just want to make sure both you and your babies, both your babies, are all right."

Judy pointed at the cot. "Baby. How many times? That's the only baby. And it's plenty. Believe me. It's plenty. Fucking hell, is it plenty." Her eyes rolled and it wasn't a pretence. "What the fuck am I going to do? I can't even afford this baby. Can you help me with that one?"

"Is that the reason, Judy? Have you passed your baby on to somebody somewhere because you can't afford two?" We understand why that happens. Really we do. We just need to learn the truth from you. For your baby's sake." The officer touched her arm. "For your sake."

Judy just shook her head and stayed silent.

"Was somebody else at your house today?"

Again, she moved her head from side to side, this time with an audible sigh.

The officer recognised the fruitlessness of the moment. Empathy and sympathy weren't working. "OK, Judy. We're going to have to investigate further though. We'll be wanting to search your house this afternoon."

Judy remembered the money in the bedside drawer. She sat up as they were moving away towards the door, instantly panicking. The volume of her voice suddenly increased. "Don't you go anywhere near my house. Do you hear? You'll do nothing till I get there."

"Of course, Judy."

"And you'll have a search warrant or you're staying on the doorstep." Her feet were suddenly touching the floor and she was sitting up. "In fact, I'm going home right now." That money needed to be well-hidden.

* * *

Four weeks on, this time it was Social Services who were concerned. "What exactly is the problem, Judy?" Angie Donnelly, a jolly, plump woman with a beaming face, a mass of grey curly hair and a relaxed but sincere attitude to all her cases, was cradling a cup of coffee, still full to the brim after twenty minutes, and lukewarm.

"There isn't really a problem. I'm just getting used to things." Judy, sitting opposite Angie at her kitchen table, was on the defensive.

The health visitor, on her umpteenth visit, dropped her beaming smile for a moment. She had done an inspection then sat down to make notes. The things she wrote today would be fuelling her judgement, a judgement that, looking around the house, might not be favourable. Angie became grave. "Judy, when I arrived, little Caroline's nappy was heavily soiled, a dual soiling. Do you know what I mean by that?"

"I think so." Judy held up her left hand. "She's had some toilet problems in the past couple of days."

"But you were upstairs sleeping. You didn't even know. That's a bigger problem. And you'd left her in the carry cot. Anything could have happened."

"It was a one-off. I don't normally do that."

Angie changed her body language to appear firm. "You shouldn't ever do that. You're taking a serious risk. How would you feel if anything happened to little Caroline?"

"I'll get better."

Angie had heard excuses and promises for the past five meetings. "How, Judy? How are you going to do that?"

"It'll happen." She shrugged her shoulders. "Just not used to being a mother."

"Did you read the booklets I left you?"

"Sort of. I'm not much of a reader."

Angie picked up a couple of them. "Do you need me to read them to you? I can do that."

"No. Course not. I can read," she said, defensively. "Just not really my thing."

The health visitor sighed. "Well, I'm here tomorrow. Not sure what time." She paused. "I need to start seeing some sign that this baby is being cared for. Cared for properly. I like you. You know I do, but the baby has to come first. I've always told you that. Actions have to match your words."

Judy smiled. "I know. Tomorrow. Things will be different."

About a week later, threee people, alongside a couple of police officers, were at Judy's door. An innocent and vulnerable bundle was soon in the hands of caring officialdom. "We have to take her, Judy."

The mother was standing with a defiance that did little to mask her desperation. "No, you don't. You have to leave her here. I'm her mother."

The social worker said it how it was. "Judy, your baby needs so much more than you're giving her. We have to take her."

"Take her? Take her where?"

"We're taking her to somewhere she'll be looked after. A nice couple who will love her. They will feed her regularly and look after her properly. Don't worry." The woman paused then expressed the grim truth. "Caroline has to have her nappy changed regularly and needs to be fed properly."

"I will do that. I've said I will."

"But you haven't been doing that. If you had, we wouldn't be doing this. Your baby hasn't been looked after properly since you brought her home."

"I've tried to look after her." Judy put up some resistance, but her voice was weakening. She had enjoyed some of the moments with this baby. There had been some unexpected pleasures from having the child. She had liked feeding her with the bottle and listening to her gentle cooing noises, as well as watching her little limbs as they moved with that absence of coordination or control.

Yet, she had a life to live. At the end of the day, this would be a problem solved. With Sweet Caroline gone, she could get back to normal. Back to the life she was most comfortable with, that sense of freedom that she hadn't embraced for a while. She wouldn't have to change wretched nappies anymore and nor would she have somebody dependent in her house. Such a development wasn't to be sniffed at.

One thing was for sure. Tonight, she was going to get wasted. It would be a phone call to a drinking pal, then a subsequent tour of the pubs in town, where she would treat herself to things that would lift her up and take her somewhere good. Consequently, with a contemptuous waving of her left arm, she gestured for them to take the infant and implicitly conceded that they should hand Caroline over to people who would give the baby the care she apparently hadn't. Bully for them.

She didn't go back into the house straight away. Instead, she watched from the doorway as the car drove away, nobody looking back, nobody caring about her, everybody only interested in that baby, a baby that had been hers. It was just as well she didn't need anybody caring about her. Just as well that she was tough and independent. That independence had been missing for a while but now it was going to be back. Tonight would be fab, she told herself as she looked around her dingy front room

Her face was instantly lowered, and she rubbed it with the palms of her hands. What had she done? Judy was struck suddenly by a sense of gloom and dissatisfaction, and an unexpected sense of loneliness. She closed the door behind her.

She resisted the urge to cry out loud. Why was she feeling like this?

That night, Judy was determined to go out and have a few drinks or more, which she was sure would make her feel better and take her away from the doldrums. She ironed her favourite blouse and a pair of jeans that fitted her now after having been too small for the past seven months. Perhaps she would go to a local pub, The Crowing Rooster perhaps, or even into town, maybe catching up with old acquaintances. A few gins would make things look rosier.

The small hand of the clock went around repeatedly. She didn't go out. She eventually found herself sitting in the dark. The dull mood of the house in darkness seemed to suit the emptiness that now possessed and threatened her, as she mused over what had happened today and the horrible quietness around her.

She tried to play a record. She stopped it before it even reached the beginning of the singing. She couldn't remember ever having done that before.

Things had been difficult with a baby. Of course they had been. Still, why hadn't she tried harder? Why hadn't she responded to Angie when she had first pointed things out to her about Caroline's care and how she wasn't being looked after in the right way? She could have made more effort. Why had it seemed easier to just let Caroline, Sweet Caroline, vacate her life and leave her sitting in the dark like this, regretful and melancholy? How she missed that little baby girl right now.

What did she have? What had she ever had? She could have changed those nappies more often, could have spent more time caring for Caroline, so why hadn't she? Why hadn't she done more to stop them taking her baby away? She had handed over the baby like she was giving her away as a gift to strangers she neither knew nor cared about. She hadn't even received any money for it. There were too many questions and no clear answers. This was not the clear-cut situation she had seen it as. What might and should have been black and white was now a depressing dreary grey. Why wasn't she more positive? When she got over this, she would be left with that freedom and would be able to go out and do the things she liked to do, with nobody dependent upon her.

The problem was that this was hurting. The pain had more in common with acute appendicitis than indigestion. These were feelings she hadn't even imagined she had.

Judy found herself sitting in a chair, paralysed. Hour upon hour passed, during which the melancholy state did not pass. By midnight, she hadn't shifted from her chair once, not even for a cigarette, not even to turn the light on. There was no chance of sleep tonight, not even a nap.

She would have Caroline back. Destiny had brought Judy this child, this vulnerable beautiful infant, beyond all expectation and even beyond any anticipation. It was fated that she would have this child, even after saying goodbye to her twin. Judy wanted another chance.

Morning found her picking up the phone. "Hello, this is Judy Lawrence. I need to talk to Angie, Angie Donnelly."

There were hoops to go through. "Yes, I know I got it wrong, but like I said last week and the week before, I've learned from it all."

"We really hope you have, Judy. The psychiatric evaluation was positive and you've been pretty consistent in your meetings with us."

"I promise. Look into my eyes and you'll see I mean this. I promise I'll be good, no, not good, superb from now on. There won't be any more complaints."

"We do hope so, Judy. You do realise that if we have to take Caroline away again, it will be permanent."

Not long after, Caroline was back in the family home. Judy

had that strong sense of relief, a sense that they would never be separated again. It was a feeling that what had happened had happened out of carelessness and there would be no repeat. From now on, she would appreciate what she had. "Things are going to be very different now," she repeatedly and emotionally assured the social workers.

There was certainly one difference she was now going to make. She decided that a move was in order. If nothing else, this would stop these over-sensitive do-gooders snooping into her business and removing the baby again. She contacted a cousin in Derby and through him she was put in touch with the landlord of a property not dissimilar to her current place. "Two good-sized bedrooms and central heating," he boasted. Judy gathered her possessions and used some of the money she had acquired from the pregnancy to finance a change in location to Danvers Rise, five minutes away from the city centre.

Having paid three month's rent in advance, Judy found herself on a terraced street in the nearby city that was not dissimilar from the one she had left, which would be home for the two of them now, and probably would be for a long time. Well, at least until an incident involving the death of a brother and sister that would see them making a hasty change of location, but that was years away.

New house, same problems. Within three months, social services, like a benevolent predator, were in touch with her again, in spite of the supposed fresh start. A well-meaning neighbour saw to that. What followed was a sequence of events that recurred several times over the next three years. Derby Social Services developed a pretty large file pertaining to Judy Lawrence and her inadequacy as a mother, with Caroline's ongoing vulnerability, so they regularly visited.

It wasn't all unfavourable for Judy. A woman called Charmaine, in her second year in the job, developed an understanding of the young mother. "I know it's hard for you. You're on your own, bringing up a baby. It'd be hard for anyone." Never without a smile, she seemed to always be prepared to give the mother a chance to make up for lost time. In her mind, Judy should be that important presence in her baby's life and Charmaine sugar-coated life at Danvers Rise in her reports to her superiors. Of course, Charmaine's line manager accompanied her to the house on a couple of occasions. Some checking and monitoring had to be done. Charmaine made these moments easier for Judy by sometimes warning her of this in advance. She was keen to stop Judy becoming a victim of the authorities and did all she could. Sadly though, even she couldn't keep things sweet enough to stop Caroline being removed occasionally from this poor attempt at a home, but on each occasion, the separation was a temporary one.

Consequently, baby Caroline ultimately managed to grow and develop under the influence of the fallible Judy. The infant was able to show energy and personality in spite of the mothering she received rather than because of it. On each of the numerous occasions when she was taken from Judy, upon the immediate return of her baby, Judy would initially be the enthusiastic and caring mother she sought to be, affectionate and responsible. However, like a child herself, her attention would soon wander to other aspects of her existence on this planet. There were too many chores, too much patience required and too much effort for a woman like Judy.

As a teenager, Judy's mother, a chain-smoker who had died prematurely thanks to her habit, had described her daughter as a 'lazy bitch'. She had found it difficult to understand or tolerate the way Judy used to just sit around all day when she wasn't lying on her bed and despaired at how her daughter only found some energy when there was something going on at night. On those occasions, Judy would roll home drunk or stoned or both in the early hours of the morning and would be outraged at being slapped across the face by her irate mother. There was no father. There never had been. Judy never did chores. She never read a book, magazine or newspaper and seemed to be almost constantly daydreaming.

Judy was still that teenager.

Things changed for her, however, when Charmaine resigned her post after a couple more years of incompetence to avoid being dismissed.

There came a knocking on the door. "Let us in, Judy."

A slurring voice. "Why? I've done nothing wrong."

"Just let us in. We need to see Caroline."

She pressed her ravaged body against the door. "You don't need to see her. Caroline's fine."

On this particular occasion, the door was forced open, and Caroline was once more on her travels to a better place. However, there was a decisive external influence. This was Tory Britain in the bitter nineteen-eighties, and Margaret Thatcher, wishing to clip the wings of the local authorities, had cut social services to its very bones, to a point where every negligent parent had to be given additional extra chances, accompanied by unrealistic ineffective encouragement. Hence, Caroline found herself once again welcomed back to her mother's home in the hope that intentions to improve could be sustained.

There were some vivid moments. Or, rather, unfortunate anecdotes. One dark miserable night, perhaps two or three weeks after the fifth parent-child reconciliation, the back door was noisily unlocked and opened, and in fell Judy with her hand holding onto the hand of a drinking buddy who had struck lucky it seemed, looming behind her with drunken hope and amorous expectation, as well as glazed eyes. They kissed passionately in Judy's kitchen, an appetiser for the main course that was inevitably going to follow, whether in the living room or the bedroom. Abruptly, she had broken off and pulled her face from his. "I just have to check on the child."

"Child? What child?"

"My Caroline. My Sweet Caroline. She's asleep upstairs." Judy made her face smile, made herself seem capable as well as accommodating.

A twitch of sobriety occurred. "Fucking what? Where's the babysitter?"

"Oh, I'm a bit naughty. I can't afford a babysitter."

"How old?"

She looked into his eyes, fearing disappointment. "You know how it is. She's very safe."

"How old is she?"

"Two. She's pretty strong."

Drunken horror had the same intensity as sober horror. Judy hadn't had much hope where men were concerned but this one was going to be another hopeless endeavour. "That's fucking crazy. I'm out of here."

There might have been no sex that night, but on other evenings like this the ending was happier. Other male suitors weren't quite so discerning. Judy would entertain the man of the evening with Caroline either asleep in her cot or stood up and looking on, no doubt wondering what her mother was actually doing.

In her pre-school and early school times, she perhaps was not learning much from her mother's carnal ways. What was happening here? Why did they make those strange noises? Why had that man hit Mummy and made her cry? Why did that other man say such nasty things to her? A variety of confusing thoughts and questions were running through the infant's head, foreshadowing the questions and answers of her later life.

CHILDHOOD WOES

Caroline, now five years old, in the denim blue dungarees that she wore most days, and this morning with a red t-shirt underneath, was enjoying sitting in one of the downstairs rooms, playing with her plastic bricks, every now and then wiping her hair from her eyes so that she could see more clearly. She was building a house. It would be a happy house, she had decided, full of happy smiling people. As she sat on the chair at the dining table, next to the window, she had a positive, hopeful expression on her face as she tried to create a colourful plastic building to match the mood and personality of the people who would live in it. The house would be a fair mixture of green, yellow and red, providing the yellow bricks didn't run out.

Unfortunately, even in this pursuit there was a harshness. The good colours always ran out. Yellow was so good, like the sun, sand and custard, all things that everybody loved and yearned for, so why didn't whoever made these bricks make more of them in that colour? Instead, Caroline was always left with the dull red bricks, dreary blocks of plastic that sapped much of the fun out of it all. Nevertheless, she persisted, determined to build. As she worked from base to rooftop, she would periodically look out of the window and notice things.

Caroline's early childhood, like those of every other youngster, was about seeing things and responding. She was normal and liked to learn things. As a young child she loved looking out of windows, watching the world go by. She especially liked to peer out through the large living room bay window, facing onto the parked cars, the road and all of the happenings out there at the beginning of the outside world. She had many questions about the world, even though she had seen so little of it.

On this particular morning, a Saturday in July, with the sun beaming down benevolently from the heavens, Caroline was in a mood for talking, especially since her mummy was sitting on the settee in the living room behind her, which was a wonderful but rare occurrence.

"Mummy. Sally's going to the seaside. She's got a bucket and a spade. Can we go somewhere?"

Judy, slouching on the sofa, was immersed in a word search. She didn't look up from the puzzle. "We don't need to go anywhere. Everything we need is here."

"She had a big yellow spade, though, and a red bucket. She said she's going to make a sandcastle."

Judy found the word 'supernatural' and circled it. "We're fine here. It's a nice sunny day. You can play with your toys in the yard."

"But the sea isn't here. Can't we go and see the sea sometime?"

Judy just needed to find the word 'magic' to complete the puzzle. "No. We don't need to see the sea. There's nothing special about the sea, Caroline."

"Oh, but I want to see the sea. I've never been there. Sally's going to build a sandcastle and she said she'll come back with a cup with a picture of the beach on it."

Judy couldn't find 'magic'. Just like so many times before, she felt compelled to raise her head to her daughter and breathe some fire. "We don't need to see the fucking beach! Now stop bothering me or I'll throw that Lego in the bin." Her voice had suddenly become shrill and her face was contorted hideously as she pointed at her daughter's brick house. "In fact, come away from that window. Go and play in your room. Best thing for you, if you want to avoid a smack." From a red and white packet she took a cigarette and lit it with the same impatience.

Of course, Caroline complied. When Mummy told her to do something, Caroline knew from so many times before that that was the thing she had to do. It always seemed to upset Mummy when she talked about other children, and Mummy's temper was scary. When Mummy smacked her, it felt like she wanted to really hurt her and Caroline became terrified, wanting it to end. She would shout and scream, "Stop it, Mummy. Please stop it" but Mummy would carry on and Caroline's legs would be red and they would hurt. They would hurt for hours after. Once they had hurt so much that she'd had to go to hospital. The people there had asked horrid questions and she'd had to tell them that she had fallen down the stairs. That had been the worst time ever. Her mummy had been so upset and frightened. She never liked her mummy being upset and frightened.

It was best for Caroline that she didn't go on too much about the other children today. And she didn't feel like building the happy house anymore. Instead, she began to take apart her toy architecture with a grim expression on her face. As she destroyed her near-creation, she deposited the bricks in the box, making sure every brick went in. Her mummy wouldn't be angry about her toys today, that was for sure.

On most days, things weren't like this. Caroline had become used to having the front downstairs room to herself. Mummy would usually sit in the back room, or in the kitchen, smoking or drinking, with the radio on. Caroline liked being at home with her three main toys, a maze, bricks and a wooden bagatelle that one of Mummy's friends had picked up at a place he called the dump, and she liked the fact that nobody, not even her mother, bothered her when she was in the front room. Here, she could be in her own world and she wouldn't cause Mummy to have to do some shouting, smacking and those horrible hard words. Well, at least most of the time.

Caroline was forming. She knew things. She knew that things weren't quite right for her or her mother. Mummy made sure she knew. "I'm sick of this rotten life. I'm sick of it. I'm sick of you. How I wish you'd never been born. I could have done something about it. I wish I had."

She sensed that Mummy was never happy, but was angry and impatient too many times. She shouted a lot, much more than other mummies. Caroline would sit and wonder why but never could understand it. She only knew that things were not nice for her when her mother was angry. That was always a good time for her to be in either the front room or in her bedroom with the door closed.

Caroline was sad that her life wasn't like that of other boys and girls. Their parents seemed happier than her mummy was. and they gave their children nice clothes, presents and birthday parties and they would have a Christmas tree. She spent time on many days trying to understand why things weren't the same here as they were for everybody else on this street and in her class. Why didn't she and Mummy have the things that others seemed to enjoy?

She wasn't always melancholy, though. After moping around, Caroline would become hardened and angry. She began to have thoughts that weren't nice, thoughts like her mummy had, and she got used to wanting things she couldn't have, wishing she could take things from those happier children on this street and everywhere else. Sometimes she didn't feel like being nice to those happier children and would have liked to make them less happy, make them more like she was.

Of course, in time the pressures on Caroline could not be comfortably contained. They would carry consequences. As she approached her seventh birthday, the misery and awkwardness she often displayed in her primary school years didn't go unnoticed. School was always going to be an awkward fit for a pupil like her. Different and alone were qualities that would always attract attention. Yet, she never missed school. Judy was keen that Caroline be at school on every day it was open. "Thank God you're in school," she would say. "You'd drive me crazy if I had to put up with your gibberish."

So it was the turn of the teachers to look after Caroline. These professionals, alongside the lunch-time supervisors and the parents of other children, were bound to express concerned opinions, even experienced teachers who had seen a lot of bad stuff in their charges.

"What is wrong with that child?" Jo Cooper, a young teacher, asked, one day during lunchtime duty.

"There's not too much right with Caroline. Strange one, she is. Arrived here a year ago and she's made, shall we say, a strong impression."

"I've been watching her for the past ten minutes. Really odd."

"Started school late. Likes her own company." Mrs Lacey was an expert on Caroline, had even written an analysis of her personality for her master's degree.

"Something's definitely not right with her. Anybody and everybody can see that. What's she like in lessons?"

"She's like an island. As far as communication goes, nothing goes in and nothing goes out. Doesn't want to talk to anybody most of the time. A classroom full of Carolines would be a silent classroom."

"That's not healthy."

"No. She's a textbook abuse case, if you ask me. Although she's not that, apparently. The head has already had that conversation with Social Services."

"The other kids don't like her."

"No. She alienates them." Mrs Lacey almost sounded like this was a normal effect for a young child to be having on her peers.

"Have you noticed how they steer clear of her? She ate her dinner today all on her own."

"They pretend she's not there. It's the same in lessons, even group work. Paired work doesn't work with her either."

"She seems content to just sit on her own."

"She's the same in some of the subjects, less so in others. She likes reading and art. In Maths and Science she seems to switch between bouts of looking totally vacant, like she's not aware of anything around her, to being totally aware. It's like she suddenly sees and understands everything. Not in a nice way, either. More like a predator."

"That sounds sinister."

"I know that. Sometimes I'm afraid. Those darting eyes of hers don't help. We need to keep an eye on her."

"And she stares at the others sometimes."

"Yep. She does that too."

"Do you think she needs to see the educational psychologist?" Jo was getting the bit between her teeth now.

"Probably. What's going on with her has to be a case of deep psychological and social issues. There's something really bad. She's utterly damaged."

"Abuse, neglect?"

"Who knows?"

"Why don't you talk to the head about arranging something with the ed psych, then?"

"We can't do that. Home's not very supportive, I'm afraid. Judy doesn't agree much when it comes to school. I know for a fact she won't agree to anything psychological."

"What's she like, her mum?"

"A strange woman. Doesn't reply to letters or messages. Loses her temper easily. She's been up here shouting the odds on a couple of occasions."

"I overheard one of the other parents talking about her. Said she did drugs."

"Possibly she does, although I've not heard that much, to be honest. Caroline wrote a piece of creative writing a few weeks ago where somebody was drunk. She described a woman who kept falling down. I'm willing to bet Judy Lawrence drinks heavily, at any rate."

"Poor little thing. Does that mean she has to suffer so much here though? Can something be done to get around the mother problem?"

"There's not much we can do. Social Services need a lot more before they'll even consider doing anything."

"It's not good though, is it? Shouldn't this place be a refuge for the children and help them as much as possible?" Jo's Christian upbringing was coming out clear and strong now.

"It ought to be. Parents have loads of rights nowadays and that seems to be the priority under this government."

"Well, maybe we could do something to help her. Perhaps get the other kids to include her more."

"They might feel sorry for her if it wasn't for the other stuff. As it is, it might just invite bullying."

"The other stuff?" Jo Cooper turned her head in curiosity.

"The stealing. That Jenny Hawthorne business. Not only that. Catherine Parker said she stole money from her too. Children don't like it when there's a thief amongst them."

"Would they forgive her?"

"I don't know, to be honest."

"It's not good. Do you think it might help, us talking to her?"

"I don't know. I've worked with a thousand children. I've seen some right cases of neglect and suffering, some really upsetting. But I'll tell you this. Caroline Lawrence is the most miserable-looking child I have ever seen. I bet you've not seen her smile."

The younger teacher thought about it then shook her head. "No. Come to think of it, I haven't."

"Caroline never smiles. In fifteen years of doing this, I have never known a child so quiet and who gives such a strong impression of needing something. She speaks when she has to. She actually expresses herself well. She's not stupid but she never volunteers anything. She just stares most of the time. A serious daydreamer. She needs something, but who knows what?"

"And what do you think's wrong? To me it's as if she's disturbed. That mother of hers has done some real damage, whatever Social Services say."

Anne Lacey smiled and held up her finger. "You've given me an idea. We could try to help her in a different way?"

"How do you mean?"

"I wouldn't do this on my own, because I don't believe it would work. But what about if we both sat with her? We could let her unpack her thoughts, get her to open up about what upsets her and makes her so miserable. She'd put up her usual wall if it was just me, but if we both try to get through to her, well, who knows?"

"When?"

"Could do it in the second half of lunch-time. Tomorrow?"

"Amateur psychology? Can we do that?"

"Yes, why not? We might even get to the bottom of the stealing."

Both women considered the idea.

Jo Cooper broke the pause. "I suppose so, if you think it might achieve something. I don't think we could do any harm. She does cut a very sad figure."

"She needs to be a part of the community."

Caroline sat at the table, blank-faced with a horizontal mouth and a head full of bewilderment. She had been asked to be in the room with Mrs Lacey and Miss Cooper and she didn't know why. She wondered if there was something wrong that she had done that they knew about. She was always careful when doing things they didn't like so it didn't seem likely or even possible.

She hated Mrs Lacey, her class teacher. She couldn't wait to be leaving her dreadful boring lessons in the summer, when she wouldn't have to hear that horrible voice and her stupid words. Worst of all, she was horribly nice to the rich kids and that made Caroline angry. She didn't really know Miss Cooper, the younger one, although she had noticed her looking at her in the dining room on a couple of occasions.

There was nothing she was going to tell them. The only reaction that was going to happen was that she would sit there enjoying the silence, while they could drink from their coffee cups.

Caroline hated coffee. The smell reminded her of her mother's dark moods on gloomy mornings. In actual fact, she didn't like most adult things, but that was something she should always keep to herself and on this occasion she would just sit there and say nothing.

"Anyway, Caroline, we thought it might be nice if we had a chat." Both women were smiling.

Caroline said nothing. She just looked at them. Her eyes slowly switched from left to right, from left to right, from left to right. To her they were just like pages of writing and pictures in the books she read, there to be read.

"We want you to enjoy your time in school."

Caroline uttered no words, keeping her eyes focused on the two adults. She was suspicious and didn't like this situation one bit, but she still had to be polite. She wasn't going to be accused of being rude because that might get her a phone call home. Her mother would be angry with her if there was a phone call home. She never reacted well to any contact from school and had even shouted at her when she had brought home a letter about a school trip.

Caroline just looked at these two adults, but they were talking and looking at her as if they pitied her. She hated that.

"Is there anything we can do to help you to enjoy it more?"

Caroline sat and thought for some seconds, but that was all she did. Her lips were still.

"Which lessons do you enjoy, Caroline?" Miss Cooper asked.

She looked at Mrs Lacey. The old witch knew which lessons she enjoyed. She had put gold stars on her book almost every week in the reading lessons, as well as repeatedly telling her that her painting was divine. Caroline didn't know what divine meant, but she knew it was something good. At this point she was able to reply. "I like drawing and painting, miss."

"Is that all?"

"I do like playing the recorder."

"And you do like reading, Caroline," said Mrs Lacey.

Caroline thought about it before speaking. "Yes. Reading's good. Well, some books, anyway."

"What books do you like?"

"Books about ghosts and monsters. Oh, and disasters."

"And do you talk to the other children about this?"

"Not about reading. I talk to Joey Mazma about my drawing and paintings. Shabina likes my music."

Anne Lacey looked at Jo then back at the child in front of her. "But Joey can't understand English?"

"I know."

Miss Cooper was bewildered. "But you don't spend any time with Joey at breaks and lunchtimes. You don't spend any time with Shabina, either."

No reply.

"Why not?"

Caroline, whose head was bowed, paused, pursed her lips and looked up at the teachers. "Because he doesn't speak English, and she doesn't like England."

Mrs Lacey became concerned. "I didn't know that. Has Shabina said she doesn't like England?"

"No. I just know she doesn't."

"How do you know that, Caroline?"

"My mummy says. She says that Shabina and people like her hate our country."

The wind suddenly flared up outside the classroom as the two adults considered how not to respond.

"What would make you happier in school, Caroline?"

"Nothing, miss."

Miss Lacey changed the tone of the conversation. "And why did you steal?"

Caroline opted for silence.

"Why did you steal from Jenny?"

Caroline remained silent.

"And did you steal from Catherine?"

"No, miss. Just Jenny. The one you know about."

"So why did Catherine say you stole from her? Other children said you did too. "

"They want to cause trouble for me. They always want to cause trouble."

Miss Cooper was becoming frustrated. Perhaps this hadn't

been a good idea, after all. "OK, then, why did you steal money from Jenny Hawthorne?"

"I don't know, miss. I just wanted to."

"Why did you want to do that?"

"You need to tell us this, Caroline, so we can help you."

Caroline kept her lips still.

"You know that it makes the other children dislike you, don't you?"

Caroline sat like a statue, as if she wanted to display a strange still defiance. After that defiance had made its point, Caroline decided to speak. "Can I go now, miss? I need the toilet." Without waiting for permission, Caroline got up and walked towards the door. She turned. Her eyes were sharply focused on both adults. "There's one thing you can do to make things better for me."

"What's that, Caroline?" Both women were smiling.

"Have a word with Sam Newton and Catherine. Tell them if they say nasty things to me again about me or my mother, I am going to hurt them. Hurt them a lot. Please tell them that, miss."

Without waiting for a reply, Caroline left the room.

The two teachers, maintaining a pregnant silence till the door closed behind the pupil, didn't even look at each other. As the door closed, Mars Lacey said, sarcastically, "Well, that went well. She actually answered some questions."

* * *

Her steps loud and frantic, Caroline was running. She had no choice. Trouble was happening so she had to move quickly. They were going to hit her, kick her and do whatever else they felt like doing to her. She knew she was in danger. This had happened before. The last two times, she had managed to get away and get home, but before that they had caught her, and she had banged her head on the pavement and had been punched.

They were angrier this time. They said she was a thief. They said she had done nasty things. Each one of the children chasing her was fuelled by a cause. Adam Porter had had his dinner money taken from his desk. Somebody had lifted his desk lid and taken it around the same time that Caroline had gone missing from the rounders game in the playground. Two days before this, Sally Chase had had her jumper ruined. Somebody had pulled the acrylic fibres apart, leaving a gaping hole, and that somebody had to be Caroline. In all fairness, Caroline had not meant to wreck the jumper. She had just wanted to work out how it was made, but nobody would ever know that or even care.

Adding to the fury of the group, last week, pages had been ripped out of Catherine's book about Greek myths. On this occasion, Caroline had wanted to trace that picture, so why was there so much trouble? David O'Sullivan and Toni Travis had lost their Maths exercise books. They had no proof that this was anything to do with Caroline, but they still kept saying it was her.

Desperately looking left then right, Caroline took a sharp turn. The trees were a help as they would block them seeing her as she desperately ran. She took shelter behind one and hoped that the threat would end. She just stood there listening, waiting for the sound of them passing. She wasn't frightened. This was exciting. If she reached home intact, that would be a great victory.

For a tense series of minutes, Caroline was sitting there breathing heavily and listening. It was either stay where she was, vulnerable but unseen, or set off running, hopefully breaking free of the chase and reaching the safety of her back door. She stayed down, thinking. After some initial hesitation, she decided to head for home, so she bolted from the cover of the foliage and continued her journey.

Bad decision. She was rumbled, finding herself on a path with angry classmates in front of her and behind. They now faced her from two directions, so there was no getting away. It was time to be tough.

The pursuers had sensed that their prey was at their mercy. Now, with loud shouts and aggressive noises, they closed in. She heard Adam Porter yell, "Let's get her." They ran towards her.

She just stood there. They swarmed. She just stood and stared. Caroline found herself pushed down onto on the ground, banging the back of her head again in the process. It hurt, but she wasn't going to show them how much it hurt.

She was now easy pickings. She endured a series of feet digging sharply into her and she felt aggressive punches to her body and head as the aggrieved children took their revenge. Caroline took it all. She uttered no sound.

At the end of it all, when the angry ones had seemingly as one all decided that enough was enough, she was left lying on the hard ground, aching and hating. She was used to the hating. There was plenty of time for her to do some hating back. She began to laugh loudly. It was better than feeling like a victim. She was not going to cry. They would never ever make her cry.

Two weeks later, it was show and tell. Caroline hadn't brought anything for it. There was nothing she wanted to show to anybody here and she preferred keeping things to herself rather than telling.

"Catherine," Mrs Lacey called out. "Don't you have anything to show us today?"

Catherine Parker walked to the front of the class with some books in her hand and started talking about her photograph collection.

Caroline wasn't listening. As if she would ever listen to a girl like this. However, she had already become good at appearing to be interested, and was wide-eyed, as if this spoilt little idiot at the front was delivering something that wasn't repulsive and monotonous.

"And that's all about my photographs," Catherine concluded.

"Fantastic, Catherine. Adam Porter. What have you got for us today?"

Adam smiled broadly and leaned over to reach into his schoolbag. Then he gave an anxious shriek and started to cry without any clear explanation. Mrs Lacey, showing genuine motherly concern, hurried over to him. He had pulled out a book, a book that was obviously old, but which, equally obviously, was covered in yellow paint.

"Oh, Adam. What have you done?"

Adam could barely get his words out. His eyes were watering. "It's my grandad's best book. He's gonna be proper angry. I told him I'd look after it."

"Did you have yellow paint from our art lesson in your bag?"

"No, Miss."

"You must have. And now it's spilled out?"

Adam shook his head. He now began crying profusely. In truth, he had no idea what had caused the ruination of his grandfather's best book. He only knew that this was a terrible moment in his life.

Caroline, two desks in front of him, didn't turn her head. She just sat there, staring ahead.

* * *

"Ah, he's cute, the old woman said, looking down into the box that Caroline had on her lap. There was a gap between the flaps of cardboard. Through this space could be seen a small tabby cat, which was purring loudly, audibly wanting to be free and roaming. That would happen soon.

Caroline look out through the bus window. Just two more stops. She watched as other people left the bus, and uttered calm coaxing words into the box to reassure the little tabby that this was a good thing.

She left the bus and walked towards the park that she could see ahead of her. This place would do.

There were only two facts that mattered today. Sally Chase had kicked her in the stomach when she was lying on the ground. This was her cat. She had heard Sally talking about this little beast like it was the best creature in the world, so it had become important to Caroline that she did something appropriate. It was dark, so nobody would see. She walked across the park, a little girl who should have been vulnerable at this time of day in a strange place, but who wasn't quite that.

She carefully threaded the cord through the cat's collar, all the time stroking it and making soft soothing sounds. She would fulfil her aim that Sally would never see this creature again. After spending so many hours waiting around to catch this little tyke, she was now going to do what she had planned for the past two weeks.

As she walked away, she listened to the high-pitched sounds of distress from the little creature and it sounded like such nice music. It was the sound of her getting her own back on someone who didn't deserve anything good. Perhaps somebody nice would end up with this little cat. Just as long as it wasn't Sally.

* * *

A month on from the chase, George Swanwick's face was a mess already. Tom Newton was now on top of him and his fists were pounding away at the younger boy's face. George couldn't do much to defend himself against this almost mechanical battering and he would have been hurt even more if the headteacher, a stern man called Mr Fraser, hadn't pulled the older boy away.

With that quality of seriousness on his face that is the essence of any teacher, he had hold of both boys by the arms and said loudly, "Right you two. My office, now."

In his office, George was sobbing and holding his face. The older boy was trying hard not to cry. He was the older boy, after all.

The head took charge. "OK, Tom. Why were you fighting?"

Tom said nothing. He preferred to keep his reasons to himself because the trouble would be the same whether he told all or not, and he didn't like this man anyway.

"I'll ring your dad and get him here. I bet you'll tell me then."

Tom looked up. He didn't want his dad here. That would be even more trouble at home. There was a pause, an impasse that had to end in Tom changing his standpoint. He gestured towards George with his left hand. "He said things."

"What things?"

"Things about my mum. Horrible things. He said she was a slag who went with loads of men."

George looked up. With tears still running down his face, he said, "I didn't, sir. I never said anything about his mum."

Fraser looked at Tom Newton. "And how do you know he said this? How do you know he said things about her?"

"I just heard he did."

Fraser became red-faced. "That's not good enough, Tom. You can't go off attacking kids because of hearsay. I'll ask you again. How did you hear this?"

At this point he decided to lie. He had sworn on his mother's life that he would never tell anybody that she had given him this information. The way the quiet girl in the year below had cried about the horrible things that had been said had convinced him that this was true, so he knew he was right to beat this kid up. She had even been so upset herself because she knew it was a terrible thing to say about somebody's mum.

This George kid would never say anything about his mum again, that was for sure.

Caroline had kept her half-smile in full force throughout the beating and for a while afterwards. It made up for the fact that George had pulled her hair while the other kids had kicked and punched her. It might even mean that he wouldn't call her names quite as much in future.

* * *

David O'Sullivan wasn't enjoying walking home that day. All the kids behind him were calling him names and laughing. He didn't like being treated like that, especially since he was on his own, his friends having caught the bus ahead of him.

A few weeks ago, it had been his idea that they all get Caroline the thief, Caroline the horrid, Caroline the weird. On that particular afternoon, he had really enjoyed shouting loudly into Caroline's ear as the other kids kicked and punched her, wanting to make her deaf with the intense abuse that he felt she more than deserved. That was OK. He, on the other hand, wasn't used to being laughed at or called names.

He carried on walking uncomfortably. The kids giving him this treatment were from the secondary school so there wasn't much he could do about it anyway.

As he reached his front door, a girl in a hood was standing across the road, a girl whose face was hidden. She shouted in an exaggerated high-pitched voice, "What do you want to write that on your coat for, gay-boy?"

Puzzled, David opened the door and went in. It was when he took his coat off that he noticed. The words 'I'm Gay' were emblazoned on the back of the coat in what seemed to be white paint.

The coat had been an expensive Christmas present. His mother would be furious.

BONDING

"When do you think the weather will change? I want to go outside."

"Sssh. I'm trying to watch this."

The predictable April rain came down, giving no respite from what had been a harsh winter. The accumulation of water created fast-flowing rivulets that rolled down the gentle gradients of the gutters that lined the roads, on which, canoe-like, floated the discarded wrappers and lollipop sticks that were the staples of every childhood. Thank God the summer was coming.

Judy and nine-year-old Caroline were having a rare tender moment watching television. Judy was sitting on the settee with a cigarette creating a warm glow in the room and had a green glass ashtray at her side, whilst Caroline was sitting on the floor with her back between her mother's legs. Well, at least Judy was enjoying it. Holiday programmes were right up her street, giving her reasons to imagine what might have been and what still might be if she got a lucky break soon. She would work on that one. She just had to get rid of this lead weight between her legs.

For Caroline, a holiday was a fantasy, something she had never experienced. The Mediterranean was no more part of reality for her than Narnia. She had read a book about Narnia that she had borrowed from the school library. She had enjoyed the death of Aslan the lion so much that she had re-read that chapter, as well as loving those moments when characters had been turned to stone. She wondered what it would be like to have power like that. The power to hurt, to really hurt. She could use power like that on people who threatened her or her mother and could use it to get what she wanted. She imagined, as she projected her own moving image inside her mind, that having that kind of strength was much more entertaining than anything on the screen in front of her, turning shop people to stone so she could have a new bike. You wouldn't have to pay for anything. The thought brought a half-smile to her face.

Caroline's daydreams were not related to the programme, which was typical, since she had little interest in most of what she saw and so it generally failed to hold her attention. She had never had a holiday, had never seen a beach and was developing resentful feelings towards people who had. Caroline liked to daydream about fearful things. In her mind she liked to create incredible stories, usually catastrophes or tragedies, often involving monsters and supernatural stuff. A few days ago she had enjoyed a wonderful moment where she had stuck the magic sword into a dragon's throat and watched the reptile's blood form a mini lake on the ground whilst she slaughtered the damsel to make the story's ending different and exciting. This morning she had enjoyed a moment of victory where a murderous man had been chasing her and she had got the upper hand. She had dug a hole and dropped him down it, never to be heard of again.

While sitting with Judy, she had been imagining a 'Home Alone' moment, a film she had seen seventeen times. In this moment, the intruder had been impaled on a spike and stabbed in the eye to make sure. Caroline wondered whether a spike merely had to enter the brain to kill a person or if it would need to go right through. She had become lost as the adventure had progressed. Three more intruders had turned up and had grabbed her mother and were holding her prisoner in Judy's bedroom, but Caroline had killed each one of them with a lightsaber and had been able to rescue her mother from her predicament. She would relive this one several times over the next few days. Her mother had been so grateful and nice, just like she was in real life occasionally, such as on the days when she cashed her giro cheque at the post office.

There was a real-life intruder approaching. Caroline felt a disturbance as, suddenly, Judy stretched her neck to see who was coming up the path. She immediately recognized the son of the woman who lived next door. Mrs Newton was in her seventies, a bit doddery, and for some reason the two women had not hit it off. Judy had only said a brief hello to her a couple of times in all the time since they had moved in.

Her son was different, however. Something of a dish, Judy felt.

She stood up, disturbing her daughter's composure and that all too rare sense of security. That same daughter had moved on from rescuing her mother. She was now sitting on a massive black throne, exercising her right to control the other girls in her class, who in turn were declaring undying loyalty to Caroline. She was sending them each on deadly missions, from which none would return. Caroline had read about Attila the Hun in a book she had borrowed from the school library, and imagined what it would be like to be able to command people like he did.

Judy smoothed her dress down and grabbed a hairbrush from the dining table. She hurriedly dragged it through her hair before she opened the door. The man was standing there looking like somebody had shot his dog.

Judy pulled her shoulders back to emphasise her breasts as she spoke. She would have worn a tighter blouse if she'd known. "Hi there."

He displayed a smile that was only momentary. Clearly, he hadn't come to ask her out on a date. "I'm sorry to bother you, but I've come about your daughter."

"Caroline? Why?" Why the fuck would he be interested in her? Judy's smile left her face.

"The thing is, yesterday, my mother had her purse stolen. It was in her handbag in the kitchen. I wouldn't have normally been here about that. It's just that a guy across the road says he saw your daughter walk up my mother's path."

"So what?"

"It just seems like a bad coincidence. In fact, it's too much of a coincidence."

"I see." Judy relaxed her shoulders and sighed as she spoke. "You calling my daughter a thief?"

"No. I don't want to do that. Listen. I just want the money back. I don't want to involve the police or anything."

Judy turned her head and yelled into the void behind her. "Caroline! Will you come here please."

"Kids do some daft things. I know I did," he said.

Caroline looked up curiously at this sombre-looking stranger. He looked down at her and clearly mellowed. Perhaps he thought that she was vulnerable and soft, especially as she had her pyjamas on, with those pink rabbits and white lambs.

"Caroline, have you stolen a purse from Mrs Newton, next door?"

Caroline looked up at her mother, switched her attention to the accuser, then back to Judy. She shook her head then bowed it.

The man breathed audibly. Then he thought of his old mother and his expression hardened. "Well, why were you heading up my mother's path, at about the same time as the purse was stolen?"

When she didn't answer, Judy looked down sharply at Caroline. "Well, you heard the man. Why were you going up Mrs Newton's path?"

Caroline looked up at the man and spoke in weak hesitant voice. "I saw a rabbit."

"A rabbit?" Two voices at the same time. Who was most disbelieving?

"I wanted to stroke it."

Judy pushed her daughter aside, appearing gentle. "She's like that. She just loves animals. Especially rabbits. Always has. She wouldn't steal from your mother. Not in a million years."

"Well, the purse went missing at the same time. It's a bit suspicious."

"There's been some teenagers hanging around a lot, you know. They're always at the bottom of this street. It's bound to be something to do with them. Would you like a coffee?" At this point, Judy brought back her most welcoming smile. There might still be a chance.

"No, I don't think so. I want to find out what happened to my mum's money. She's a pensioner. She can't afford this kind of loss."

"I know," Judy said. "Some people are so horrible. I bet it was those teenagers, you know. They were hanging around the shops. They have a horrible look about them. One of them looked like he was on drugs the other day. I bet he's got something to do with it."

The man was unconvinced but, whatever was going on in his mind, he was forced to admit that he wasn't going to get anywhere on this doorstep.

Judy watched, slowly closing the door as the man walked back the way he had come. Straight away, she followed Caroline into the front room and turned off the television set. The Costa Brava beach vanished. "OK. Where is it?"

Caroline didn't reply.

Judy lowered herself to her daughter's level and put her hands on her shoulders. "Where have you put that purse?"

Caroline stayed silent.

"I'll ask you one more time. Where have you put that fucking purse? Tell me, or there is going to be serious bastard mayhem. D'you want me to run after him?" She gestured outside with a movement of her head. "Tell him you've taken it?" At this point, Judy had that menacing scowl of hers that showed her resolve.

Caroline raised her head and looked into her mother's eyes. "It's in the garden. I put it in the back of the shed."

Judy's expression changed. "Smart thinking." She left her daughter and went out through the back door. Within a minute she was back. "We have to leave it there for a few days, then we can do some spending."

"Was it bad what I did?"

"It was bad and good. I'll get you some sweets."

Caroline looked at her mother, gave a half-smile, and nodded in agreement.

* * *

Sharon, Judy's cousin, was about five years older and well-worn in face and body. She had caught a train from Alfreton to spend the afternoon in Derby, making it a kind of adventure. Since this was one of the rare periods of time where she and Judy were friends, she had taken the effort to catch up. No doubt they would fall out again soon, probably for some stupid reason or from some misplaced jealousy. For now, things were harmonious.

"It's easy."

"It's not that easy. My George gets caught every time. He's on first name terms with the store detectives at Asda and Morrison's." Sharon was wearing the same tired maroon jumper she seemed to wear every time she visited, on this occasion with hideous grey jogging bottoms that made little contact with her arse and legs. Somebody should have advised her to steal some new clothes for the journey to Judy's.

Judy laughed scornfully. "Well, he would be. He's a fucking idiot."

"Hey, not so insulting if you don't mind. That's my fella you're calling names."

"Yeah, I know. He's your fella all right. The same fella who beat you black and blue last year for going out without him. A real good guy."

"Well, you'd know all about that. You've had your share."

"I know. I never said I was any better at pickin' 'em."

"So how is it easy then?"

"It's not. They come over all smooth and we fall for it."

"I didn't mean that. I meant the shopping."

"It's dead easy, like shooting fish in a barrel."

"OK. Don't be coy. How?"

"Well, it's a piece of piss when you've got a glamorous assistant. Well, an assistant of some kind."

"Who? You gone into partnership?"

"No, daft lass. It's Caroline."

"Caroline?" Her face was a mask of incredulity. "The little one? She helps you nick?"

"Too right she does. A vital part of the operation."

"How? Does she distract them?"

"Not quite. She wears that black coat hung up over there. Go and have a look at it."

With a heaving sigh, Sharon dragged her tired body, on the

wrong side of comfortable by three stones, over to the black woollen coat hanging on top of the door. She pulled it down and held it in front of her, studying it. "OK, what's special about it?"

"Try the inside."

Sharon turned the garment around and surveyed the lining. "Christ. The pockets are massive. Have you done that?"

"Of course. With my own fair hands. I put some real effort into it. It's Caroline's nicking coat."

"So she does the lifting, then?"

"Yep. She seems to think everything's free." She cackled. "She's dead good at nicking. Dead sly. Like a magician. I distract the assistant and she does the taking."

"And you get away with it?"

"Every time. Do you know what? Think I've given birth to a master criminal."

* * *

"I don't know why you've dragged me in here. I've done nothing wrong." She looked at them like they were two thugs she had caught putting graffiti on her house.

The two men were very serious. One was wearing a suit, with a plastic badge with the words 'Store Manager' on it, with some other writing at the bottom that was difficult to read. The other man was in double denim with a jumper, looking so much like an ordinary member of the public, which was how he made his living. "We think you do. We want your child to show us the contents of her coat."

"What the fuck do you want with her? Are you fucking perverts or something?"

"Miss Lawrence, if that's your real name, your daughter has been stealing meat from our shelves."

"That's it. We're leaving. We've stolen nothing."

The denim-clad man positioned himself in front of the door. There was going to be no escape.

Judy sighed. In her mind she was accepting that this meant more trouble coming her way. There would be an appearance in court. This would be another fine she wouldn't be able to pay.

At that moment there was a high-pitched noise coming from beside her that took Judy by surprise. Caroline was crying. The whine went on and became an utterance. The child looked up at the store manager. "Mummy has no money. I'm very hungry. I only took this meat so that I wasn't hungry anymore. Mummy gives me her food. The meat I've taken means she won't die from not eating." She began crying more loudly as she uttered the last word. The couple of sentences she spoke after that were almost indecipherable, each syllable being suffocated by the child's intense emotion and the all too obvious pressure this family was under.

The two men looked at each other. Then they both simultaneously looked at Judy, who had immediately adjusted her demeanour to one of impending tragedy and the previous position of defiance had faded.

Of course, it was this beautiful sad child who had the most significant impact.

The manager looked at his colleague. "OK. Consider this a warning. I'm letting you leave. Just empty your coat pockets so that you're not leaving with any of our stock."

Caroline did as instructed, intermittently wiping the tears from her face to maintain the emotional effect. Judy's mouth tightened and she groaned inside. It was a lot of meat being placed on the table by her daughter's tiny hands. There must have been a week of meals. She winced as a large steak was placed on the desk but tried to appear shocked at discovering this. "Oh, Caroline."

"Is that everything?"

Caroline nodded.

The manager looked at Judy and gestured to the store detective to open the door for them. "I'm warning you, though. Next time you come here, it'll be a police matter."

Judy held her daughter's hand as they left ASDA. She maintained the pretence of them being a vulnerable family with hearts of gold. As soon as they were in the car park, Judy looked at Caroline with real censure in her face.

"How did that happen? Are you getting careless on me?"

Caroline didn't reply, but in her mind she was working out why they had been caught.

She wouldn't have long to work it out.

"Let's go to Tesco. Their chicken's better anyway."

DATE NIGHT

So many years on, it's Friday night. There's that start-of-the-weekend buzz in the air. The mood around is full of positivity and vigour, and for many people, memories are about to be made. There's a real energy aboard the buses and taxis, carrying people to the city centre and the opportunities it affords for enthusiastic socializing.

On this particular evening, for two particular individuals, there's a more compelling vibe. It's simmering below the surface of the obvious. What is implicit is the strong sense of possibility.

One of the taxis pulls up outside the Portland Hotel, Nottingham, and a glamorous blonde in her late twenties gets out. The accentuated curves, the elegant shoes and the beautiful flow of hair all declare a successful combination of femininity and money. The young woman looks radiant in a smart black number with everything optimised so that shiny accessories like Alice the bracelet enable her to look like the treasure she needs to look like if she is to acquire the treasure she seeks.

Caroline is keen to go inside. The 'keep the change' she utters to the cab driver helps her to generate the mood and the feeling that she needs to pull this off. She steadily and surely walks into the hotel, a shiny construction of new brick and glass, and disappears from sight, all clothes, confidence and purpose.

Outside, in one of the hotel's car park spaces, some way from the building, but within plain sight, somebody is watching. It is somebody with the same level of purpose, somebody who knows and someone who also hopes to gain. Leoni, with a packet of Mayfair cigarettes and a flask of coffee, is prepared to wait. She knows the demands of her role in all this. They have gone over it so many times. For her part in what's going on, there needs to be resourcefulness and initiative, and these are things she has in abundance, so there is no problem. She reads her copy of 'Vogue', knowing that the beep of a text at some point will signal the beginning of her work this evening.

Inside, Caroline has the mindset of a visiting marauder. She approaches the bar as though she has been there a hundred times before, even though she notices straight away that the furniture and carpeting are clear signals of a place classier than any bar she has visited before. She smiles sweetly to the barman and orders a large white wine, with the intention that she will only have one alcoholic drink this evening, or perhaps two at the most. Senses need to be razor sharp, so there are no mistakes.

She surveys the large room without appearing uncomfortable, and considers where to locate herself, knowing that every choice she makes from this point onwards has to be thoughtful. There are several empty tables. She decides to sit at one that is situated towards the rear of the room, choosing a chair that faces away from the bar so that she doesn't look expectant. Any appearance of being attainable will not enhance her value tonight and may lessen her chance of total success. She feels it is sensible to not make herself too available at this point in the operation.

She types 'Fab place. X not here yet' and sends the text to Leoni.

Leoni replies, 'Blonde suits you.'

Without facing the bar, she knows when he has entered. She hears a male voice and knows it is him. This is the consultant surgeon. Leoni has done some research. Bruce Callaghan is married with two children and for him this is a naughty away fixture, for which he is using a bogus name whilst realising the value of keeping his job description as the only evidence of his identity. She, however, intends to be much naughtier.

"Excuse me. Are you JoJo?"

Caroline smiles the fullest of smiles with all the sweetness she can feign, just as she has rehearsed in front of the hallway mirror. It is her working expression, utilised to good effect since her teens. Deep down, she has never got used to the name JoJo, probably never will, but she is more than equal to the demands of this role. "I am. And you must be Mike." She takes his hand. I'm very pleased to meet you."

"Not late am I?" He is a handsome man, Caroline has to admit. Just like his picture, not that it makes any difference at all to anything. On the contrary, she despises handsome men but this one will never know that until it is too late. She knows he is looking at her with keen interest. The trap is set. He's already in all kinds of trouble but he just doesn't know it.

"No. I've only just arrived."

"Have you been here before?"

"Never." She turns her head to look around. "It seems like a nice place."

"Yes. Came to a wedding here a few years ago. It's very spacious. It has a large function room upstairs."

"You look like your photo."

"Is that a good thing?" His eyes don't shift from hers.

"Not bad." Caroline is determined to play nicely. She checks out his suit, the rings on his fingers, and draws conclusions.

"So what made you go on the website then?" he asks.

"I guess I'm looking for someone to be nice to me." She has to play well.

Mike's eyes give him away. He doesn't realise anything, but Caroline sees through the glass of his personality and attitude. As far as she is concerned, he is yet another one who can be read like a children's book from the first second and thus, like all the others there have been and are going to be, can be manipulated, seduced and broken, as and when she desires. She just has to say the right things and seize the right moments.

"Aren't men always nice to you?"

Caroline sees through the question and knows what he means by the word nice. He isn't thinking of nice smiles, nice words or even nice gestures. He isn't thinking of bunches of flowers, walks in the countryside or scintillating sensitive conversation. By nice, he means sex.

She conceals her repulsion. This is business. "Usually." She is purposely looking away from him. At this moment, she pushes away from her mind the idea about how unpleasant this work is and eclipses that idea with the knowledge and expectation that she is going to be well paid.

"What kind of nice do you like, then?"

"You know." She looks into the distance, appearing dreamy. "Someone who makes me feel valued. Somebody sensitive. A man who is good to talk to, and intelligent." She pauses, deliberately. This is the first meet, so there has to be a balance. "Obviously, a good lover too." Well, she does need to bait him a little, sow some seeds.

"Well, I guess this is me being pretty forward, but here I am." He spreads his arms wide to support his words. "I suppose I'm looking for the same."

Caroline notices that he has no ring on his wedding finger but that there are white tell-tale marks. Did he stash the dead giveaway jewellery in his car's glove box, she wonders, or is it at home somewhere? Perhaps he'll let her know the answer to that one when the sting comes.

They have an hour and a half of conversation. At the end of the ninety minutes, Caroline knows that Mike Parker's best friend is a heart surgeon called Rory, that he grew up in Huthwaite and that he drives a Merc that he bought last year. She knows all about him splitting his head open when he was five and how he once went foxhunting but didn't enjoy it. He has given out a hundred facts but the only fact that matters to her is his bank balance and he's not given her that explicitly, although she can read between the lines.

She leaves the hotel with him and agrees as they part that a second date would be nice. She waves gently as he departs, appearing to be about to make her way to the taxi rank. The surgeon obligingly makes his way to his sapphire Mercedes and is in it and away in a minute, although not without an enthusiastic wave through the open car window. Caroline waves back. She senses that this one is going to be the easiest of prey.

Half a minute later, Leoni passes in her car. Caroline watches and nods to her as she leaves the car park in the same direction. This is where Leoni has to show and develop some expertise. They know where he lives, but Leoni will find out where he goes from here anyway. Any additional addresses will give extra leverage. Caroline hopes she will maintain a reasonable distance. It could ruin everything if she is rumbled.

* * *

"That's absolutely priceless. Are you sure?"

"Totally. No mistake. Got photos to prove it." Leoni smiles widely, like anybody taking pride in her work. Everything is going to plan.

"We're definitely going to make some money out of this one. It was always going to work out anyway but now it's guaranteed. We can even increase the amount we're after. We just need to find out some more about him."

"What do you mean?'

"Get more info about his domestic situation. I need to know just exactly how much leverage we're going to have. I want to know more about his relationship with his wife and kids."

"Why?"

"Because it will strengthen our hand. I want to know just how vulnerable he actually is. How close are they? How much would the wrong information actually threaten his very existence?"

"I'm not sure I can find out that much. I'd have to infiltrate his life for that to happen."

"Well, just learn what you can, then. Knowledge is power. The more we know, the more we can hit him for."

"Babe, we can make a mint out of his workplace alone. We can discredit the fucker big time if he doesn't co-operate and he won't want that."

"No, Lu. Look for the domestic stuff too. It could be his weakest link."

"Don't you think he'll pay anyway?"

"I'm sure he'll pay. He certainly seems like he'll be a good payer. Let's just try to make him an even better payer."

* * *

Three weeks later, Caroline is sitting in Wollaton Park, Nottingham. A gentle breeze is passing through the trees and this seems so calm that it can't possibly precede a storm. She is sitting there studiously reading various Facebook postings on her phone, doing far more despising than admiring. Every so often she looks up from her browsing to consider her surroundings. She pays particular attention to the trees above her, hoping to see what birds are perched in the branches. She can't tell. Why are the birds always so unclear?

Inside she has steeled herself for the coming moment. This is the point that all of the work has been leading to. She is as relaxed as can be, this state of being supported by her attire, which today is jeans and a red top, a reflection of her wanting to appear relaxed and in control. For some indecisive moments that morning, she has half-considered a suit, but has dismissed power dressing on the grounds that it will make her conspicuous in a park. She is prepared for whatever is about to take place.

Mike approaches. He is confident and assured because in his mind, this woman is his. He comes and sits, surprised that she hasn't got up from the bench to greet him with a kiss of some description, as she has done on their previous meetings. This doesn't fit with how they have been with each other, but so be it. He is ready to be cool. "You asked to see me. You said it was urgent."

"I did, and it is." There is no eye contact. Caroline doesn't even face him. Her head is temporarily turned in another direction, looking away from him and into the distance, where the grass ends and the road and houses take over. Mike senses that something has changed. Caroline, on the other hand, is distracted by a child on the next bench, a few metres away, nagging her mother, probably about sweets. She remembers a time when she used to nag her mother, not that it ever did her any good.

"What's this all about?"

Caroline hands Mike a piece of paper. At no point has she looked at him.

"What's this?"

"I'll get straight to it. That's how much you're going to pay me."

"What?"

"The account details are on the other side."

He speaks louder. "What?"

"Like I said, you're going to transfer to that account the amount I have written on there."

"What the fuck?"

"No, not quite. You'll transfer it."

"Why will I?"

"The alternative's not nice."

"What alternative?"

"A horrible one. Having your life destroyed won't be very nice."

He has reddened. "What? What do you mean?"

"You've been enjoying yourself, Mike. OK, so it's only sex, I know, but unfortunately for you, it's sex with me, and on top of that, as if I'm not enough, sex with Evie, fifty pounds an hour Evie. That in itself might be OK. The problem for you is that you have also been sharing a bed with that dear wife of yours. Sweet Grace Anne, bless her. You know, the one you supposedly love."

"Why are you bringing Grace into this?"

"I don't know. Didn't you make some vows when you married her? Oops."

At this point he wants to speak, but Caroline raises her hand to signal that he should refrain. "It's OK. You can do that. I don't mind you sleeping with the woman you married. Evie doesn't upset me either. I can cope with the rejection, the betrayal." Here she puts in the same effort as she used to put in during her drama lessons at school. "But it comes at a cost."

"I'm not paying you."

Caroline nods. "Oh, you are."

"I won't. It's blackmail."

"It's worse than that, Mike. Oh, I forgot to tell you. I knew there was something else. I have photographs."

"What photographs?"

"Good ones. Put it this way, I don't think you'll have kept a space for them in your family album. Pretty colourful pictures, if you ask me."

"You never took photographs. You're bluffing."

"You're giving me some serious attention, really serious attention. These are strong images, powerful enough to shock your employers and make you a figure of fun for all who know you. Pictures with me, and even a couple of telling pictures with Evie. On our first date, Mike. How could you? You don't want trouble, Mike. We're not worth it. I'm not, at least. Evie might be, although I doubt it. You know you'll be ruined. Poor Grace Anne."

"You can't do this."

Caroline shakes her head slowly then stops and looks him straight in the eyes. "I can. In fact, I believe I can totally destroy you. And you know what? I might even enjoy it."

"This is evil."

"No, Mike. It's business."

"Why would you want to do this?"

"Because. That's why. Don't look like that. It's not all doom and gloom. There is a way out of this for you. Obviously, if you pay the money, you avoid the shame."

He gathers strength and sits back. He can ride this out. "You're a liar. You don't have any proof."

She opens her black clutch bag. "Don't I? Well, here's one. What do you think?" She tosses a photograph into his lap, all the time appearing to be looking a hundred yards away from him. "Better still, what will that sweet lady you married think? I don't think she'll like that picture, Mike. Do you think she'll like it?"

Mike is silent. If he's trying to find an exit strategy, a way out of the financial loss or shame, there isn't one. He stares into space for a while then stares at her. She keeps her left hand in her coat pocket. If he attacks her, he will die, and she will hastily exit the scene with the sunglasses and the blonde wig hopefully protecting her identity.

"OK, so now that I have your serious attention, the amount on the paper will be paid into the account number on there. It's pretty clear, in big black letters. You need to do this within the next five days, Mike. Pretty reasonable, if you ask me."

"Are you kidding? I can't raise that kind of money in five days."

"Well, you'd better. Otherwise I start wrecking your life on the sixth day."

"Why would you do this?"

"Why not?" Caroline stands up. "Like I said. It's business. Strictly business."

"I could go to the police."

"You could. But then, you'd definitely have no life left. And six months later, I'd cut out your heart with a knife. I'm good with a knife."

A few seconds elapse before she decides it's time to leave. "I've somewhere to be now. Bye, Mike. Payment in five days and you can enjoy the memories we made. Otherwise it's big trouble."

* * *

Two evenings later, Caroline is standing in front of the television set. "He fucking paid, Lu. He transferred the money. We're fifty grand to the good. I knew he was good for it."

CONQUERING JACOB

There are others.

Men are money.

Here's another one. They come along like trains, but most are more predictable than National Rail and more enthusiastic than public transport has ever been. Caroline, now twenty-seven, has seen Jacob once a week for the past four weeks. Throughout that time, she has entertained his urges, catered to his demands and has always put in plenty of effort to optimize his pleasure in her company. Jacob appreciates it. He loves her keenness to please. She has made Jacob think she will do anything for him, any sordid act, regardless of how distasteful to other women. She does not enjoy one second of it but puts aside any sense of revulsion, so that he is now convinced he has her utter devotion.

Jacob likes devotion. "Anything for you," she says. "I want us to do everything together." She smiles, oozing sincerity and using the touch of her hand on his to indicate that she is his, and his totally.

It's the first time she has done it with a man with a beard in a long time. Back in her younger days on the street, she remembers a guy with a thick black bush of hair who always liked her to go down on him. He would pay her more than the going rate for the trouble, but the most memorable aspect of that liaison was his keenness to kiss her after proceedings were completed. Although this was never kissing with tongues, since that was always a no-no in the working night, he would insist on planting his lips affectionately on her cheek afterwards and she would endure it with reluctant willingness, even though the whiskers on his chin irritated her beyond belief. In short, Caroline did not like beards.

Once again, it is payback time, just like it has been for Edward the accountant and Paul the company director. They have been discoveries on the so-called elite dating site that is home to aspiration of various kinds. The two young women seek out the ones who might be rendering themselves vulnerable in some way. The bigger the hypocrite, the bigger the potential. With Leoni's diligence and growing resourcefulness online, as well as the research she undertakes in her car and through investigating key locations on foot, they acquire the means to make money, the information that will create opportunity. Someone once said, 'Knowledge is power'. Too true.

"This Tony looks like a good prospect. Send him a message."

"Tell me about him again."

"He lives on his own. Rarely leaves his flat. Lives off his inheritance."

"No family?"

"No family."

"No sick parent or child anywhere?"

"Nothing, Caz."

"No point meeting him, then. No leverage. Let's look for another one."

Seven months ago, Edward the taxi entrepreneur willingly paid up the-five thousand pounds in cash demanded of him.

Too willingly in fact. Caroline could hardly believe it when he arranged a meet two days after the sting and brought a blue sports bag full of the money demanded. That night, she and Leoni had enjoyed sitting in a bath full of twenty and fifty-pound notes.

Stammering David, on the other hand, was more reluctant, but Leoni had done some effective dealing and negotiation on that one. He paid eventually, especially after a brown envelope had been delivered to his boss at his place of work, giving him palpitations that he didn't need as a man in his sixties with a heart condition. A sheet inside was blank apart from a single statement. 'This is what I could do – David Henderson', it declared. Clearly, his boss would have read that and summoned poor David into the office. That must have been an interesting conversation.

It was time to leave the internet alone for a while. They had ridden their luck well, made enough money to have plenty stashed away for the future, and they both felt the need to be out of cyberspace for a while. They had switched off the computers a month ago to go 'real life'. If they operated in the same way perpetually, they might be caught out. It was time to try a different tack.

Hence, Caroline and Leoni have travelled thirty-five miles to get here every week. Leoni has researched some appropriate places. The first few times have been speculative, just a young woman and her friend looking for an opportunity. They have needed to locate a victim, somebody they can take maximum advantage of and make some significant gain from. Of course, there are several flops, men who give themselves away thanks to Caroline's developing sense for potential and her intelligent subtle questioning. After a series of hotels and several cocktail bars frequented by the well-heeled, Caroline has encountered the latest gold mine.

"I must have a hundred antiques at home. They're well-insured, of course. My ornaments in the living room alone must add up to half a million. And their value is going up every month." The bearded Jacob Moore, six feet three in height and built for putting a ball through a basketball hoop, is a local businessman who has made a couple of millions building houses for young aspirational professionals. Jacob loves money and he loves to monitor and talk about his growing bank account, his numerous stocks and substantial shares. He also loves to talk about the vast array of valuable artefacts that he has collected over the years.

Most decisively, he also loves sex. Not quite as much as he loves money, but not far behind. He's not that big on boundaries either and seems to be lacking when it comes to control. He even thinks he might be falling in love with Caroline. "Unfortunately, my wife's not bothered. She always tells me it's difficult for her now," he confides in her. "We've been married a long time. I don't suppose I get her blood racing anymore." He laughs as he says this, as if he is being ironic.

Caroline laughs with him, but she has no sense of any irony. She is all ears with Jacob, sometimes flirting with him and regularly displaying a mischievous smile.

"Me, on the other hand, JoJo, I have these needs. Guess that's why I'm sitting here with you. You understand my needs." Here was Caesar's, a smart and classy bar, with an adjoining restaurant and a popular dance floor, a place with a reputation for high prices and extravagant customers, bang in the centre of Birmingham.

It is here he has met Caroline. It is here he has gone on to meet her a second and third time. Following on from this, they have met in some different places, which have always been classy, spending evenings that have ended with them leaving for a four-star Birmingham hotel room. A man made visually distinctive by his dyed straight brown hair that is swept across his head, Jacob turns the clock back in their late-night activity and feels he is recapturing the passions of his university days in his sessions with this beautiful younger woman. Of course, she hangs on his every word, and that helps too.

Obviously, Caroline has had to indulge this man. She has had to show him the kind of time that will have him coming back for more, all the tricks of her trade, and he loves it. In Jacob she has planted the seeds so that he cannot help himself coming back for more. Obviously, being a man, he is proving far from immune to some weakness in judgement, and is displaying a profound and misplaced willingness to take a risk. This is most welcome. This is what Caroline is hoping for.

"We need to find out when his house is going to be empty. He's told me all about the security, even gave me the password for the alarm." She laughs. "His wife's first name and twenty-one after it. Can you believe that?"

"We just need his wife gone."

"Or else we take care of her." Caroline rubs her fingers on the sharp jewels of Alice. "There's a lot of money at stake here, and we've invested a lot of time."

There is a welcome new opportunity. No one has to die it seems, for there is to be a change in setting that will develop this relationship. This is going to be a different kind of sting. To their delight, Jacob's attachment to Caroline is reaching new levels. He is ready to take a risk. This means a liaison at his home. It is so much desired by him, a liaison that will be taking things to an edge that Jacob will derive massive pleasure from. He knows how much of a thrill it will be for Caroline to be pleasing him in his marital bed. He doesn't say whether he will be changing the sheets afterwards, and Caroline doesn't care to inquire.

She is excited. She totally desires that liaison at his residence too. There could not be a more opportune moment to strike and have a successful evening. "Circumstances have favoured us," Jacob tells her. Fortunately enough, Jacob's wife has gone to visit family this week, and Jacob, the wonderfully treacherous soul that he is, has indicated to Caroline how they can both have the time of their lives. She has shown him a serious level of enthusiasm, suggesting that the sexual pleasure he will enjoy will be beyond mortal measurement.

"Hi, honey," he says, as she gets in his car.

She fastens the seatbelt and smiles at him, alert to what she is about to do. "Did you have a good day?"

"All right. But never mind that. We are going to have a fantastic night. I'm so hungry for you." He's stroking her thigh. She puts her hand on his.

They drive through double gates and pull up in front of an imposing detached house that serves as confirmation, if she needs it, that this is a world of money. Jacob is fifty-one, and Caroline wonders if she will be as wealthy as this at fifty-one. She is certainly working on it and tonight could be an important stepping stone to that level of luxury.

She plays it like a visiting professional, as Jacob has insisted, perhaps a physio or a legal adviser, and has walked behind him into the house. All the time she has been anticipating how much they're going to make from this caper. "I'll prepare the drinks," she says, seeing the bar area at one end of the lavishly spacious room. "You take care of the curtains. Will you turn down the heating. It's a bit warm in here."

He retorts by suggesting that soon things are going to get much warmer, while Caroline plays the bartender role.

She insists that he tells her all about the house. He describes the refurbishments they have made, such as the Elizabethan fireplace and the forty-thousand-pound carpet. Caroline listens, knowing they really have only one thing in common, and that is being driven by money.

Nothing is to happen until he has finished his drink. "I want you totally relaxed,' she says, "so finish it."

Once his glass is empty, Jacob, an excited puppy of a man, jumps on Caroline, starting to undress her and she reciprocates, kissing him, undoing buttons and a zip and all clothes are soon removed and strewn on the floor of the living room.

"God, you're sexy!" he can't help exclaiming, his voice an octave or two higher than normal. "I just so love doing this with you, woman."

"Well, show me how much you like me."

He ends up on top of her on the living room sofa. She wants him to come quickly so the hard bit for her is over. She is in luck, for tonight he cannot hold out long enough for that planned experience of his at the top of the stairs. This means that he is in his final throes above Caroline, giving what he thinks is the good news to her as she waits for the bad news to come to him, courtesy of her good friend Tammy. Having reached his climax, he falls onto her. They lay together, with their bodies entwined.

He reaches for a remote and turns on some music. "Do you like classical? Have a listen to this," he suggests. Chopin. She recognizes it instantly and is relieved that it isn't Mahler. Last thing she wants is to be reminded of this loser every time she listens to one of the great man's ten symphonies.

Within half an hour of what to Caroline is pretence and tedium, he has sunk into unconsciousness. The Tammy has worked well.

What this means practically, however, is that she has to disentangle herself, which she does. She leaves him unconscious on the settee while she gets dressed. While he dozes, Caroline unlocks the front door and in comes Leoni, beaming, and with her eyes flitting from side to side as she takes in the opulence of this punter's lifestyle. Leoni knows antiques. She has been learning about Jacob's possessions for the past month and even has a contact. She knows what can be fenced, with a little help from a couple of people she knows, and she knows where the big money can be made.

"Get that picture. There's ten grand in that. That vase is worth a bundle too."

Caroline, having the sense to bow to her partner's newly found wisdom, is out of her depth. "Everything should be worth loads. He's a fucking antiques dealer."

Jacob carries on sleeping, oblivious to his life's achievement now being all but eradicated.

There is no pressure of time, so they do an effective removal job. They put as many valuable things as possible into the Renault they have borrowed, which has fake plates, adding to their security, with the car being parked just beyond the reach of the security camera. They anticipate being able to fence these expensive items without too much trouble and are envisaging a load of money. Perhaps they will make enough to finance a few expensive holidays or even buy some property.

As they drive away that night, with Leoni having now disabled the cameras from inside, the boot and back seat of the car are full of treasure that should guarantee their comfort for a while. Both the young women are smiling. Jacob, meanwhile, is still unconscious. He will be wiser when he wakes.

PREPARING KALEEL

Things are looking better. After two leisurely months away from internet dating, their attention has been diverted for a while, and the gains from the Jacob business have become even more clear with the fencing of the items raising nearly two hundred thousand pounds. Much of the money has been securely stashed in bogus bank accounts, with about eighty grand under the floorboards of the house and ten thousand under the floor of Caroline's old bedroom at Judy's. Of course, she hasn't told her mother anything about that. That would not have been wise. She has looked after Judy, though, money-wise, and her mother asks no questions when Caroline gives her the three thousand in twenties and fifties to look after herself for a while.

"Why do you do it?" Leoni asks. "After what you told me about her, and how you were treated by her, I don't get it."

"I don't either, so let's not go there. I guess it's just something I want to do. Judy's Judy." Caroline can only shrug her shoulders.

Caroline is in no mood to stand still. It's time to work again. She wants to move further up the spectrum of imaginable wealth. She wants that buzz again, the buzz of money being accrued, the sense of moving further and further away from that poverty that is all she ever knew growing up.

"Do we have to go again?" Leoni asks, less motivated by the idea. "We've made loads."

"Of course we have to. We need to make loads more. Don't get hung up about it. It won't go on forever. In time, we'll have enough. We'll be able to buy a really nice house and live there for the rest of our lives, probably after a long time on some beach abroad somewhere."

Leoni accepts the argument, slowly nodding. Yet, she is curious. "So how long do you think then? Before we retire?"

"Two years. Maybe three. Could be sooner. Nine or ten real money-spinning deals should do it."

"Let's find those lucrative deals, then." They're soon back studying the screens of their laptops.

Leoni spends some time absorbed. "There'll be somebody here who'll do the trick."

"Well, obviously there is. We just have to find him."

"I don't want us to waste time on somebody who just isn't going to pay out serious money."

"No, and we won't. We don't go ahead if there's no potential." Caroline clicks and, within seconds, a profile is there in full colour on her screen. There is a series of photographs, a portrait and three full-length. He is wearing a suit in all of the pictures and in the third picture, the setting looks classy. "What about this one?"

Leoni looks, pauses, then gives her verdict. "He looks like an ape."

"Well, apes aren't that bad. You can make friends with an ape. You can manipulate an ape."

"This one might be bad though. We could be in danger from a bloke like that."

Caroline gives her the look of an admonishing parent whose child has expressed a fear of Santa Claus.

"We won't be in any danger. He'll be the one in danger."

"In an ideal world, that's true, but we're not in that world. Something could go wrong. A powerful bloke could hurt us if we make a mistake or don't take care of everything."

Caroline strokes her arm. "We won't make a mistake. You're missing the point, Lu. If he has the money, we're going to do fine. So fine."

"Let's look for somebody else." Leoni clicks and reads. "Hey, this bloke has a Rolls Royce and runs a security company. What about that?"

Caroline leans over and scrutinises the image and writing. "Let me have a look...Well, he certainly qualifies money-wise. Let's see what else he has going on."

"Leicester. That's where he is."

"That's cool. That's a city we've not worked yet."

Together they read the profile, a detailed one. Leoni breaks the silence. "Kaleel. He's an Indian guy. Do they like shagging?"

"He's a bloke, isn't he? He'll like it."

"Whatever he is, he's looking for something. Think he'll go for you?"

"Don't you think he will?"

"Well, you're beautiful. Will that be enough for him?"

She becomes circumspect. "Thanks, babe. Maybe he will. Maybe not. Don't know until I try. I suppose if he didn't go for me, we could always put you out there. Swap roles."

"That wouldn't be as good."

Caroline has a twinkle in her eye. "Why wouldn't it? I can keep an eye on you for a change."

"You could. But I'm nowhere near as good as you at that, and you know how prone to disaster I can be. Don't you agree?"

"Perhaps," Caroline replies.

"I'm better as back up, taking care of the technical side of the operation. And I'm better at the researching."

Caroline looks at Leoni, takes her cigarette from her then takes a puff, before saying, "You're right. You can get on with it, Lu. Today you can find out about this lovely Kaleel. I'll message him and see what information I can get through that. See how much spin he does."

* * *

The first impression is positive. Kaleel Begum is a pleasant handsome man with impeccable manners that would impress most people he meets. At their first meeting, he wears a smart suit that is clearly tailored, and from the off he is something of a gentleman, inquiring after Caroline's health and how her week has gone thus far. "It's interesting how we both feel the same. It's always a bit nervous." He speaks standard English with no trace of an Asian accent, which suggests to her a public school education. Caroline has no problem taking advantage of the advantaged. It is why she exists.

"We just need to learn some things about each other. I'll start. You can begin by telling about your life. Did you grow up in this area?"

"Yes. I grew up in Loughborough."

"Where did you do school?"

"I was sent to a horrible boarding school near Birmingham. I hated it totally."

"Why?"

"It was full of idiots. Hated every minute, but you know what parents are like."

"They wanted the best for you."

"That's it. They wanted the best. That's how I deal with it.

How I get past the horror of it." He laughs. "They thought they were doing their best."

Obviously, Caroline has the advantage of her date on this first meet. Thanks to the diligence of Leoni, she knows that Kaleel lives with his mother, an elderly woman with a serious health condition, who inhabits the bottom floor of the house they share and who uses a wheelchair. He also has two children from a previous marriage who live with their mother close by. It is all useful information, as is the knowledge that Kaleel visits his brother at his family home on the outskirts of Loughborough every week. There are definite angles for leverage once they get the material together.

"Tell me about you," Kaleel says.

"There's not much to say," replies Caroline. "I work in the antiques industry, if it is an industry. Most of what I do is from home. I buy and sell stuff. Whatever it is, I earn enough money to pay my way in the world."

"That's very clever. I know nothing about antiques."

"That's fine. I know nothing about security. To be honest, I don't know all that much about antiques but I just go by my instincts most of the time."

"Well, security is probably easier than your business. I just take a fee from nightclubs and concerts and then subcontract the work to various family members and family friends. I'm pretty well-established in the area now."

"Is that what you always wanted to do, then? Did you always want to beat people up outside nightclubs?" Caroline smiles.

Kaleel has become deadpan. "That's not what we do. I think I need to educate you a little. However, the answer's no. I wanted a career in mathematics. Well, my parents did."

"And you ended up running bouncers."

Kaleel laughs. "Exactly. Life's a strange thing. It's a good job I like the bouncers, as you call them. Most of them happen to be family members or friends, which makes things easier."

One and a half hours later, Kaleel is on his way home, trailed by Leoni, but this yields no extra information. She stops twenty yards behind him and watches. It is quite a home, a huge house with a tennis court alongside and is dimly lit, except for a downstairs room. Leoni watches as Kaleel locks his car and heads into the house. She notices that no upstairs light goes on. Maybe he's gone to check on his mother, perhaps to tell her all the details of his wonderful date with this fabulous respectable woman he's met. Leoni laughs.

* * *

"It's not working." Caroline speaks in her usual calm voice that belies no small amount of frustration. She fastens her seatbelt and faces Leoni. Leoni looks at her like this is inexplicable and unimaginable. 'Let's just get home."

"What's going wrong? You losing your touch or something?"

They have had five dates. They have been positive pleasant experiences for Kaleel, she feels, with plenty of smiles and that flowing conversation, yet none have led to anything decisive that will yield that serious money. Caroline manages her half-smile. "No. Well, at least I hope not. We might just have to rob this knobhead at knifepoint and leave out the sex stuff."

Leoni laughs. "How are you going to rob him, if you can't get him horizontal? Anything else'll be too risky."

Caroline doesn't reply. A thoughtful silence prevails in the car, as she looks at the houses they pass for some kind of inspiration. "I need a stimulant."

"A what?"

"A stimulant. Something to get him going. Something I can slip in his drink."

"Where are you going for that? The chemist?"

"Have a word with your brother. See what he can get."

"What do you mean? Viagra?"

"Something like that, but more potent. It has to get him hot to trot. A guaranteed tonic. I don't want to waste much more time on this idiot. He's already getting on my nerves."

"Will do. Do you know what? Think I might become a pharmacist when we retire from this."

INTRODUCING PETER –
A GOOD STEP?

Things had been so different three decades ago. So many years prior to wanting to sort Kaleel out with some appropriate medication, Caroline could be found in her bedroom, still in her school uniform, reading 'The Wasp Factory', a book he had stumbled upon in the library. On this particular night, at about Eleven-o'clock in the evening, she was just lying there on her side with this book of disturbing ideas that utterly fascinated her. If she had had a larger bedroom, she wouldn't have minded building a wasp factory. It would have been such fun to watch the little creatures meet their fate in such an imaginative variety of ways. Being a private creature who mostly liked to dwell on things alone, her door was closed, as it so often was these days. There was just Caroline, her imagination and the imagination of Iain Banks. Mahler's Second was playing in the background, performed by the Berlin Philharmonic. Some combination. It was so good that that music teacher had introduced her to the wonders of Gustav. It had been love at first listen, made even more alluring by the fact that Mahler always included death in his symphones, something that made his music essential listening to Caroline.

She heard sounds from downstairs that unsettled the harmony of her reading and its musical accompaniment. It was the unmistakable irritating sound of her mother laughing. How she hated her mother's laugh. Too high in decibels, too high in pitch and about as far from Mahler as any sound ever could be. If she had her way, her mother would never laugh out loud again and would never do anything more noticeable than quiet speaking.

The laugh ended, however. Next, in the dullness of a floor below, she heard a deeper voice in response. Caroline's heart sank. Not again. Another man. Caroline sighed. Judy hadn't done this for a couple of weeks and she had been hoping she wouldn't again. There was only one thing to do. She would put her headphones on and turn up the music, since the alternative meant enduring the sounds of adult intimacy. Far too much ridiculous information.

This happened every once in a while. Of course, it was always drug and alcohol fuelled. He was here for sex. That would be the only reason a man would come back here. Caroline could not recall Judy ever bringing anybody home sober, and always the two would be in some state of drunkenness. To escape the sounds of her mother's sex life, she turned off the symphony and instead she selected the radio and turned up the Radio 4 news programme she occasionally listened to. This drowned out all surrounding sound with the welcome but grim reality of another uninteresting war in the Middle East. Whilst occasionally listening, she was simultaneously reading the Iain Banks book that had gripped her for the past two hours.

The night went. Morning came. Caroline's eyes opened and she raised herself straight away. When she went downstairs, her mother was already there. She was sitting at the kitchen table opposite a man Caroline had never seen before. She had seen so many men at that kitchen table on so many mornings and some of them looked at her like they wanted another helping, but this time from a younger version of Judy. At best, they said hello and then vanished, never to be seen again. This one, the latest instalment, was a tall, dark-haired man, probably about her mother's age or a tad older, a man who smiled as he was introduced to her.

Caroline was used to humouring her mother's friends. She gave some semblance of a smile back at him and let her mother do all the talking while she put two slices of bread in the toaster.

"This is my pride and joy, Peter. My beautiful daughter, Caroline. Sweet Caroline, like the song." In a show of enthusiasm, Judy started to sing the Neil Diamond song.

The teenager cringed and wanted to bury herself in a deep hole, since stabbing her mother in the heart wasn't exactly possible at this moment. Judy sometimes behaved like this, demeaning herself in front of a new man, over the top and disgusting, making Caroline want to run either at her or well away from this shedding of dignity. Away was an attractive proposition. Yet, escape would not be easy. Where could she go? She would have to continue struggling along with this embarrassing woman. "

"You know what, Peter? She's really clever, this daughter of mine."

Caroline smirked, embarrassed. She was surprised too by the compliment. Judy rarely said nice things. It just wasn't in her nature, so perhaps something was different about today. She hoped not. However, it was clear that this man was somebody Judy really wanted to impress. As the toast popped up, Caroline was hoping this was just another one-night thing as she took her breakfast onto the living room. The last thing she wanted to happen was some dope who fancied Judy cluttering up the place. Thus far and thankfully, most of the men Judy brought home in recent years were very temporary affairs, strangers who had come for some drunken pleasure in Judy's bed and who would return to their rat-holes the next morning.

Still a virgin, Caroline's only sexual experience had been to let Sammy Fairhew put his hand on her chest while they had snogged behind the church. That had been after the school trip to the theatre to see 'Our Day Out', when Sammy had made his move by sitting next to her on the coach, taking advantage of Caroline's isolation. Sammy, a confident soul, street-wise for thirteen, had charmed her, offering to walk her home. Caroline, curious, had accepted his offer. She'd not been snogged before and wondered how she would feel. However, even she knew the dangers. Hands exploring was OK, but that had been the limit.

She had taken something significant from the experience. She mused over the fact that she had gained no thrill from any of it. Her hands hadn't gone anywhere, but had just remained at her sides, and she had gone to bed that evening wondering what the fuss was about. She had seen passion and lust on films and late-night TV but had felt none of it with Sammy. For her to snog anybody else, they would have to pay her money, she had decided in an overnight decision.

After finishing the toast, Caroline brought the plate back into the kitchen. Immediately, Judy chose to focus on her again.

"OK. I'll say it before you do. You don't believe I'm old enough to have a daughter as old as this," the mother said. Peter's hand was on Judy's knee, tensing and relaxing his grip, and Caroline rinsed her hands, dried them on the tea towel and wanted to flee the scene. She wondered if he was going to be a fixture round here, and in which case how much of an irritation he would be. She inwardly considered the idea. Was the scene in the kitchen real? Was it just a happy finish to a one-night stand?

Could it be that this Peter, whoever he was, was just putting on an act before making his exit like so many before him?

However, this one made an effort at conversation with her. "Your mum says you like drawing."

Caroline wasn't comfortable with this strange man knowing stuff about her. The hold he might have on Judy had nothing to do with her. She wanted to be kept out of it. "A bit."

"That's brilliant. I can't draw to save my life. I once drew a cavalier from the English Civil War and the teacher said it looked more like a snowman. Imagine that."

Lingering in the doorway, Caroline couldn't help herself and laughed, only slightly, and for Caroline that was all it would ever be. It was only the briefest of approving sounds, but she couldn't help herself. Judy looked at her. A laugh of any kind from Caroline was a rarity. Caroline was wondering if Judy had actually met a human being for once. As she walked upstairs, she thought about what had just taken place. The bloke seemed normal, not like the arrogant morons she usually went for. In Caroline's minds was a catalogue of the beatings and abuse Judy had taken through the years and it had produced steel in the teenager. Nobody would ever treat her like that. Not in this lifetime.

Judy and Peter didn't turn out to be a one-night affair. Things developed.

Peter was there two nights later, breakfasting again the following morning. After that, he stayed with Judy all the subsequent weekend. In fact, Peter began to be at the house with increasing regularity. He started coming with takeaways for all three of them and began taking Judy out on dates two or three times each week, and within six months, Caroline's world was profoundly different. Her mother was seemingly becoming involved with Peter, who worked as an electrician on the days when he wasn't drinking tea and smoking in their kitchen or lying watching late-night or morning television in Judy's bed. It had become something of a relationship. Also, to the daughter's chagrin, this meant that they could sometimes be found cuddling each other on Judy's sofa, in front of the TV. He even sat and listened when Judy played him her Neil Diamond albums. "He's pretty good, this guy," Peter said.

"Pretty good?" Judy punched him affectionately. "He's an absolute fucking legend."

There was a downside of this for Caroline. It meant that she had to spend more time hiding away in her bedroom, although she begrudgingly went from accepting Peter's presence in the house to actually welcoming it. Surprisingly, he was fun, always cheerful and funny, and he did say nice things to her. Sometimes he looked at her in a sustained way that made her uncomfortable, and Caroline didn't exactly enjoy the way he often touched her when he was talking to her. Caroline dismissed these things as just the way adults communicated. She had teachers at school who were like this. There had been no man in Caroline's life, ever. Although she remained on her guard, she couldn't help appreciating the novelty of this and wondered whether Peter would be the first male in her life to have a decent impact.

Most importantly, and this trumped any downside, he seemed to get on well with her mum and this in turn made Judy easier on Caroline. Perhaps, with him in her mother's life, things would be better for both of them. She smiled a lot more, didn't shout at her so much these days, or throw things. Even better, Judy cooked sometimes now. She didn't just expect her daughter to run to the chip shop or tear off the polythene cover of a ready meal. OK, so it was hardly cordon bleu, but chilli con carne or stew beat packets any day, and Caroline had to admit that the lentil soup her mother occasionally made was pretty tasty.

In the general scheme of things, Judy and Peter were

together most of the time and they were pretty passionate. Caroline could never imagine her mother in a relationship that wasn't pretty passionate. There was always sex at the heart of stuff for her, especially when she'd had a drink. Caroline didn't get it. Thankfully, it wasn't genetic. Her experience with Sammy had convinced her of that. She cringed at the very idea of sex with a boy. She wondered what would become of her, since she had decided resolutely that she would never be in a relationship, that she would be single to the grave. She was nothing like her mother.

Sometimes, particularly in the early evenings, Peter would emerge from Judy's room and come and talk to Caroline in her bedroom. He would stand in the doorway, leaning on the door frame, and talk to her about the posters on her wall, school, and music and always asked questions about why she never went out.

"No need. Not much happening," she would say. She couldn't offer a more developed explanation, because there wasn't one. If she had been totally truthful, she would have told him that she just didn't like people, never had.

However, there was a chance that Peter might yet prove to be an exception, even if he failed to understand her love of Gustav Mahler and his ten symphonies. "I'm a rock man myself," he told her. However, he seemed to accept that Caroline wasn't a typical teenager. "I guess you feel more yourself with your own company."

There was something about Peter that made Caroline feel relaxed. Maybe it was his soft voice, or perhaps it was just that he seemed to care about her and was the first person who actually wanted her to be happy. She could switch off her hate for the human race when he was talking to her, because it reassured her that he was bringing stability to her mother's life and that was actually making Caroline's life better too.

She also liked how he seemed to understand her. "Yes. That's it. I'm happier when I'm on my own. Besides, I don't get on with many people. I can talk to them for as bit, but then I get fed up and they start to irritate me. Really irritate me."

"I get that. I had times like that when I was your age."

"You were never like me. Nobody is like me." Although she kept her cards close to her chest, and always would, behind her expressionless face, she was thinking that in this dreadful life that she had led from birth, perhaps this bloke in her mother's life would provide something good and give her a reason to have less negative thoughts about life with her mother and life beyond her mother. She had never had any kind of hope before.

Something that Caroline couldn't quite fathom was how there were some times when Peter seemed to be more interested in Caroline than he was in Judy. What was weird were those moments when Pete, as Caroline now called him, helped her with her homework. For her this was surreal, as before Peter's arrival at the house, she rarely even did homework, never mind expect somebody to help her with it. She would face the teacher square and just say, "I haven't done it," especially if it was science or maths. She never cared about consequences and would quietly sit in detention as if it was her natural habitat. However, Peter kept telling her he thought she was great and could do brilliantly. He believed in kids working hard on their studies and repeatedly told her he was always happy to help her with her school work if she found it challenging.

In fact, challenging was Peter's favourite word. He would say things like, "That was a challenging game for the Rams," or comment on how the wind or the rain was "challenging." When he did a crossword in Judy's kitchen, that was always challenging to some degree and he often used phrases like "challenging problem" or "challenging situation". Caroline never remarked on this to him. It would have irritated her if it had been anybody else.

Consequently, with Peter's help, Caroline would apply herself. She did wonder, however, why, suddenly, she was being encouraged to work hard on that laborious school work. "I don't mind English and art. They're OK. I don't care about the other subjects, though. Most of them are boring. So boring."

"Well, you should care about your studies," he insisted. "All those subjects could help you make something of yourself. It's my one big regret, I'll tell you."

"What? Not doing homework?"

"School full stop. Truanted every week and did as little as I could get away with. Hated lessons."

"Like me, then."

"Yeah, but I wouldn't hate them now."

"But you've done OK, haven't you?"

Pete laughed. "No love. Not in a million years."

"But you have money. There's always money in your wallet."

"That's not as much money as it looks. Real money is never seen. It hides in bank accounts. It's there when you need it but the rest of the time it sleeps. Like a dragon, when you wake it up, it breathes fire into your life."

Peter would sit on the end of Caroline's bed and look at her affectionately. Caroline wondered if he was seeing her like a daughter. He was very tactile towards her and he was always asking her about boys and what she had been up to. She didn't want that protective thing going on, but she tolerated it. Of course, she had told him all about the Sammy experience and he had asked her lots of questions, which made her wonder whether it was all about protection, as it made her slightly uneasy. "So, you're still a virgin, then?" he had asked. She didn't like him asking her that question and paused before giving an affirmative response.

CRYSTAL SPURR
(A SHOW OF POWER)

Crystal Spurr had arrived early to school that day. With four versions of her school uniform hanging in her wardrobe, Crystal had plenty going on and nothing at all. A pale freckled girl who had met up with her friends at the end of her road, she had a pretty smile and enough curly hair to fill a small suitcase.

All five walked through the school gates, Crystal and her four close confidantes, all of whom could have been clonish replacements of herself in attitude and personality. She led the way into the school building with the kind of confidence and security that comes from having two loving parents who spoiled her beyond belief. Fate, or the God that Crystal's mother and father believed in, had decided that this first child would be their only child. Of course, a child as special as this would want for nothing. Occupying pride of place in the comfortable, positively detailed picture that was Crystal's life there was also a well-groomed horse, a beast she treasured and talked about incessantly. Appearance-wise, today, like all days, she was always immaculately dressed. She wore a designer version of the otherwise dull black and white school uniform that the others emulated, and always sported expensive shiny black shoes, with a schoolbag to die for. Everything shouted sophistication. Equally loud was the cry of over-indulgence with consequences.

She was sounding off to the others about how great her weekend had been and how the Lake District was something else. This had not been a typical weekend for Crystal, which would normally include plenty of riding on a Saturday morning, when she would take Hunter galloping around the field that her family leased. At other times during the weekend there would be the regular trip into town and at least one restaurant meal with her family or friends. "Back to normal next week," she said. "After I've done some riding, we can all meet up and hit town Saturday aft."

"Can we have another sleepover?" one of the others had suggested.

"Why not. With a bit of luck, Mum and Dad'll go out somewhere."

"Wild party," one of the others said.

Crystal laughed. With the kind of control she liked to exercise, a wild party would never happen.

All five settled in the form room, listening to Eminem on a portable CD player, another of Crystal's favourite possessions. Crystal and her friends were competing to remember the lyrics of the song being played and were laughing at each other's mistakes.

Crystal was sitting in the back corner with April, her best friend, next to her, whilst Joanne and Paula, two others in her group, were sitting opposite. They were all such confident souls, and why wouldn't they be? They were all nice-looking, fashionable and sociable and for them life was not far from a dream. Of course, they all followed Crystal's lead. She was the one with the fabulous life and the wealthy family so why shouldn't she be the leader?

Nice-looking but hardly fashionable, and certainly not sociable, Caroline Lawrence was sitting two desks in front of them, drawing a picture of a gargoyle smoking a joint in a notepad while she wondered what it must be like to appear on a chat show like 'Parkinson'. Why was it that he didn't ever interview interesting normal people like herself? Why was it that the people he interviewed were never asked tough questions? "Tell us about your latest film, book or album? Next, talk about something you want to talk about? Finally, let's have a silly moment that will amuse the morons watching." Not a probing question in sight. Utter trash.

She would never open up to anyone like those freaks did on his show, she mused. No one would ever understand the thoughts she had. If she held up this picture she was currently creating, would the dumb audience of a tedious chat show all sigh in shock or would there be somebody sitting there somewhere who would get her, who would appreciate her mind. It was an intriguing question. She would never know the answer.

She was sitting on her own next to the window, two rows away from the group at the back of the classroom, which was always the case. Caroline had continued in the same vein as in her earlier years, barely doing conversation, never mind school friends. This was Year Nine. She would be commencing her GCSE's next year, not that that meant very much to her. There were some stains, stresses and strains in Caroline's clothing that matched her relationship with the learning environment. She intended to leave school at the earliest opportunity and try her luck in the outside world.

Crystal, who always had plenty to say, was holding court at the back of the room, talking about her pride and joy, her horse, which was her most frequent topic of conversation. "I just love him so much. I don't think I'll ever need a boyfriend while I have him. He's just so wonderful."

Of course, the girls listening were indulging her. This was a school composed of pupils from a variety of social backgrounds, but not many of the pupils in this area owned horses and most certainly could not afford to rent fields for those horses. April, whose father was a dentist, said, "Do you think you'll still own a horse when you're older? Do you not think you might grow out of it?"

Crystal became dramatic, giving April a look of incredulity. "I could never grow out of horses, April. Are you serious? I could marry a horse. More reliable than any boy, and it would probably give me more fun."

At this point, Caroline laughed. Perhaps she thought it was a silent laugh, like most of her laughs were, one that would pass unheard. It wasn't a loud laugh, to be fair, since Caroline never did loud laughter, but Crystal, who despised Caroline for her quietness and awkwardness, as well as her clear social inferiority, was alerted to the sound because she had been looking in that direction as she had spoken. In fact, she had been waiting. Part of her actually wanted this girl, whom she had despised and detested right from her arrival at the primary school, to come up on the radar and make herself prey. Perhaps it was because so many details of Caroline screamed disadvantage, whether it was her shabby uniform, her clear shyness, or just her insulting solitude. Then again, perhaps it was due to the fact that there had been problems between them for a long time and perhaps it was time for things to come to a head.

The two girls had recent history too, Crystal making snide comments and spreading rumours about Caroline and her home life, making her friends giggle. "Imagine a girl who's a dirty smelly slag, with a mother who's a dirtier smelly slag." They would all laugh out loud.

Caroline would seethe but would ignore the indirect abuse, knowing she would be outnumbered and that no good would come of it. She hated Crystal. She knew, had known for some time, that one day she would show Crystal how much she hated her, but for now she soaked up the ill-treatment. It was notable that, perhaps knowingly, none of the other girls directly insulted Caroline and her home life. Maybe they sensed that this lone wolf of a girl might have teeth, or were they merely worried that she would become tearful and involve the teachers? Was it even possible that they had enough morality to restrain their cruelty? It was difficult to say.

Today, Crystal did not have that morality. She was now roused, and the communication was direct. "I think I'd laugh if I was you. I'd definitely laugh at myself. Somebody lend Lawrence a mirror. We can watch her look of horror when she sees herself." There was a chorus of callous laughter, even though the joke was ironic. Caroline was hardly lacking in the looks department. She had overheard a Year Eleven by describe her as the prettiest girl in the school with the most horrible personality. She had quite liked both elements of that comment and had walked with a spring in her step for the rest of that day.

Caroline turned to face that back corner. She uttered no words, but the look she gave said everything. She glared at Crystal as if she was the only one there, clearly understanding the power dynamic of the group, staring as if she was looking through the spoilt girl's eyes into the back of her head. Caroline had powerful patience, had developed it through the troubled years of her childhood, but the clock was ticking. Maybe it was ticking faster now. Crystal looked away.

Caroline picked up her bag and her pad and left the room. She left behind a silence and in her mind was the sense that a line had been crossed.

Joanne spoke first. "That was some dirty look. Does she think that's OK?"

Crystal now became keen, staring at the doorway through which Caroline had disappeared. "Knowing that scrag-end, she might do. She probably needs to be taught a lesson."

The girls alongside Crystal nodded. It was wise to co-operate with Crystal. Crystal had once been in a fight with a girl three years older than her and had all but clawed her eyes out. As far as they were concerned, Caroline Lawrence, even though there was something uncomfortably strange about her, was small potatoes compared to Crystal, and small potatoes, like tin cans, could be kicked up the road and out of sight.

The first lesson that day took place in the girls' changing room. The girls had been playing netball in the gym.

Caroline, in the midst of changing back into her uniform and dressed only in her underwear, suddenly realized her period had begun. She grabbed a tampon from her schoolbag and rushed to the changing room toilet.

Of course, this left her school uniform and her schoolbag exposed. "Right. Let's have a laugh," Crystal said. She grabbed Caroline's coat and placed it on the shoulders of one of her stooges. "Girls, grab her clothes."

Within seconds the others soon had the entirety of a girl's school life in their hands and they formed a procession of spitefulness going out of the changing room.

In five minutes, with much accompanying shrill laughter, Caroline's bag and clothes had been tossed into a skip full of cardboard and other school waste at the edge of the yard.

When Caroline emerged, she found her spot in the girls' changing room now empty. Clad in only bra and knickers and realizing the futility of any attempt to save her dignity, she realised her predicament. Fortunately, Miss Abrahams, a young PE teacher, came into the changing room, somebody Caroline knew was soft and sensitive, qualities that were normally anathema to her. "What's happened here? Caroline, why aren't you dressed?"

Caroline, concise as always, said in a bitter voice, "I don't know. My clothes have been taken, haven't they?"

The young teacher was quick to act. Within minutes, she was able to supply the scowling Caroline with some new uniform from lost property. The blood inside the girl had reached boiling point.

Her anger was still bubbling unpleasantly at lunch-time, when she went into the school canteen. Nevertheless, she took possession of her pasta bowl and bottled water, placing both on her tray, and found a place at the end of a table. Normally, an older boy or two would come and sit with her and they would exchange pleasantries, in which Caroline was never all that forthcoming. The girls in her year might not have found her to be their cup of tea but for some reason, boys in the years above wanted to get to know her better. Caroline never understood why but she didn't really need to. Nothing that happened in this place had any relevance to who she was.

One such boy was James Furniss. During those lunchtimes when he wasn't with his friends, James, a handsome sporty youth with dark brown straight hair, would sit near Caroline and try to engage her in conversation. He didn't get more from her than anyone else, grunts and nods and little else, yet he was very confident in approaching her, especially since he was a key athlete for the school and he thought that might make her more positively disposed to him. In truth, she liked his sense of humour, but she just didn't trust boys. They either lied or pretended, and they always wanted to take advantage of girls who were gullible. She had heard enough male conversations to make her despise older boys and the snippets of male absurdity had given her an immunity from gullibility.

However, James seemed to like Caroline. She hoped he talked to her and smiled at her because she was quiet and strong-minded. If he had hopes of anything else, the bitter disappointment would be all his.

Strength was needed. Whilst Caroline and James were at the end of a long table, Crystal and her 'gang' came and sat down in the seven or eight seats at the other end. Each of them glanced at Caroline, nothing more than that, as they placed their food down.

Crystal made the first move. She called across without turning her head, "I hear you lost your stuff, Lawrence. That's really sad."

Caroline didn't move. She didn't even respond. She just stared ahead and continued to sip at her can of cola.

Crystal had the bit between her teeth. "Well, really, you don't need those clothes, you know. You're better off looking like a slag in lost property."

Caroline noticed James look across at Crystal challengingly but knew that he was never going to say anything or try to stop them. He had too much to lose from this malicious bunch. They were well-known as trouble-makers and James wouldn't have known what to do if he had become a target. No boy or group of boys even could hope to gain anything from a conflict with this bunch.

Caroline continued to sip her cola as if she wasn't hearing the toxic words. She appeared to be scrutinizing the writing on the can.

James tried in vain to make eye contact with her, shaking his head in sympathy. Caroline didn't do sympathy, neither giving nor receiving it.

She was on her own and in her own zone. The temperature in that zone was rising. She didn't need or want anybody else. James had become no more than a blur.

Crystal continued. "Where did you get those clothes from, anyway? The food bank? Or did that mother of yours shag somebody to buy them for you. How's life in Slag Central anyway?" Crystal laughed out loud and her friends echoed her.

At this point, Caroline continued to stare ahead. She barely noticed when James signalled to her with more shaking of his head to continue his show of sympathy. She registered nothing when he flashed another look at them to show his disapproval, as if it would achieve something this time.

She stopped the staring and found a purpose. Caroline got up and put her chair under the table. She made sure everything was on her tray and took that to the collection area where she slowly and carefully disposed of everything as if nothing had happened. Just like normally, she placed the empty tray on the pile.

Now her hands were free.

She slowly and seriously made her way to where Crystal was sitting. They were all still half-laughing and grinning. No doubt Crystal thought that Caroline had gone, that she had taken her humiliation and gone away to hide from it. Perhaps she had found some quiet place and was upset and wishing away the insults and bullying.

Suddenly, the girls facing Crystal looked shocked. Caroline was ready to fight them all. She settled for showing her chief tormentor that any assumption she might have had about Caroline's state of mind was misplaced. With the meanest of scowls on her face, she violently dragged this leader of bullies back by the hair and slammed her head down on the tiled floor. From the expression on her face, she could see that Crystal was shocked to learn that her strong sense of superiority was not happening for her today. She had her head held the ground and she found herself exposed and vulnerable. The quiet girl was astride her now and her face was all menace. Caroline's fists were now pounding, hammering down repeatedly, and there was the crack of a nose breaking. This was her moment. Caroline worked quickly, perhaps sensing that she would be pulled away soon, and was keen to have maximum impact in the time she had. To Crystal's friends, it looked as if she was intent on killing Crystal.

She was intent on killing Crystal.

James stood up, horrified. Was this Caroline? Was this the girl he had sat opposite in this dining hall so many times who had seemed peaceful and calm, if a trifle on the quiet and strange side? He had been shocked by Crystal's provocation but the level of violence being dished out by the quiet attractive girl was shocking and sickening. He had a horrified look on his face. Somebody had to stop this.

At that moment, just about unconscious, Crystal, as well as everyone in proximity, knew that she had made a disastrous mistake in her choice of victim. With shrieking voices, the teachers were soon dragging a dishevelled but satisfied Caroline off her and Crystal's supposed friends were left sighing and uttering sounds of horror at the mess that had been made of their leader's face.

Soon Caroline was in the headteacher's office. Mrs Collins, an experienced school manager who had a photograph of her two sons on her desk along with a paperweight containing a small lizard, had read Caroline's file several times and now wanted answers. "Why did you hit Crystal like that?"

Caroline sensed a severe punishment coming her way. She suddenly became tearful. "I'm really sorry, miss. She said horrible things about my mum. My mum has been seeing the doctor and I've been worried about her. She might have cancer, miss. I just lost my temper because my mum's been so poorly."

Despite the disturbing level of violence, the woman found herself feeling sympathetic towards this girl. She knew quite a lot about the personality of Crystal Spurr, and her parents had caused trouble for the headteacher on numerous occasions, objecting to the curriculum, objecting to the school's catering arrangements, objecting to the limited extra-curricular activities. It was clear that she had to act, but at the same time she had to show some understanding of the pressure young Caroline was clearly under. "You can't go about hitting people, Caroline, whatever they say to you."

"I know, miss. I'm sorry." She kept her head bowed.

"I'm putting you in isolation for three days, then we'll make a decision after that. I have to warn you that if you do anything like this again, the punishment will be a lot worse. You'll lose your place here."

The next day, Crystal didn't come to school. In fact, she didn't return until Wednesday of the following week. She didn't look in Caroline's direction once that day.

Caroline's problems with Crystal were over.

Crystal's problems with Caroline weren't.

A couple of weeks later, Crystal was missing from school again. Caroline, who had arrived earlier than usual that day, overheard the conversation from her seat near the front of the classroom.

"Where's Crystal?"

"It's Hunter. Crystal's horse."

"What's happened?"

"She went to feed him this morning and found him dead in the field."

"Poor Crystal. She'll be so upset."

"How did he die?"

"They don't know. He was just lying dead in the field."

"That's terrible. Poor Crystal. She'll be so upset."

Caroline smiled. Mission accomplished.

THE FUN OF KALEEL

Quietly, she closes her eyes as he lays on top of her and moves up and down, driving into her with the usual heavy breathing and grunting. She forces out quiet noises of approval as he gives her what is probably the best he has to offer. He no doubt thinks he is giving her the time of her life, giving her something she will look back on with awe, something momentous and unprecedented for her.

Caroline's mind is on the money. Caroline's other thoughts are about the gap in the curtain to the left of her. She is hopeful that the gap will be sufficient to enable a photographic masterpiece, as well as some powerful video footage This will be enough to guarantee the big pay-out.

Before they have got into the bed she has made sure that they are side on to where Leoni is positioned and waiting outside this ground level room. Just Leoni and her camera. As he undresses her prior to that, Caroline has been secure in the knowledge that Brett's aphrodisiac powder has done the trick, that meeting in this hotel has been a sound idea and that this little moment is going to be a serious money spinner.

To be fair, Kaleel has been easy company. While she has anticipated and contemplated, he has talked about places he likes, asked her about places she likes, and has expressed a keenness to take her to other bars and places in this town. Obviously, Caroline has not deterred his interest in this. It's all part of the set up. The bottom line is that she needs him giving it to her visually and audibly in the downstairs room she has provisionally booked. He is now meeting that need.

She makes an addition to his drink while he is in the toilet. "This will have him so hot to trot, he could run the Grand National and shag every one of the fillies after the race," Brett had bragged.

Two drinks later, his expression and body language have both shown that the formula is a winner.

She has taken control this evening. "I think we're ready for some privacy."

"How do you mean?" His eyes now have the glazed look of co-operation.

"I've booked us a room here. The thing is, I really like you and I want us to have a bit of intimacy."

"Oh, you do, do you?" He grins as if he is the one in control this evening.

"Yes, I do. Let's finish these, and we can have a nice time. We don't have to have sex or anything, but we can at least kiss each other without it being public."

Not protesting, Kaleel stands up. Handsome. A well-toned body that suggests many fruitful hours spent in the gym. However, Caroline would rob Adonis or Quasimodo in the same way that she is going to rob this one and would be just as unmoved. "OK. Let's get to the room."

A BITTER STEP

The mood in the house had changed. Over the past three or four months, everything had lost its relaxed momentum and there was no joy, or anything approaching it. The whole atmosphere downstairs particularly was tense these days. Whatever force it was that brought contentment and positivity had left the building, leaving behind something gloomy and doubtful.

Visually, not much had changed. The untidiness of the house had been constant in recent months, just as it had been in the years before. There were still the all too often unclean surfaces of the dining table and the kitchen worktop, and the carpets had continued their gradual deterioration. The removal of grime took effort and industry, whilst carpets were expensive to replace, and Judy was prolific in putting things off and feeling no shame. Also unchanged were other, more polluting, features. The cigarette smoke was still relentless, and the sounds of the television or local radio continued perpetually, either simultaneously in their different rooms or in relay.

What was different was that there was more shouting now, more swearing and more antagonism.

At first, Caroline, who had made a point of not celebrating her fifteenth birthday six weeks ago, couldn't help but sense the transition in her home but, not understanding it, had her defences up. She was not prepared to be a victim of this new gloom. She found herself ready to stand up to Judy at every point, believing that her mother was doing her usual, putting Caroline last, taking everything out on her, and actually showing the hostility to her apparent daughter that she had shown on so many occasions. Never much of a mum, Judy blamed Caroline for all her woes. These days she chose to adopt an almost permanent parental scowl. "It's your fault I never have any money."

Caroline was ready for her. "How can it be my fault? It's not as if you ever spend money on me. Just look at the shit clothes I have to wear. I've had this uniform for two years. It's uncomfortable now I've got tits. This blouse is way too tight. Don't you get that, Judy?"

"Don't you dare speak to me like that. I didn't raise you up to be a twat."

"Didn't you? Just exactly how did you raise me? Anyway, I'm not being a twat."

"You are, so don't be one."

"I won't be anything as far as you're concerned."

There was a pause. As if the silence was achieving nothing, Judy chose to break it with a further attack. "It's you who's causing all these problems for me. God, you make me so angry."

"How am I causing the problems? Things don't go right for you and I'm to blame. That's stupid."

"Peter and I can't get on properly with you distracting him all the time." Sitting on the armchair in the living room, Judy cut a miserable form, and with the ashtray resting on the chair's arm, she took a deep drag from her cigarette.

Caroline got up from the settee and walked towards the door, not wanting to say anything.

"Think of all the things I've done for you."

Caroline stopped. "Hey, I know everything you've done for me. I've written it all down. It's what gives me fucking depression."

On other occasions, this would go on for a number of minutes. It ended either with blows or with somebody storming off, most likely Caroline. At this point, Judy was stronger, physically, which was usually decisive, but the older woman knew that the creature she had brought into the world was developing a powerful anger and, when she could be bothered to think about her, she wondered what that daughter of hers might do with this anger. She was a realist. Her physical supremacy would not last much longer. The day would come when the violence she had displayed to that girl in school would be turned back on her. And then what?

On this day, however, Caroline realized that the conflict wasn't really between her and her mother. The trouble was between Peter and Judy. She was being caught in the middle of another of her mother's problematic relationships. All of Judy's relationships had been problematic, so why was this one ever going to be any different? And her mother might be right. On the days when he spent time here, Peter was talking to her more, looking at her and touching her when talking to her. Caroline had come to dislike that touching. She was beginning to sense that something wasn't right.

Things had changed with him in other ways. The man who'd had a positive influence six months ago had undergone a change in attitude that even Caroline couldn't help noticing. He hadn't had much electrical work for months and this had taken its toll on his state of mind. He had, over the weeks, reverted to somebody not quite so trustworthy or reliable, somebody who no longer showed the same interest in Caroline's homework, never mind helping her with it. He seemed more interested in her personal and social life. Caroline didn't like talking to him about the personal stuff. She never had.

In fairness, Peter had sought something within the house, living amongst this dysfunctional pairing that could not be called a family, something that he had never had – the ability to feel good about himself. For a while, things had seemed positive and the relationship between him and Judy had been happy. But, the pleasant picture had faded, as had the sense of novelty created by regular sex, and his enthusiasm for the relationship had been replaced by disinterest and dissatisfaction. Now it was dragged down further by the economic challenge of neither of them having money. The novelty had more than worn off. It had disappeared. He no longer derived any happiness from any of his time in this house and was beginning to despise Judy. He was now feeling just like he had felt in every other relationship he had ever had if he could have been honest enough to admit it.

Caroline, for her part, had made a decision that morning. She wanted this intruder, for that was how she saw him now, far out of her vision and reach at the very least. Judy's bloke needn't make any further effort to ingratiate himself with her daughter, as if that would make up for his abusive outbursts and negativity towards her mother. Any bridge that might have existed had burned in a miserable and predictable fire. From here on he would only encounter nonchalance or mild hostility. He was just another man for her to despise. He could cut out the funny looks and the staring at her too.

Later that evening, Caroline was perched on the settee watching some silly kids' show. She wished something else was on for her to watch, perhaps a documentary or game show. Even a decent movie would have been worthwhile. At least it wasn't a soap. Even the ridiculous primary colours and artificial smiling presenters were better than those programmes. She had imagined a script where a small nuclear bomb had fallen on Coronation Street. Now that would have been some storyline. She would have a go at writing that one.

As she watched, her attention was interrupted by Judy's shrill voice in the back room. "I'm fucking sick of you too. I want you to move out." There was a pause, just as Caroline had turned down the television slightly. "I'm going for a very long walk," she heard her mother say. "Be gone when I get back." Clearly, he had annoyed her again. He was always annoying her.

Why hadn't he gone with her? Caroline had heard the front door slam and decided to make her way upstairs and get out of the way, in case Peter had the ridiculous idea of talking to her about it. There was nothing to be had staying downstairs this evening. When her mother returned, she would probably start on her again and that would be another fight, another outbreak of shit that she didn't need. Not today, anyway.

Abruptly, she ran upstairs, firmly closing her bedroom door behind her.

Within five minutes of lying there looking out of the window, she heard somebody ascending the stairs; the footsteps became increasingly audible and she remained transfixed, looking out of the window.

He knocked on the door and opened it simultaneously. "I take it you heard?"

Caroline refused to turn and face him. "Heard what? I'm not really interested."

"We've had a bit of a row, Caroline. Do you mind if I sit and talk to you?"

She minded. "I'm really tired. I want to have a sleep."

Ignoring her protest, Peter came into the room and sat on the edge of the bed, his back at a slant with his head above her horizontal form.

She put more force into her words. "Look, will you go. I want to sleep."

"I just want to talk to you, love." He reached out and touched the top of her leg. She was wearing her school uniform, and had taken off her tights, so his fingers were underneath her skirt and touching her bare flesh.

She half raised herself and pulled herself away from him, colliding with the headboard. "Fuck off. Get the fuck off me!" Her voice was sharp and defiant.

His expression changed. The pleading look had been replaced by a look she'd not seen before, something sinister, and Caroline, even with her limited experience, recognized the primal urge in his face that she herself sometimes felt. She sensed threat. She could smell alcohol on his breath and his eyes were glazed over.

He struck. Slamming himself down on her, he pinned her down to the bed. The difference in weight between the two meant that she could do little about it. "Look, I don't want to hurt you. I just want us to be friends."

Caroline sensed the danger but opted for defiance. "Get the fuck off me." She tried to knee him in the groin but he was wise to that and had positioned his legs to avoid it, as if he had done things like this before. He now gripped her leg firmly.

Anger took over. "You're an ungrateful bitch. After all I've done for you." With no shortage of force, he punched her in the face. He was a big man, and she felt sharp spasms of pain that engulfed her entire head. She was in the grip of an overpowering dizziness, like a helicopter inside her head was careering into the walls of her skull.

"Come on. You know you fancy me." He started kissing her, on the lips, with an aggression that hurt. Caroline could do nothing as he took control of her. His body odour made her almost retch as he was on top of her. She wanted to bite his face off and would have done it, but he must have sensed this, since he kept her face away from his. The inescapable reality was that she was far too slightly built to shrug off a man three times her weight so all she could do was grit her teeth. She would take his worst. She wanted it over.

All the time he was thrusting into her, her expression was fixed. He had made a terrible mistake. She was no pitiful victim and wasn't going to scream or cry or anything like that. What she was feeling as he finished was the feeling of extreme malice. She silently reassured herself that she would get serious revenge. Nobody could do this to her without huge consequences. She had so wanted to stay a virgin, untouched and independent. Did he know what he had done?

As he raised himself, he had a swagger of arrogance. "I'm getting out of here, now. I'd keep quiet about our little friendship if I was you. I don't think Judy would be impressed."

As he closed the door behind him, Caroline shed no tears. She stared at the ceiling as if she wanted to tear holes in it and bring all the plaster and wood crashing down on her. Against her wishes, he had taken from her that which she would never have given to him or to anybody.

She heard the slam of her assailant leaving the house. He was a condemned man, did he but know it. He had probably done this to others before her, probably to weak little girls or women who couldn't do anything. Perhaps he had enjoyed watching them beg him and squeal, and maybe he had enjoyed their tears afterwards.

There and then, she vowed. In fact, she more than vowed. She knew. It was a fact. That rapist fucker would die in absolute agony for the moment he had just enjoyed. He would not enjoy his death, that was for sure. She would spend hours, months planning it.

She heard the front door; Judy was back. It would be difficult getting to sleep with this anger burning inside her, but

Caroline was not going to leave her bed till the morning. As she mused, tossed and turned all night, she consoled herself with the fact that the house would be better now with just she and Judy in it.

BRINGING THE STING

Caroline has not been fifteen for a long time. Twelve years, to be precise. Life for her is much better now as she careers through the second half of her twenties. She has more choice and power and she has Leoni. On the radio behind the café's counter there is talk of the recent terrorist attacks in London and somebody is droning on about how people have to be resilient and how we all need to stand up to terrorism. A cabinet minister declares how totally safe it is to travel on buses in the capital during these troubled days.

In contrast to all this seriousness and this national need for reassurance, Caroline has opted for a can of Diet Coke to wash down the toast. This is a café that specializes in vegetarian cuisine and that does nothing for her, but the ambience of the place makes her feel relaxed. Not that she is a fan of MacDonald's, Burger King or anything like that; it is just that she likes the taste of meat so why should anybody tell her she shouldn't eat it? This is one thing that she and Leoni always disagree about.

"How can you eat an animal?" Leoni says. "It's gross and it tastes gross."

"Tastes good to me."

"You just like the idea of something being killed for your benefit. It's the hunter in you."

"Nothing wrong with hunting."

"No. But that animal hasn't been hunted. It's been kept in a factory. Never seen sunlight. Might get a glimpse of sunlight when it's slaughtered, but that's all."

"Maybe. I've never thought about it. Do you think I should slaughter the animals myself?"

Leoni doesn't answer. She's said these things too many times.

Caroline muses over the idea in the café. She has no problem killing animals, especially for the dinner plate, has killed animals on occasions in the past. She recalls the strong image of a stray dog that she briefly befriended before tiring of it. The killing on that day had been easy and pleasurable. However, the thing deterring her doing it regularly would be the mess and all the cleaning up afterwards. No. Let somebody else do the killing. She can't be quite so dismissive when it comes to ending the lives of troublesome humans, since the pleasure that comes with that is beyond food.

She looks up from her drink as the door opens and closes. Kaleel smiles as he walks over and kisses her on the cheek. Caroline realizes he is pathetically falling for her, as so many do in this working life of hers, just like they do on rubbish TV programmes and in daft stories. The kiss itself seems utterly inappropriate. Caroline feels like rubbing forcefully at her cheek to wipe away any trace. "For you," he says, handing her an equally inappropriate and ironic colourful bunch of flowers that are never going to have the intended impact.

Kaleel sits down. "Do you want anything?" Caroline declines his offer, so he orders tea for himself.

Caroline keeps a serious expression on her face. She will play her role consummately as always. This is the moment when an angler, realising he has a fish nibbling at the bait, strikes with the rod in a vigorous sideways direction to have the fish inescapably hooked. This is the moment of striking.

"I have something to say. No, don't speak. I need you to listen."

He sits there, all ears, doubtlessly expecting some romantic announcement from Caroline, perhaps a declaration of love and commitment.

"I need some money from you."

Bewilderment takes over. "What do you mean? What money? Are you in trouble?"

"No, Kaleel. You are."

"Babe, I'm confused. What do you mean?"

"I'll make it easy for you. I have photos. Very embarrassing photos." She pauses. "Here's the thing. Twenty thousand in cash, that's what it takes. That way, your mother and employer will never get to see them or the video footage."

He sits there, only capable of staring at her. Caroline has become used to this response. It's like so many of the stings she has done before. She expects nothing different.

"I promise you they will never be seen by anyone on the internet, either."

"You're blackmailing me then?"

"You could call it that. On the other hand, you could call it the price you pay for being so free and easy with your affection. But I do promise you, pay the money and others in your family will never know about your dirty times with me."

Kaleel shakes his head. "Do you think I'm a fool?"

"No. And that's why you'll pay up. You can call it an investment."

"Investment? Investment in what?"

"An investment in you still having a future."

"So it all meant nothing. The times we've had meant nothing to you?"

"No. It meant something. It meant this."

There is a silence that lasts about half a minute, during which Kaleel is looking out of the window. He turns to her. "I'm paying you nothing. There are no photos. You're lying."

Caroline is prepared. This has happened a couple of times before. She reaches into her jacket pocket and pulls out an envelope and passes it to him.

He opens the envelope and takes out a small photograph. He only has to glance at the picture for a split second for a severe frown to appear on his face. He puts the photograph in his pocket. He turns to her, with a look of suppressed anger on his face. "I need time to think about this."

"You have seven days. Within seven days, you text me on the number on the back of the photograph and we'll arrange for you to hand over the money. Don't have any silly ideas, like contacting the police or not paying what you owe. It's so easy to make sure the whole world will see your bare ass and your intimate adventures in the Harvey Hotel. You'll look great on YouTube."

"How can you do this?"

"If I haven't heard from you by this time next week, then I'll destroy your life. Don't look at me like that. This isn't personal. It's strictly business."

* * *

"He's not paying."

"It's not twelve o'clock yet. He could send a text at eleven-fifty-nine."

"It's half-ten. He's not going to pay."

"We'll give it the time anyway."

147

At that moment, the mobile phone begins to vibrate. Caroline picks up the phone and just says, "You have the money?"

"I can't get the money. Not the amount you said. I can lay my hands on eight."

"That won't do, I'm afraid."

"We had sex once. That's still a huge amount of money. If you hurt me, you'll get nothing."

"That's true. But if I get nothing, that means I get the wonderful pleasure of destroying you, and I'm more than happy to do that."

"I beg you not to do this. You won't just hurt me. You'll hurt everyone around me."

"Tell me about it. Now can you have the 20k by twelve or not?"

"No, I can't. Please accept the eight. It's all there is."

She looks across at Leoni, who is frowning. "I'm sorry. It just won't do. You'll be hearing from us. Goodbye." Caroline disconnects, as Kaleel begins to raise his voice in desperation, but in vain. Methodically, she takes the sim card out of the phone and takes some scissors from a drawer and cuts the card in two.

"Send out the photos. Put the footage online."

Leoni looks at her. "We could have accepted the eight grand."

"No chance. He has the twenty. He's just trying it on. He needs a lesson so he's getting a lesson." She shakes her head. "You're too soft sometimes."

* * *

"Which photos shall I send? I was thinking that one and that one."

"They're both great, but we need to send one that does some serious damage. That one's pretty explicit. That'll send a message out."

"A message. But to who?"

"To a couple of people connected to him. It's a message for ourselves as well. We don't take shit. We give it."

Leoni grins. "Well, in that case we should include this one in the message," she says, pointing at one of the thumbnails on the screen, one graphically revealing more of the seriousness of that hotel room activity.

Caroline nods. "Those three should do the damage. I've had a thought. Email them to Kaleel, his mother and his brother. On second thoughts, send a printed picture to his mother. At the same time, we need to get a message to him. Tell him for ten grand, that's the extent of the damage. Nobody else sees them. Nobody gets to see the video." She has a sim card pack in front of her. She tears apart the cellophane and passes Leoni the card inside. "Give him this phone number."

"That's a good idea. You know what? I think we're becoming sophisticated."

"Exactly. And ten grand will still come in handy."

* * *

Five days later, Leoni comes rushing downstairs with the laptop in her arms.

"Kaleel's dead."

Caroline looks up from the book she's reading. "What do you mean, dead? How?"

"I was just searching online for some trace of him after that email and it was on his cousin's Facebook. There's a big report in the Leicester Mercury. 'Tragic deaths,' it said."

"Deaths? Plural? What do you mean?"

Leoni passes the computer to her. "Read it yourself."

Caroline reads the online news report and learns how an old woman has had a heart attack and, unable to cope with the death of his mother, her son, Kaleel Begum has taken his own life. Her heart sinks. Now they won't get the ten grand and she has done all that work for nothing. It has all been a complete waste of time. "Oh fuck. Why did he have to do that?"

"It's obvious, Caz. We killed his mother. We caused the heart attack."

"You don't know that."

"I know it. The shock killed her."

"That's just you guessing."

"No it isn't. And he felt guilty about it. There's no other reason for Kaleel to top himself. If you read the last two paragraphs, the police are mystified."

"Well, that's good then."

"Good? How do you mean?"

"It means they're not onto us. The photos probably were hidden away somewhere. The brother is probably keeping quiet about it out of shame."

"But if they check his email account?"

"A bloke like him will have several email accounts. It's not a murder mystery. I bet the police don't even check his computer."

"We don't know that. It says the investigation is ongoing."

Caroline scoffs at that. "Yeah, and that means two cops and a typist. Shit. I had plans for that ten grand."

SWEET SIXTEEN
(A GIRL'S GOTTA DO...)

"Where you off to tonight?" Judy asked, calling from the living room as Caroline checked herself at the bottom of the stairs.

Caroline was sitting on the edge of her bed applying eye make-up, trying to ignore her mother's presence.

"I'm going to the cinema."

"Oh yes? What you going to see?"

"Don't know." She paused. "Whatever takes my fancy. Might see 'The Matrix'."

"You going alone?"

"Of course."

"You're not going with some new boyfriend then?"

"Of course not." Why was Judy bothering her like this and not minding her own business?

"Where did you get that dress?"

"My job paid for it." Caroline had on a little shiny red low-cut number, revealing her pale shoulders.

Judy had left the living room and was now standing in front of her. "I don't get it." She felt annoyance as her mother felt the material. "You can buy dresses like that, game consoles and god knows how many books from a couple of day's decorating?"

Caroline had on her best poker face. "That's about right. I could buy more clothes and things if I didn't have to pay you board."

"Perhaps you should pay me more board, since you seem to have so much money these days."

"No chance. I pay too much as it is." Caroline grabbed her handbag and her jacket from the bottom of the stairs. She pushed past her mother, who had a look of doubt and disbelief on her face.

"You're a bit dolled up for the cinema, aren't you?"

Caroline didn't offer a reply. She slammed the front door closed behind her and went into the night.

* * *

The following week, with the house in darkness, Caroline quietly unlocked the front door and wandered into the living room. She fancied watching some late-night TV before retiring.

As she switched on the light, she saw her mother had been sitting in the darkness and was waiting for her. "Did you have a good night?"

"Not bad. Boring film. Why are you still up?"

"What was it you saw?"

"Some film trying hard to be scary. 'The Blair Witch' something or other."

Judy stood up. "You're a liar."

"No, I'm not."

"I saw you. I knew you were up to stuff. I followed you. On Bradshaw Street. You're on the game."

Caroline was silent.

"I knew you weren't painting houses. What a story that was. You've been shagging for money."

Caroline changed her mind about watching television. "Well, fuck you, Sherlock Holmes. I'm going to bed."

As Caroline made for the staircase, Judy grabbed her and pushed her hard against the wall, banging her daughter's head in the process. The reaction was instant and instinctive. Caroline sprang back against her and within seconds had pushed her mother onto the carpet below her and had the sharp point of a blade digging into the older woman's throat. "Now listen here, Judy. Listen properly. Don't, don't, don't ever question me again. I do what I want. I pay board, and for you that's enough. If you ever follow me again, or lay a finger on me like that, I will rip your throat out. It will be the last thing you do. Do you understand?"

Judy lay there, still and petrified, but didn't respond. This was the world turning.

"I said do you understand? I'll end your life now if you don't."

Judy nodded. She was shaking now. "Yes." It came out like a whimper. I get it."

Caroline calmed down just as quickly. She sprang back. "Right. I'm going to bed now. I think you should do the same."

Judy remained shaking for over an hour after her daughter had gone upstairs.

INTRODUCING LEONI

She was walking. She did a lot of walking. Caroline found that the world was easier when she wasn't still and liked it best when she wasn't at home. At her own steady pace, she was very comfortable moving through the world she inhabited and found the town she lived in to be a much less intolerable place. She enjoyed walking around with her permanent sense of alertness and liked to take in the details of things she saw. She admired the nice cars and the impressive trees and flowers, whilst frowning at the tasteless curtains and pathetic behaviour she encountered. The miserable rain was refreshing, the raindrops kissing her face as she went past countless shop windows, where she noticed deplorably cosy couples, wretchedly hand in hand and equally deplorable loners (ugly, stupid or dirty), and dumb men who leered at her, dangerously (for them).

When out walking like this, Caroline maintained her gentle grip on the handle of the knife in her coat pocket, ready to act. Since the Peter incident three years ago, Caroline had felt the need to be strong, the need to be able to fight back if cornered, the need to be able to harm any attacker, even make a necessary first move against somebody threatening an attack. She had acquired the knife, a pearl-handled affair with the sharpest of blades, and it made her feel like Zena the Warrior Princess. When she had started working Bradshaw Street and the roads around the park, she had discovered that a blade was always useful for those punters who threatened trouble. And then there was that pimp she'd had to deal with in Nottingham.

Fortunately, she hadn't had an occasion to use it recently, this weapon initially bought on the internet to be used on Peter the rapist when she caught up with him. She had gone looking for him on a number of nights, but he seemed to be elusive. Either that, or he'd died, or he could even be in prison, perhaps for another perverted act. There was no way of knowing.

She was more than ready to cut up any rapist or any punter who dared to attack her, but killing Peter would be special. Regularly, she had practised moves with the weapon in her bedroom, bringing the blade out quickly, swift arcing movements, powerful forward thrusts, merciless dragging motions, doing these moves over and over like a soldier preparing for the battlefield. She had even studied anatomy and knew where to strike for instant death, where she would connect terminally somewhere decisive, particularly the carotid artery. One day she would bring forth that powerful spray of blood and create a masterpiece. She would enjoy the splash of colour. Caroline imagined herself drinking the colour and screaming with delight.

Two years had passed since the turning point of her relationship with Judy. Judy had known to watch her step with her ever since. Things were actually better these days, since Judy now gave her respect, something the younger woman had never had from her mother. Now that she held the upper hand in the house, they could co-exist without Judy getting on Caroline's nerves so much, and Caroline had her privacy.

Of course, she had never bothered to tell Judy about the rape. Why would she? Judy was hopeless, more of a nuisance than a mother. Strangely, with the new deal she had now established, Judy was the ideal mother for Caroline right now. She had been forced to give up the idea of having any authority over her, had a vague moral compass herself, so couldn't, shouldn't and wouldn't engage in any conflict of values with her offspring. The fear actually made Judy a better person as far as her daughter was concerned. That was not to say that there weren't still problems, since Judy was often incapacitated in some way, either from prescription drugs, gin, or a combination of the two. Caroline just let her get on with it and enjoyed free reign over her existence.

She turned a corner, past MacDonald's and heard shouting. She was curious, and scurried forward, beyond the lit window of the fast food restaurant. Two people were in some kind of a scuffle. Caroline moved forward, keeping out of their vision whilst eyeing the scene.

"Where's my fucking money?" The man, with short cropped hair and a face that was creased up with anger, a Union Jack tattoo on his neck, had hold of a petite blonde woman by the back of her neck, his face against hers.

"I never took your money. You must've lost it."

"Don't fucking lie to me, bitch. I want that money back." His hands had moved dangerously to the front of her neck so that he appeared to be preparing to strangle her. She had her hands on his arms as if to resist.

"Stop it. You're hurting me."

"Hurting you? If you don't give me my money back right now, I'm going to kill you, not hurt you."

"No, you aren't." This was a voice now immediately behind him, a calm certain voice that took him totally by surprise, a young voice, yet one with an intent beyond her years, and it was a voice that had a close relationship with a sharp blade that he now found pressed against the side of his neck. It was a voice devoid of emotion.

"What the fuck?"

"I'll tell you what the fuck. You've ten seconds to get away from here or I am going to cut out every piece of you I want for the human jigsaw I'm making. In a moment, I will give you a push. You should run. You'd better hope I don't come after you." Caroline was excited. She had been waiting for a moment like this. She was ready to strike decisively. Her hand gripped the knife tightly. Part of her hoped he would be awkward and give her the reason to do it.

However, the man had lost his aggression. It had poured out of him like water through a hole in a bucket. He relaxed his grip on the blonde girl and stumbled away from the blade of Caroline's knife, all the time looking back at her with hate and fear in his eyes. He looked far less formidable now, as if the touch of Caroline's blade had removed that surplus of energy and emotion.

Left behind was this young blonde girl, a similar age to Caroline herself but not as tall, still astounded at how she had been rescued from this predicament. She watched as her assailant vanished around the corner. "Thanks for that. He would have killed me. He was warming up when you started. I'd better go." With that she turned and started jogging away.

Caroline casually placed the knife back in its pocket and continued her walk.

DOING THE BUSINESS

The driver indicated that they were on Hattersley Park Road, another part of the town that carried a reputation for some that meant a business opportunity for others. Caroline got out of the cab and was careful not to catch her heel on the kerb, like she had done earlier that week. This was her second night working here. Last night, she had done three jobs and felt that that was a pretty good start in a new venue where she wasn't known. Business had needed to move on from the previous workplace for a while, where a couple of pimps were flexing their muscles and had beaten up a few of the girls. Caroline was not going to have her face ruined or face time inside for stabbing a pimp if she didn't have to. Tonight's success had shown that the move might be a profitable one anyway.

Another girl approached. Short black skirt, open white top and fishnets gave a not so subtle hint that this would be competition. It didn't matter. Three other girls had been working this part of Hattersley the previous night and it wasn't as if there wasn't enough work to go around in this deprived place.

Caroline was thinking that there was something familiar about her and then she realised who it was. It was the girl she had rescued the previous week. She'd bailed her out and the bitch had rushed away with the most meaningless of thank yous, as if Caroline owed her, not the other way around. The size of that brute, she had probably saved her life, with that intervention preventing her receiving a savage beating at the very least.

However, this was another time. Furthermore, this was business. As she always did with the competition, Caroline nodded to her and there was a space of about twenty yards between them.

Suddenly there was a flash of recognition twenty yards away and the blonde approached her. How Caroline did not want this. On working nights, Caroline did not do conversation, not unless it was with a punter.

"So you're a working girl too?"

"Caroline nodded, then turned her head away from the enquiry.

Undeterred, the blonde continued. "You're too pretty to be doing this."

Caroline almost laughed, but it really wasn't funny.

"If I'd known that you were like me, I'd have thanked you properly, rather than running off."

"That's OK." Caroline sensed that she was not like this one. Not one bit. They breathed oxygen. That was probably their only real similarity.

"Your first time on Hattersley?"

Again, Caroline nodded. Why hadn't this idiot moved away? This was work, after all.

The girl's expression changed. "Oh shit. Here they come. Police."

Caroline looked where the girl was looking and could see the unmistakable form of a police car a couple of hundred yards away.

"This happens sometimes. Come with me."

Reluctantly, Caroline followed. With gentle jogging on high heels and no small amount of clip clopping, she was led around the corner and down a side road. About twenty yards on, they turned along a lane that ran alongside the front of a series of garages.

"Quick. Nip in here."

Within minutes the two women were between two garages. The petite blonde pulled a cigarette from her bag. "Here. Have one of these. I'm Leoni, by the way."

Caroline would keep her identity to herself. "I don't smoke."

"Me neither. At least, not from next week. You might like these. They're menthol."

Caroline shook her head. "How long do we stay here?"

"About five minutes. I usually have to do this several times a night when they're in that kind of mood. The advantage of this road is that you can see them coming up the street long before they get here. They don't like us working here because of them." She indicated some place somewhere beyond the garages.

"Them?"

Leoni became emotional. "The poshies. Those people on that side of Hattersley with their big houses and their big gardens. Hoity fucking toity, the lot of 'em. They don't like us working here. They've complained so much about us that most of the girls have gone. Driven out."

Caroline looked at her watch. How long was five minutes?

"I want to get back out. It's Frank's time at half past."

Caroline looked at her. "You know the names of punters?"

"Sometimes. You get more business if you're nice to them. Take an interest and stuff."

"I never want to know their names. I despise them." Caroline felt superior to this one. There was something grubby and low about her and it wasn't just her broad accent or her inability to say a proper thank you.

"I only learn the names of regulars. Helps me to remember. Frank just wants a blow job every week. Says his wife's not interested. I'll just pop out and see what's happening."

Caroline stood there and waited till Leoni returned.

"Fuck. They've parked up right next to where we were. Looks like there's been more complaints than usual this week. I'm going home."

Caroline didn't answer. She was glad to see the back of this irritation of a girl. She decided to brazen it out. She decided to walk right past the police car, go further along the road and see if somebody like that Frank fancied some female attention.

Three days later, Caroline was back on the same street corner. She had an uncomfortable feeling in her stomach and supposed that that was due to not having had anything to eat since lunch. The thing was, the fish and mushy peas she had eaten had sat heavily insider her, and she had decided the best thing was to fast until the morning when she would go to the Whitegate Café on the high street and have egg, beans and waffles. Best meal of the day, that was.

She was dropped off again by some guy with long hair who had sucked her tits while she wanked him. The money he had given her for that service would buy her food for the next few days. Another punter now would enable her to buy some new lingerie. Two or three after that would finance a jumper and a top she had seen in Top Shop.

Suddenly she felt a sharp pain.

Everything went hazy. Caroline lost consciousness.

* * *

She awoke and looked around at a white world with splashes of light and dark blue that eventually became disappointingly clear. "What am I doing here?"

A nurse was at her bedside, looking down. "You've had a narrow escape."

"Why? What happened?"

"You nearly died. I'm afraid you had a burst appendix. Your friend saved your life."

"Friend?"

"Dialled 999. Little blonde girl. Pretty. Lots of people die from what you've had so she did well. Came in the ambulance with you. Had you both been to a party or something?" She touched Caroline's black mini dress, which was hanging over a chair. "Been a while since I wore finery like this. Too many weekend shifts."

Caroline surveyed her surroundings. Four beds in this small ward, each one occupied by somebody a good bit older than she was.

"Are you going to ring home now you're conscious?" the nurse asked.

"Perhaps later."

The phone call wasn't made, and Caroline, having spent another night in hospital, was allowed to leave. "We can book an ambulance for you," the doctor said.

"No need. I'll get a taxi."

"Well, to discharge you we need to take you to the taxi in a wheelchair. Are you sure there isn't somebody to come and collect you?"

Caroline groaned.

It was just after noon when Caroline was able to plonk herself in her bed at home. The previous night, she hadn't slept much, not in a ward rich in coughing, snoring and farting, so she needed to catch up.

The clock said seven. Caroline needed to go out. She had been full of thought in the hospital and needed to see someone.

She found her on Hattersley Road.

The blonde girl looked shocked but pleased to see her get out of the taxi that pulled alongside. "So you're alive."

"What's a burst appendix when you're the best blow job in town," Caroline said.

"Good for you. Are you here to work then?"

"No. Not for a week or two. I've come to see you. Thanks to you I'm alive. You could have left me for dead, but you didn't. You've quite surprised me."

"Surprised you? Did you think I was a selfish bitch or something?"

"Something like that. Anyway, there's a pub there." She pointed to a building with a sign hanging outside about fifty yards along Hattersley. "I want to buy you a drink."

"OK, but I don't have ID."

"Who the fuck needs ID?"

Within ten minutes, they were sitting in the bay window of The Grapes Inn, each wondering if this was the beginning of something.

"Anyway, you never told me. Why did that wanker attack you?"

The girl, who had introduced herself to Caroline as Leoni, spoke as though it was utterly trivial. "Oh, I did a shag on him a few weeks ago and nicked his wallet. Nothing major."

The girl said it as though it was normal. Caroline didn't smile, but she enjoyed the honesty.

"Do you do it a lot?"

"What? Stealing or shagging?" Leoni laughed.

"Both. Obviously, I've done plenty of the sex bit myself but you steal as well?"

"Yeah. If the opportunity arises."

Caroline nodded. "That's impressive, getting some extra like that. Perhaps you can show me how you do it."

"Impressive? Except when they catch up with you. Like that night."

Caroline looked into an imaginary distance, at a place where men were lining up waiting with their sick moronic faces. "It's no less than they deserve anyway. I'm sick of servicing these cretins for thirty quid a time. "

"Thirty quid?" She raised her eyebrows. "I always charge fifty."

"Fifty? No wonder I'm popular. I'm charging more when I'm back working."

Leoni seemed to go defensive. "I don't always do it. Rob them, I mean. It's a bit dangerous."

"Yeah, I bet. I saw that. I'm actually keen to learn more from you." She felt electrified by this striking confident girl fate had brought to her. "I've never rescued anyone before. Never had the urge to rescue anyone. I want to know something? Is Leoni your real name?"

"Yeah, it's Leoni. Punters call me Lulu, though. They don't know Leoni."

"Why Lulu?"

"Got to preserve identity. The people in the ambulance wanted to know who I was so I gave them a false name too. Keep identity for family and friends. Not that I have much of either."

"Me neither."

"Well, in that case, it's good that we chose each other to start our life-saving careers, then. If I'd known you were like this, I wouldn't have rushed off that night like that. Sorry for that."

Caroline patted Leoni's arm. "And I'm glad you did what you did for me. Massively. Tell me more about how you managed to rob that knobhead though? I'm fascinated. Was it easy?"

"Well it varies. Sometimes it's easy, but at other times you have to make it easy."

"So you do it regularly?"

"Once or twice each month. It pays pretty well. Better than just giving them sex. Just a bit more dangerous. As you saw. And you have to move around a bit. You do the same location and they get you if they come looking for you."

"So how did you manage to rob him then?"

Leoni had her head down looking into her glass like it housed a worthy secret. After a few seconds, she raised her face, as if to allow the secret to float out of the glass. "Let me explain how. Are you sitting comfortably?"

"As well as I can with a burst appendix."

"The thing is, it only really works with overnight stuff."

"Overnight? How does that happen?"

"I get the John to take me to a hotel. Doesn't have to be a nice hotel, just somewhere with a bed. Can even be their house or flat if they're single. Do the work, paid beforehand of course. I tell him I won't charge for extra services if he stays with me till the morning. So there's no rushing off, no line of punters. I just do the one. Make him feel special. I wait till he's asleep. That's when I do some sneaking around and empty the wallet. It's the risky bit of the whole business. Believe me, that takes more skill than the sex. If he catches me, I'm probably gonna have to fight my way out of there." She held up her fingers. That's why I have these sharp nails. Anyway, when I've found what I want, a few crisp notes, it's time for a hasty exit."

Caroline displayed her half-smile. She didn't meet many people she liked and her dislike of this girl had left with her appendix. "I can already think of a better way."

Leoni looked puzzled. "A better way? A better way of what?"

"A better way of making some money from these bastards. The work has to involve having a drink or a meal with them, though, so it's that kind of punter. An all-night job. What we do is, we load their drinks so that they sleep properly."

"You mean spike them?"

"Why not? Have you never thought of doing that?"

"No. I always thought I could pull stuff off naturally. Never really considered getting them pissed."

"Well, what happened that night should show you otherwise. Get the fuckers so drunk that their brains are so clouded over that they can't even remember you properly. Could even drug them."

"Rohypnol?"

"I'm not sure that's the name for it. That's the date-rape drug, so not really that one, but something like it. We'd have to find something that works. Perhaps stick with the spiking first. See where that gets us."

Leoni put her glass down and leaned back, keeping her eyes firmly fixed on Caroline's. "You said we. Are you wanting to go into business or something?"

"I don't see why not. Never been in a team with anyone. Might be fun." Her smile gave way to a more serious expression. "Just don't let me down." Caroline patted her coat pocket. "You know what I'm like with a knife."

A SEVERE CONSEQUENCE

They were running. It was the only thing to be done right now. Caroline, some metres ahead, kept looking back. Her friend was keeping up, but only just. "Come on."

Leoni was panting, and the words came out ragged. "Aren't we safe yet?"

"We just need to get to City Square. Once we're in that taxi, we can relax.'

Leoni stopped running. "Who do you think might come after us? He won't be doing much."

Caroline slowed. "I'm just being careful," she said, turning to face her as she continued moving. 'Now come on, get moving. Unless you fancy being in a cell."

"There's no way I'm doing time." Leoni found a new determination and resumed running.

Three weeks prior to this, at around the same time, they had been on the Norton Road, just like tonight, but the mood had been different. The two were working. Somebody had pulled up alongside them and Leoni had got herself her first punter of the evening. Caroline had waited for her to return just like she always did, since the way they worked it, there was always one of them watching out for the other. Well, as far as they could in this risky business of theirs.

Leoni had been gone an hour, and that was usually more than long enough for these sad cases. If he took her to a hotel, that was different, and in that case, Leoni would send her a text from the bathroom saying as much.

Hotels were the best deals, but they were rare. 'A night inside', as they called it, might pay dividends, unless the punter rushed off. While he slept off the sex, emptying his wallet in the early hours was a possibility. If he gave signals that he only wanted the hour and then would be off home, as most did, they were left with just the payment for the service. It was all money.

She looked again at her watch then looked into the distance in both directions. Still no sign. Where was she? Caroline's record with a punter, her personal best, was ten minutes. On that particular night she had looked particularly professional and the bloke, who was enjoying his first night off the oil rig, just couldn't control himself, which actually Caroline preferred. That was one thing about this job. Punters often got too excited and it was over pretty soon after it started. It meant she didn't have to have the degenerate arsehole inside her for long. It was even better if he wanted to rush off. A spent male meant no need for further action, and she wouldn't have to perform the act longer than she had to, although it was a repulsive act that paid well, as her wardrobe testified. She was good at this now, and unintentionally made these hopeless Joes feel better about their impotence or premature finishing through smiles and reassurance. "I love an early happy ending," she said, but not to the customer.

Leoni had been gone over an hour. Caroline checked her phone again. Nothing. Leoni was good, meaning that a blow job was often done and dusted within ten minutes, while a shag could last anything from eighteen seconds to half an hour.

In Leoni's case tonight, to last an hour, that probably meant somebody was wanting some company, some sad Herbert who had an inadequate life and wanted to pay for a friend for sixty wretched minutes. Caroline always cringed. It never failed to shock and disgust her when these pathetic characters wanted to talk, like Sam, a regular late-night punter who always wanted a conversation after she had wanked him off. The bottom line was, she despised all of these wretched arseholes and could gladly have killed most of them if they didn't guarantee her lifestyle. They were just an insult to themselves and humanity.

She noticed movement at the end of the road, next to the chemist's. Somebody walking this way and in a hurry, by the look of things. The bright red mini skirt gave her away. It was Leoni. Caroline moved towards her and within a minute they were within reach of each other.

"The bastard didn't pay."

"No. What did you do?"

"What do you think? Told him I wasn't moving until he paid. The shit started hitting me and pushed me out of the car."

"Wanker. Did you get his reg?"

"Of course. He wasn't a regular. I've seen him before, though."

Caroline's eyes narrowed. "Well, we'll be seeing him again."

An hour ago, that same punter had been cruising the Normanton Road. Leoni and Caroline were standing in their usual spot, and Leoni's face had lit up when she had seen a car approaching with the registration that was ingrained on her brain. "That's him. The non-paying shit from the other week."

"Hang back." Caroline went up to the car and he wound down the window.

"Special offer tonight, love. Two of us for the price of one. Maximum pleasure."

He looked uncertain. "I'm not sure about that."

Caroline put on her most wicked of smiles. "Hey, we can please you like you've never been pleased. Do we know how to be a tag team. "

The man's uncertainty fell away and his eyes lit up. "OK. Sounds interesting."

"It will be. We're going to give you a night you will never forget."

The wig had been a good idea, as had been the sunglasses. He hadn't given a flicker of recognition as Leoni had seated herself in the rear of the car, with Caroline, confident and assured, in the front. "Just drive us to a good spot, somewhere we can have a party. You're in for the time of your life."

He was a short guy, slightly built, dressed in double denim and wearing glasses with thick lenses, with that same depraved look that so many of them had."

"What's your name, sweetheart?"

"Paul. What's yours?"

"I'm Lisa and this is Sammi in the back. We're going to show you something really special."

He had driven them into an area in the town where factories stood all around, a place that would have been busy and thriving in the daytime, but which was utterly deserted at this time of night. Ideal, in other words.

Caroline looked around her and approved. "Hey, this is great. What a fab spot. How about this, Sammi?"

Leoni made an approving sound, opened her handbag and was ready and waiting.

Caroline gave her a look. "I'll tell you what. I'll go first. You can come in after I've warmed him up. That suit you, Paul?"

Paul nodded and sat back in his seat, as Caroline manipulated his zip. Initially, her head went down, and Paul closed his eyes to enjoy the moment. After about thirty seconds she came away from him, leaving the blade of her knife touching his bare flesh and ready to strike. He thought… Well, who knew what he was thinking? Caroline didn't care. Was he thinking he could be treated this nicely and not have to pay for it? Was he thinking that he could attack both of these women and remove them from the car with some rough treatment? On the other hand, was this an occasion where he intended to pay for the services he was given?

Caroline was looking at his face with utter contempt, milling the situation over. She now had her nails firmly digging into the side of his neck, drawing a small trickle of blood which seeped onto the collar of his light grey polo shirt. She moved back and gestured to Leoni with a slight movement of her head.

Leoni pushed herself through the gap between the front seats and had her face next to his. As Caroline held the blade at almost arm's length, poised to do serious damage, she said, "Do you remember me, Paul? We had some time together. It was a few weeks ago."

Paul was too busy being petrified to give a significant reply. Wide-eyed and wondering if this was the end, he could only mumble, unintelligible and child-like.

Leoni opened the car door, went outside and opened the driver's door. She was above him now.

Leoni continued, leaning in. "The thing is, Paul, you never paid me. And then you were really rude to me, and that's just not on." At some point, Paul began to utter the word "No" and to this day, the two women can't decide whether the screams were a result of Caroline's blade cutting into his groin, or caused by the swing of the small but weighty builder's hammer that Leoni inflicted with a righteous fury on Paul's head and face. Either way, it was quite a spectacle. Not that anybody saw it. Leoni gave three angry blows to the side of Paul's head and he fell to the side. That was enough. He was down and staying down for a while. The cut to his groin was not fatal but was deep enough to leave a memorable scar.

Paul was left unconscious and bleeding, with severe indentation in the skull and lower abdomen as the two young women left the scene. They held hands and ran together from a man who was possibly dying or dead. Who cared anyway? Leoni laughed out loud in the knowledge that nobody would hear her in this protective darkness. The only thing on both their minds was getting far away from here. Caroline knew that if he was dead from their dual attack the shit would hit the fan, so it was best they get home to Leoni's flat.

* * *

"Time now for an appeal for help. Detectives in Derby need your help after a vicious attack not far from the city centre. I'm joined now by Detective Inspector Jim Matthews from Derbyshire Police. Jim, this was a dreadful attack."

Caroline and Leoni loved 'Crimewatch'. Usually, it gave them ideas and inspiration, but tonight's episode was special.

"Yes, but thankfully one that is extremely rare. The information that we have is that on the twenty-seventh of May, James Bennett, a local man, picked up two women in his car. He had offered them a lift home from a night out."

"So, he was being the good Samaritan, then?"

Leoni cringed.

"Exactly. Anyway, one of them, a woman, going by the name of Lisa, sitting in the front of the vehicle, put a knife to his throat and made them drive them to a deserted area, where they attacked him in what can only be described as a savage fashion. He was left needing hospital treatment and is now recovering from a fractured skull. The second assailant was introduced as Sammi. She was particularly brutal and used some kind of blunt instrument in the attack."

"So shocking. What do you think was the motive for an attack like this?"

"We think it was random. Obviously, we want to catch these individuals. We have artists' drawings of the suspects, which everybody can now see. The victim says these are both good likenesses. He described them as women in their early twenties, both with long straight blonde hair. The one called Sammi has a broad Derby accent. I don't think that Lisa or Sammi are their real names and people out there might know them by different identities. These are two highly dangerous women. If anybody out there knows these individuals, they should ring the number being shown on the screen right now. We are really determined to find these violent women. They clearly need to be caught. We have to warn the public, however, that they are highly dangerous and should not be approached."

"Looks like we're famous," Leoni said.

"Guess that's the end of our time on Normanton Road," Caroline said.

"And the long blonde wigs," Leoni replied, dragging her hand through her curls.

"Those drawings look nothing like us. We'll be old and dead before they catch us."

IN CONVERSATION

"How did you start?" Leoni asked her.

"Start what?"

"Doing the work. What else?"

"It sort of happened by accident."

"What? You fell into a punter's car and accidentally started giving him a blowie?"

"Obviously not, Lu, totally unexpected. I found myself at a party one night and was in a bit of a difficult situation. Needed to get a taxi home."

"I bet I can predict the rest. I've been there. You offered sex to pay for a taxi."

"That's what happened. I offered two arseholes blow jobs if they would give me a tenner each. They were drunk, but not too pissed to hand over money." She laughed. "That's how I started. I was sixteen. Still at school, although I wasn't going there much. I got home and I put the change from the taxi on the table in my room. I actually had money. That was fucking massive, having money. And you?"

Leoni gazed into the distance. "With me it was different. I'd left school. Was at college. Two girls on my street were working Park Road. Suppose I wanted some independence. I soon realized that I could earn more money doing the street than I would ever earn from going to college."

"What did you do with the money?"

"Just spent it on clothes. I've the best wardrobe on the whole estate."

"Yeah. There's no getting away from it. It pays."

"As long as neither of us gets a habit going."

"Yeah. Some of them are working for nothing virtually."

"And then there's the pimps."

"Bloodsucking leeches. Hate those twats. Did a stint in Nottingham and ended up drawing my knife on one."

"Fuck. What happened?"

"Demanding money. Said it was his turf and I should pay him. Had me in a corner. Got me by the neck. I don't take that from anyone. He got one in the stomach. I was out of there sharpish. Don't know if he bled to death or survived."

"Is that the nearest you've come to actually killing someone?"

"So far. I know I will kill sometime. I only left school two years ago so there'll be plenty of opportunities ahead of me. It's just a matter of where and when. If life's taught me anything, it's that you have to stick up for yourself. You want to know the best way to stick up for yourself?"

"Go on then."

"Be explosive about it."

"What does that mean?"

"Do it like you mean it. Do it like you love it."

"Just like the sex?"

"Exactly."

SETTLING THE SCORE

Caroline switched off the TV. "Right. That's it. I'm bored with staying in. Let's go out."

Leoni looked at her like she was insane. "What? We were out last night."

"That was different. That was work."

Leoni had spent the previous night with a bloke called Terry at a Holiday Inn, with Caroline hanging around just in case. She'd eventually emerged with a hundred and twenty pounds and the almost poignant words "That was shit" as she'd joined Caroline in the car. "OK, I suppose I quite fancy a drink. But if there's any hustling to do, it's your turn."

"No. We won't be doing any of that tonight, but we can talk about it. Call it a business meeting."

An hour later, the two young women were in The Liquorice Parade, a wine bar in the town centre. Caroline had ideas. "Listen. It's a waste how we're doing this. We could make much more money than we're making."

"How?"

"Their cards. There's so much more money in their wallets

than the ten and twenty pound notes. Why don't we try to steal a credit card or two and do some real damage? If we play it right, we could hit twenty shops before the mug even realizes."

"Be even better if we could learn the punter's pin number."

"We could try for that."

Caroline held her index finger vertical in front of her face. "I have an idea. When I talk to the idiot, I'm going to let it slip that I use my mother's birthday as my pin but I have trouble remembering even that. I'll ask whether he uses a birthday for his."

"Do you think that will work?"

"Well, if he says yes, he might be dumb enough to say the number."

"That won't happen. Who'd be that stupid?"

"I guess the big challenge then would be trying to find out key birthdays around him. His wife's or kid's would be the main ones."

"You'd have trouble getting that info on a date. You'd give yourself away."

"I know. That's the sticking point. We have to find a solution to that."

Leoni smiled. "I could do that. I always fancied myself as a detective. You could text me some details from the ladies' I. go online then, and find out what I can."

"Great idea. I could do that. And if he doesn't use a birthday as a pin number, we go to plan B."

"Plan B?"

"A bit trickier. It involves a pair of binoculars and watching him when he uses a cashpoint."

"That's tricky. I'd have to be in position somewhere, perhaps in the car. The car would have to be parked in the right place or I'd have to be standing where I could see without being seen."

Caroline felt really positive. "That's right. I'm sure there's a real devil in that detail, but it can be done if we put enough thought into it."

"There's one drawback. As soon as the punter wakes, he'll know he's been hustled. He'll ring and get his credit card cancelled straight away. We'd be reported and arrested before the morning comes. I'm not doing prison."

"I've got an idea about that. An idea I had a while back. That's why I asked you to get Brett here."

They weren't waiting long, since Brett, Leoni's brother was sitting at their table within fifteen minutes. All Leoni had told Caroline about him was that he was into drugs and 'a load of dodgy stuff'. Plus, he had some pretty useful contacts. Five years older than Leoni, he had already done stints inside, on two counts of robbery, with one or two drug offences also taken into consideration. He was pretty mean-looking, sporting a closely shaved hairstyle, with a long jagged scar below his right ear from a knife fight. He had been known to stroke the scar with his finger, declaring, "A fucking victory scar, this is. The wanker who gave it me's a vegetable now." Learning about Brett and his specific knowledge and connections had reminded Caroline of an idea she'd had a while ago.

Within seconds of landing at their table, Brett had made a point of putting his hand on Caroline's, which had been greeted with a choice phrase that he recognized from his own repertoire. Oh well. He sat back and listened to what his sister and her highly attractive friend had to say. He could still do some business. "You want sleepers. I can get you some, but it'll cost you."

"What's the sleeper and how much?" Caroline had taken an instant dislike to this brother of Leoni's, but needs must, so she stayed quiet and let his sister do all the talking. She had that blood hold over him that would be more likely to lead to a successful outcome.

"It's Temazepam, shortcake. Tammy for short. Half a teaspoon in a drink will fucking knock somebody out for about ten hours. What do you want it for?" Brett was clearly intrigued.

"Caroline here has trouble sleeping. She stays awake all night and it's making her tired in the daytime, really tired."

Caroline raised her eyebrows, then nodded. "I really need knocking out or I do no sleeping at all."

"How old are you?"

"Twenty."

"You look older. You tried the doctor?"

His voice had a sarcastic tone that made him even more irritating. Was every single man on this planet so totally annoying?

"Of course. Nothing works. Pretty powerful insomnia, I've got."

"Well, this bastard will definitely knock you out." He winked at his sister. "And anybody else you want knocking out."

"How much?"

"Give me two hundred quid and you can have enough to last you a long time. A half teaspoon will take care of anybody."

"Caroline looked hard at him. "We'll give you a hundred and twenty."

Brett looked back at her but knew he had met his match. "Hundred and forty. I have to make something on the deal."

Caroline was unflinching, while Leoni looked on, fascinated. "Ok. Get the Tammy to us here tomorrow and it's a deal."

Brett looked confused. When Caroline left to go to the bar, he looked at his sister. "Hey. What's happening here? That's still plenty of money to be spending on Tammy. You got a scam doing, or some sugar daddy I ought to know about?"

Leoni smiled. "None of that. Let's just say, Caroline's a friend in need."

When Caroline returned, carrying three drinks, Brett said, "Great that my sister cares about you sleeping. Always thought she was a bit of a selfish cow."

Leoni took hold of her friend's hand. "You got me wrong. What I won't do for a friend." She looked straight into Caroline's eyes and Caroline knew.

Brett took a large swig from his beer before returning to their business transaction. "Well, don't take too much of that stuff. Half a teaspoon will have you sleeping for more or less a full day. A full bastard knocks you out for ten to fifteen hours. You have any more than that, and you might need an undertaker."

Brett left the scene. Caroline's mind was already racing through scenarios. "So the plan is, we get a punter, hit a hotel or whatever, we drug the punter, we ravage his credit card. We need to sort out the details. Getting that credit card number will be the thing."

"This is where I come in. I'll do what you suggested, in position somehow so that I can observe the punter when he goes to a cashpoint or attempts to pay for something with the card."

"So we've decided that's your role from now on? Observer?"

"Not exactly. More observer and researcher. I'll keep my eyes open and use the car to our advantage. All you'll have to do is the sex bit, and I'll do the other stuff."

"All I'll have to do? Did you really say that? There's nothing easy about entertaining these knobheads."

"But you don't drive."

"True. I am working on that one, though." Caroline had been having driving lessons for the past six weeks. She had seen how even a little car like Leoni's gave her so much freedom.

"You can look after yourself better than me anyway. You give them the Tammy at a convenient time, maybe slip it in when they go for a piss or something or when you ask them to go back to the bar to get you a different drink. You probably won't have to do much anyway. And you know how most of 'em don't last very long anyway."

Caroline pulled a face, then shrugged her shoulders in begrudging acceptance. "OK, I guess that role is more me. As long as you do your bit. I don't like it, but I guess it's better me than you."

"You don't have to like it. You just do the dirty stuff and wait for the John to fall asleep. As soon as he's knocked out and snoring, you extract the goods. After that we meet up somewhere close by and do some shopping. "It's win, win, win. I won't be far away."

"OK. I get it. We'll need a variety of masks for when we raid the cashpoints though, and some kind of disguises for hitting shops. We'll go to Northampton or Leicester tomorrow and buy some wigs."

"Just think of the money, Caz."

Caroline's attention was drawn to a neon sign she could see in the distance. "Do you fancy a dance?"

They'd been in Crazy's for about ten minutes when Caroline spotted him.

She had felt an inward shudder and had stopped dancing almost immediately. Without saying anything, she walked a few steps away from her friend, then turned to look again, all the time keeping out of sight. She made a gesture to Leoni and went to the bar, where she ordered a Tia Maria with plenty of ice and reassessed the evening. She knew at that second that the night now had a different flavour.

Leoni joined her at the bar. "What's wrong?"

"You know I'm doing the sex stuff from now on."

"Oh. You're not changing your mind about that?"

"No. Not from tomorrow onwards. I just need you to do something for me tonight."

Leoni's heart clearly sank. She groaned. "Tonight. No, Caz. Not on our night off."

"Yeah. Look to the far side of the room. The edge of the dancefloor. Don't let him see you."

"Who?"

"You see that bloke there in the black waistcoat, with two others. He's in the middle."

Leoni surveyed the dancefloor, and her eyes settled on a small group enjoying the music.

"I see him. The older ones."

"Well, he's an old friend, and I want to surprise him."

"Well, can't you do it then?"

"No. That's not happening. Let's say he's not so much a friend."

"What do you mean? Who is he?"

"Peter."

"Peter. Stepdad Peter? Rapist Peter?"

"Yeah. That's Peter."

Leoni gave a quick glance as she drank and then looked back at Caroline. "The one in the waistcoat. That's the bastard. Yeah?"

"That's him."

"And you have an idea?"

"Yeah. I want you to go over there, show an interest in him, then get him to take you back to his. Do everything you need to. Get him to take you back to his."

"Where will you be?"

"I'll be watching from a distance. Just make him an offer he can't refuse."

"What if he refuses?"

"There's no need for a plan B. He won't refuse."

"Does he have money?"

"He might do, but we're going to do the plan a bit differently this time. Don't mention money."

It was easy. Caroline watched as Leoni approached the three. She would be making sure Peter sensed that it was him she was most interested in. Leoni adeptly managed to disentangle the trio and within the hour, she was discreetly signalling to Caroline with a behind-the-back thumbs-up gesture that the objective was achieved.

He'd had plenty to drink, so once the door of his flat was closed but not locked, Leoni did the work. She undressed, trying to appear excited despite the obvious squalor of her surroundings, throwing her garments onto each other on his sofa. Peter looked like a child getting a new bike as she undid his buttons and unzipped his jeans, both of them giggling as he led her into the bedroom. Naked, he fell back onto the bed. She was immediately astride him, grinding away meaninglessly and soullessly, making enthusiastic and encouraging noises. She added vigour to her movement, waiting for him to come so that she could end this chore. After he gave a grunt of completion, she got up. "I need to go to the toilet. Won't be long."

A minute later, she had entered the bedroom.

It was very dark as the silhouette of her form approached. It was dark enough to hide everything.

For about thirty seconds she just stood there in the darkness, a shadow looking down at him and remembering.

She recalled him on top of her, hurting her, then pushing her aside like he had the right to do absolutely anything. She recalled his hard brutal words and the way he had punched her in the face.

Well, here was payback. She had always known this time would come. She just hadn't expected it to come tonight.

For the second time that evening, a woman was astride Peter.

She struck quickly. She flashed the knife across in a way that would have been spectacular if anybody had been able to see it.

Force and speed, just like she had rehearsed so many times. Peter the rapist screamed as his penis was instantly dismembered. "This is what you get for what you do," she said, as she held the blade aloft in front of her. She looked down at him, writhing and bleeding, wondering whether she should finish him. He did deserve to die, after all. She would have killed for so much less. It wasn't as if this man had any real right to live, especially after what he had done to her. In her mind, nobody could do anything to her if he wanted to carry on breathing.

As he squealed and screamed intermittently, Caroline decided on a U-turn. Killing him would deprive him of the half-life he would now be forced to lead. This would be far better revenge. She put the knife away.

Caroline left the room, carrying his lost appendage in a supermarket bag she had found on the floor of Peter's kitchen. She kept running until she found Leoni waiting in the agreed spot. She held up the bag. "He's not having this back. It's going in the canal." Challenging or what, Peter? she thought.

LEONI LOSES

Leoni wasn't happy. "Why me?"

"You pulled him. I didn't. Next time you're meant to observe, just observe."

"I guess it was habit. An opportunity was suddenly there in front of me."

"That's right. And now you're gonna make some money."

"How do I look?"

"You're getting there."

"Just tell me I don't look like a schoolgirl trying to get into a pub."

"What? You don't look like that. You look pretty good."

"You would say that. You look about twenty-five, but I don't."

"You look good. That's enough."

"OK, but we both know you look better."

"No, we don't. You're missing the point. You're the one in the driving seat tonight. Enjoy the moment." Caroline managed a smile. "Anyway, you look old enough. When you go to work, it won't matter. Let's just make sure that one of us nails the card number."

This time the venue was the Britannia Hotel in the centre of Manchester. After the incident with Peter and the earlier incident that had got them on national television, it made sense to avoid Derby for a while and do other towns. This was the third long weekend they had done in Manchester. It was a city rich in potential and possibility. They just needed to discover the fruit that hadn't made itself available during the earlier weekends.

Tonight, Leoni had lined herself up to do some business with a business-type who had taken a shine to her the previous night while she had been stood at the bar. Ironically, she had been keeping an eye on Caroline, who had eventually drawn a blank with a tall European guy who had appeared interested but who really probably would have been more at home on Canal Street.

"OK, so how are we doing this? I presume it is a 'we' thing?"

"Well, if you can get him to a cashpoint or a keypad and one of us can see it, we're laughing. I'll be watching and trying to see. You do the same. More likely he'll have some money on him. Tens and Twenties. The cards are the big prizes."

"I get that. I'll be giving him the Tammy as early as possible." Caroline had used the temazepam on three occasions and it had worked a treat every time. She was developing the technique of inserting it surreptitiously, so the punter would have no sense of the deep sleep that was coming to him. And what a buzz it was afterwards. It was so satisfying and enjoyable, robbing while the victim was completely out of it.

Caroline was in the hotel already in position when Leoni arrived. She had seated herself in the rear of the main bar area close to three empty tables, one of which would serve as their destination. She was enjoying a large coffee when Leoni walked in. There was a gentle ambience in the bar area and Caroline found it easy to relax as she ate the complimentary nuts.

She watched as Leoni approached the punter, all tits and a big smile, Caroline felt her heart beating faster. She couldn't take her eyes off her, especially since she looked so stunning in that turquoise two piece with a long black curly wig, looking to everybody around like this was a date to be enjoyed rather than a working moment.

Laughter. They seemed to be getting on well. It was easy to see why. Anybody could get on well with Leoni in that divine dress. Caroline could see nothing but smiles, and the body language from the punter looked promising. It would be a good thing if Leoni could occasionally take the lead in situations, and do the dirty stuff when needed. Perhaps tonight she could make money as well as Caroline could, as it would give them that sense of equality that she knew was good for their relationship.

After an hour and a half had passed, she watched as Leoni went with the punter towards the lift. This meant that things had gone well, that she was getting a result. Unfortunately, she had been unable to get card information, so she presumed Leoni had managed something, otherwise this would be a cash deal.

Caroline didn't feel good, and it was nothing to do with money. As the doors closed, Caroline felt something negative, something that wasn't in their plans. Caroline was jealous. Impossible. She didn't do jealousy, since that meant weakness. However, watching Leoni go in the lift like that had felt like she was losing something, letting go of something precious. This was a complete first. Was this how somebody in a relationship felt?

She ordered another drink, a gin and tonic this time. She sipped from that and then sipped some more. She ate the rest of the nuts that were in the dish in front of her. She began to feel like someone who was in the wrong place at the wrong time. Everything about tonight now seemed wrong. She even found herself now hating this hotel.

Two hours later, with the bar now closing, Caroline finished the drink but she was concerned. Something was wrong. What had happened? Had something gone wrong with the Tammy? Had it not kicked in yet? Why wasn't Leoni out of there? Why was she still in that hotel room? Everything should have been done and dusted by now. If she was staying till the early morning, she would have texted, surely.

She sent a text. 'How are things?' it said. She took a seat in the hotel lobby and kept her eyes on the phone for a reply.

Ten minutes later, she hadn't received one. She pressed a finger to make a call but resisted the impulse. The last thing she wanted was to endanger Leoni. Listening intently, nothing to allay her concerns happened. The plan had been for Leoni to leave the hotel as soon as the Tammy took effect, which should have been an hour ago.

Caroline decided it was time to move, having the sense that her friend's life might be in some kind of danger or that she might be hurt in some way. That was not going to happen.

She was soon at the lift. Leoni knew the risks, but so what? Her text had said room Three hundred and sixteen, so Caroline got out on the third floor. As the lift doors opened, Caroline burst through. Her hand was already on her knife. She was one hundred per cent committed to a violent defence.

She hurried along the corridor, scanning the numbers as she went. 328… 326… 324… She quickened her pace.

The door of 316 was open, so Caroline rushed through into the dimly lit room, the blade of her knife horizontal next to her waist, ready to strike. She looked ahead of her and was pained by the sight. Leoni was laying on her back on the bed, looking as if she had fallen asleep, although the purple marks on her cheek and left eye were a dead giveaway.

Caroline rushed to Leoni's side. She prayed that the unthinkable had not taken place.

It hadn't. Well, not quite. Leoni managed to utter words. "It went wrong, Caz."

"What happened?"

"He saw the Tammy. He got a bit angry."

"Didn't you have your back to him?" They had gone through this so many times. They had even practiced at home.

"Yeah, but somehow he saw it. I think it was through the big mirror. He just went crazy."

"Where did he go?" Caroline surveyed the room, hoping for an enemy but sensing that there would be no immediate revenge opportunity. This would be someone angry and desperate. He would have vacated the area and might not even be in the city centre anymore. Caroline wanted to be face to face with this bastard. She wouldn't want to leave Manchester until she'd caught up with him.

"I don't know. He must have knocked me out. He was just hitting me...over and over. I thought this was it. That I was being killed."

Caroline lay on the bed and, for the first time in her life, hugged someone. She held Leoni close to her and it was unclear whether it was to reassure and support Leoni or to express her own relief that she was alive, if battered.

They parted slightly still holding each other and their eyes met. Almost at the same moment, their lips met. Their open mouths were together and this was not a kiss of friendship.

Caroline found herself overwhelmed by an intensity of feeling that her life thus far had not prepared her for. There had been hints of something, sensations that up to this point she'd dismissed on so many occasions. Now, she was overpowered with the promise of something brilliant.

Caroline was stroking Leoni's hair as she continued to kiss her. Leoni reciprocated, albeit weakly. Before long, Caroline stood away from the bed and undressed. Leoni watched.

Caroline stood there looking down on the battered and beaten woman whom she loved beyond anything and then lay down next to her, never shifting her gaze. In Caroline's mind was the promise that nobody would ever hurt this woman again. She wrapped herself around her. At last, and utterly unexpectedly, Caroline was experiencing those feelings that had evaded her for so long. The strength of feeling was not hers alone either, she knew. For the first time in her life, Caroline knew mutuality.

She momentarily left Leoni on the bed to close the door. She didn't want them to be disturbed.

* * *

Two days later, Caroline was again sitting in a bar. This time it was the Midland Hotel, the place where Rolls had met Royce before the creation of their legendary cars and engines. This chocolate-coloured building, not far from Deansgate, the main hub of the city, was a well-recognised landmark as far as most Mancunians were concerned. The bar area was pleasant and spacious and she savoured the classiness, even if her reasons to be there were not quite so sophisticated.

She had left Leoni back in a hotel room they had booked, recovering from that severe beating she had taken and seemingly enjoying the fact that she was now in a relationship that wasn't just a business deal or even merely platonic. Both had everything.

"I love this," she had said, holding Caroline's hand tightly.

"Me too. Didn't expect it, but I'm glad. I'm sorry it took you hurting so much to do it for us but…"

"Every cloud." This was not the first time Leoni had finished Caroline's sentence and it would not be the last.

Arranged online that afternoon after a Facebook chat while Leoni had slept, the man she was waiting for was going to be wearing a suit and would be sporting a red tie, so she kept her eyes peeled. She tried to tell herself that his was just another job. In reality, she was still deeply seething about what had happened. They would make enough money from this to pay the mortgage for a month, or longer, and the price for doing it was going to be minimal. Just a bit of sex.

She was sitting there, sipping away. Sipping was a prerequisite in this line of work, since more committed drinking would lead to a lack of control and more chance of a disaster like the one that had befallen Leoni.

On her own at the table and wearing a red dress, she was very distinct and the man who approached her certainly felt that way. "Are you JoJo?" he asked.

"I am," she replied, trying to appear amenable and friendly. More importantly, she was concentrating on a role that would earn her money.

He took a seat next to her. He was confident and clearly was the man of money his Facebook profile had suggested, judging by the way he called over the hotel staff and requested a rum and coke. Caroline enjoyed meeting up with men of status. It made the victories even more satisfying.

She saw through this man, whoever he was, and wanted an early outcome. "You know what? I've always wanted to stay in a room here. Shall we do it?" It was a gamble, but she needed a quick result. She looked at him in the knowledge that her eyes were full of meaning.

He smiled. "Crikey, you're a woman who knows what she wants."

"Yeah. I'm like Lady Macbeth. Full of purpose."

He stood up. "OK. Why not." Grinning, he left his seat and went to sort out the room. Caroline took advantage of the situation and put a smaller amount of temazepam into his vodka and tonic. She wanted him drowsy but not asleep. This was a different kind of plan.

Once in the room, the medication had begun to take effect as she undressed him and secured him, tying his hands together, then his feet. He wasn't going anywhere.

"What are you going to do to me?" he asked, with an expression on his face that seemed to be encouraging her to do her worst.

No problem. She would definitely do something close to her worst.

* * *

Caroline threw six hundred pounds in twenty pound notes onto Leoni, who was still horizontal but looked better than earlier.

"Fucking hell, Caz. How did you get that? You only just met him."

"Yeah. Did it differently this time. Made him squeal a bit."

"Squeal. What? Sexually?"

"No. The opposite. Totally sexlessly, if that's a word. Used the knife. Had him at my mercy, all tied up and that."

"I bet that took him by surprise."

"Put it this way. He won't be wanting bondage ever again. Real easy, he was."

"Tell me, Leoni urged.

"Started by introducing him to the blade." I said to him, "This is your saviour this evening. He must have thought I was one of those religious nutters or something." As she said this, with her elbow resting on the bed, she held up her arm, causing her silk sleeve to drop down and a red stain to be dramatically visible. "I drew a little blood then I gave him a choice. I told him he could have no money or no life." Caroline moved her hand from left to right across her neck to make the point. "Obviously, he chose the first of those."

"Good going. At least one of us made some money in this city. Better than my disaster, at any rate."

"I enjoyed it. Somebody needed to pay for what happened to you. He coughed his bank details like a little kid giving up his dinner money. It felt good."

Leoni looked serious. "He'll tell the police."

"He may do that. So what? We're going back home soon so they can search for us in Manchester till the end of time. Besides, the way he looked at the end, I don't think he'll go anywhere near a police station."

"How can you be sure? He'll have recovered by now."

"I told him that if he did that, I, or somebody connected to me, would kill his wife and daughter then I wouldn't care one bit if they caught me or not 'cause I'd enjoy that so much. I had his wallet photo of them in my hand as I said it. 'I know exactly what they look like. And where to find them,' I told him. His face looked a picture. I'd made a bit of a mess of him though. Lots of blood."

"Brilliant. Well done, babe." Leoni held out her arms invitingly. "I missed you."

ANOTHER JUDY CHOICE. (MOTHER'S NOT SO LITTLE HELPER)

A few weeks after Manchester, with a light heart, Caroline pulled up outside the house. Before going in, she wanted to look at some living room furniture on a few websites. She took out her mobile from her jacket pocket. Sitting there, she looked for a sofa that would suit Leoni's flat, which to all intent and purposes had now been home for Caroline for over two years. She reckoned that black leather would look really good in there.

"Leather's no good for sofas. Cold in winter, hot in summer."

"I think that's a heating issue, not a furniture one. Leather always feels good."

Moving out from here had been inevitable. On the day she had done it formally and technically she had been unemotional. Caroline had been packing clothes into a suitcase in her room and filling a large box with books and compact discs when Judy had discovered her. "You're moving out?"

"Yeah. I'm moving in with Leoni. There's no reason for any of my stuff to be here anymore and it seems right. I am nearly twenty-one, you know. I've been with Leoni all these months. I should really have moved my things before now."

Judy had been clearly disturbed by this, even though she hardly saw Caroline at the house these days. "So you're leaving me on my own then?"

"That's right. Don't worry. I'll still visit you sometimes."

"So I'm going to be on my own. It's a long time since I was on my own."

"I've hardly been here. Knowing you, you won't be on your own for long."

"I don't know about that."

"One thing, though. Got some good news for you. I'll continue paying you board."

Judy had had a surprised look on her face. "You will?"

"On one condition. You keep my room as it is."

"What? You want it as your bedroom still? Even though you don't live here?"

"Exactly that. You'll have security, money-wise, and I'll have a just-in-case room. A hidey-hole."

Judy now found it easy to assent to that arrangement. "OK. If that's what you want."

Moving out certainly hadn't taken long. There were no longer many of Caroline's things at the house so, one packed cardboard box later, completed within an hour of informing Judy, Caroline no longer lived with her in any sense. An era of her life was over. She had embarked on a better one.

Tonight, eight months later, there was a strong smell emanating from the kitchen of that same house. Judy had cooked. Fortunately for her, after Caroline's exodus, just as her daughter had expected, she had managed to find some male company that she reckoned had potential. This time, it wasn't somebody she didn't know. It wasn't some dodgy individual who would pretend to be nice for the novelty of some easy sex. It wasn't somebody who would shock her with hostile unpleasant behaviour and a scornful attitude. It wasn't someone with no intention of forming a relationship. She'd done the negative stuff so many times. It had never proceeded well and had never ended well. The last thing she wanted now was another relationship that wasn't.

This time she had gone for familiarity. Her current beau was a man whom Judy had known in her youth, a man she would have been wary of when he was a boy, when he had been known to be something of a rogue. He had been to court a few times, with the occasional spell inside for violence that had never been his fault. He just stuck up for himself, he claimed. Moreover, all these years on, Jim had a new maturity about him and he was prepared to spend the night with Judy on a regular basis. He was also prepared to share his skunk with her and smoke her cigarettes. What was there not to like about Jim?

Like a lot of good questions, this one had a not-so-good answer. What was not to like about Jim was his dark side. He worked hard to hide the consequences of a pretty tough upbringing that had included a severe father with hard hands that he was keen to use on his children, and a neglectful mother hooked on painkillers. All too often she had been out if it and ineffective as a mother, so it was easy to understand why Jim was like he was and how he might not have held women in the high esteem that they might desire.

Perhaps Judy would be the answer to his questions. Perhaps these days he spent with her and these passionate nights were changing him, giving him a more positive opinion of the fairer sex.

Not today. On this particular evening, Judy had pushed him just that little bit too far.

Their relationship had developed quickly. After a period of late night hooking up over recent months, he had been staying at Judy's house quite a lot these days and tonight Judy had been in one of her rare cooking moods. The rarity of this could be best summed up by the fact that Caroline had not even experienced any home-cooking until her twelfth birthday, when Judy had had a rush of blood to the head and left the packets in the freezer compartment in favour of a chili con carne. This had been one of the three meals Judy knew how to make, if the truth be known, the others being spaghetti Bolognese and beef stew.

The Italian meal was the delight she had prepared for Jim to accompany the six o'clock news, which he watched religiously, even if some of the news reports had him shouting at the television set.

Things had started promisingly, with a conversation about the weather and a promising horror film on the TV that evening. Bringing a lull in the mood had been Jim's assertion that spaghetti Bolognese was a boring meal. Judy had ridden that one, but then, Jim had said something about Judy's choice of clothes. "You should wear sexier stuff when I'm coming here."

"What do you mean?" She was sitting at the side of him, taken by surprise.

"Just nice clothes to get me going. Don't you know that at your age?"

Judy, being Judy, paused to consider his words then she had felt compelled to make a suitable reply. "And you should wear sexy clothes too, then. Baggy jeans don't exactly get me going, you know."

Not long after that, the spaghetti Bolognese was all over the living room floor, and Jim, fuelled by seven pints of beer that afternoon, three games of pool that he had lost money playing, and a tablet that somebody had suggested would take him out of this world, had a shrieking Judy by the throat. He had her pushed painfully against the back of the sofa. "Don't you ever give me mouth like that. I've had a shit day. If you know what's good for you, you'll keep a civil tongue in your head tonight."

A tearful Judy was visibly shocked. "But, Jim. I cooked it special. I don't cook very often, and now you tell me it's boring. Then you slag off what I'm wearing. How am I supposed to react?"

"You react by keeping your mouth shut." At this point his demeanour softened. He relaxed his grip on her and returned to his side of the sofa. She was allowed to recover.

Outside, Caroline, who had seen plenty of furniture that would look great in the flat, had heard the commotion inside. She was considering her position, not exactly sure what to do. This was a surprise visit. She had come to pick up a few items from the bathroom that she had left behind, but judging by the noise coming from within, she sensed some kind of domestic going on. She hadn't yet met her mother's new beau, as she only ever called there in the daytime once every two or three weeks.

Caroline had a good idea what kind of relationship Judy had landed herself in. She recognised it as a situation not too far removed from earlier ones that she too strongly remembered. Caroline felt herself becoming lost in painful and horrible memories.

In the living room, Jim had taken command. "To make it up to me, get this shit cleaned up. Then we can watch that film."

At first, Judy, red-faced and breathing heavily, appeared meekly to surrender and began to put things right, scraping the food back onto the plate.

Then she stopped. "You should clear it up. You made the mess, not me. That's only fair, Jim." She left the wasted meal where it was and left the room to go into the kitchen. She needed a cigarette.

She didn't get there. Like a bull, he charged after her and in the kitchen doorway he gripped her tightly by both arms, forcefully enough to guarantee severe bruising and tight enough to have Judy squealing with pain. She could do nothing. When she looked into her boyfriend's eyes, lust and acceptance had been replaced by hatred and contempt, a disdain for her that was all too familiar. His hand flew up to tightly grip one of her cheeks. His scowl deepened.

The brutality stopped.

With a sudden and painful realization, Jim turned. Contempt in his demeanour had turned to shock.

He found himself looking into the cool staring eyes of somebody he had not yet met. It was somebody who was going to be the last person he would ever meet. His hand dropped to his left side where the handle of a knife was protruding, held firmly and being twisted by an assailant he had not been expecting. She was unflinching. Caroline coolly watched the pain in Jim's face, continuing to stare at him with intent and contempt as the life begin to leave him. In a vigorous movement, she pulled out the knife and thrust it in again, creating a new hole next to the one she had just made. Blood was spreading through his clothes on that side. It began to run across his hand, which was now at his side.

Judy could do nothing but stare in horror with her hands pressed to her face.

Jim began to totter. Caroline backed off slightly and pulled out the knife. Away from him, her mother watched with a twisted expression on her face as he fell to the ground with a resounding thud. Judy, paralysed with disbelief at what she was witnessing, looked like she was seeing some final horrific scene in a horror movie.

A red pool began to form around his body. Caroline looked down at it, wondering whether the red liquid would cover the entire kitchen floor. That would have been a great photograph, she thought.

"Oh fuck. What have you done?"

Caroline stared at her, showing the ruthlessness that Judy herself had played such a big part in creating. "I've finished him. That's what I've done."

"Why?"

"Why? Why do you attract dogshit like this?"

Judy, normally hard-faced, was visibly shaken. "What are we going to do now? You fucking stabbed him. What the hell did you do that for?"

"Because I wanted to, and because he wanted me to. He asked for it."

Judy was almost hysterical. "What? Asked to be stabbed?"

"Yeah. That's right. Starting like that when I was coming visiting."

"But we didn't know you were coming."

"We?" She looked down at his corpse. "You and this thing hardly looked like a we."

Judy moved to the kitchen chair and sat down, not once taking her eyes from the corpse on her kitchen floor. "And now we're going to go to prison. Nobody is going to believe it's self-defence. I can't do time."

Caroline was up to the new challenge. "We're not going to do any time. We're going to get rid of this knobhead while it's dark and then we'll clean up. Who knows he's here?"

"Nobody. He had no close family. He mixes with people in The Globe and The Swan, but that's it."

"Great. Your usual type, Judy. Thought he would be. I'm just gonna make a phone call."

"Who're you ringing?"

"Just you put the kettle on. No sugar in mine."

Half an hour on later, a rolled-up carpet, secured by loads

of silver duct tape, was being carried in a clumsy fashion to the waiting car that Leoni had driven here, a BMW estate that she had managed to borrow from somebody who owed her. Once the carpet and its mortal contents were safely contained in the back of the vehicle, all three women got in the car and they drove out to a wood they knew, about ten miles from the town of Mansfield, where Judy said there was a lake.

"This is like the movies," Leoni said.

"Which movies?" Caroline enquired.

"Those old movies. Black and white. Doesn't a murderer put a corpse in the water in that one about that motel we watched the other week?"

"No. You've got that wrong. He put corpses in the cellar, like Fred West."

"He puts his mother's corpse in the cellar. Other corpses go in the lake. Just like we're doing."

Judy's anxiety had subsided as Caroline had done a sterling job in convincing her that death was the best thing for this brute. At one point, she had actually laughed. She joined the conversation. "Some of the best films are black and white."

Caroline liked to disagree with Judy, even pretend to disagree. "Rubbish. They're unbearable."

"No they're not. Hitchcock films and Laurel and Hardy are back and white. They're fabulous."

"Hitchcock!" Leoni exclaimed. "It's one of his films I was just talking about. He has a body in a rolled up carpet in it, I seem to remember."

Caroline turned to face Judy. "She's talking about 'Psycho'. Like that twat in the back. One serious psychopath."

Fortunately, the area they headed to was deserted. "This would make a good film setting," observed Leoni. It was a dark evening with a thin crescent moon and a total absence of stars, and together they dragged the carpeted corpse from the car park, in and out of a cluster of trees to the edge of the lake, which was tranquil and still, totally at odds with the three women and the mission they were now undertaking. At the water's edge, they tried to ensconce stones inside the carpet to act as weights when the corpse was thrown into the mass of dark rippling liquid. With enough stones put in to guarantee a successful sinking, they once again picked up their trouble and tried to carry it, but this was an even more difficult task now, due to the added weight of the stones.

Like slapstick in a television comedy, Leoni and Caroline both ended up falling, collapsing into the water and the carpeted corpse dropped with a loud plop and a large necessarily heavy stone escaping out of the open end. At this point Leoni started laughing in a way that contrasted the eerie darkness. Both were kneeling in the shallow water now, yet they couldn't ignore the urgency of covering up Jim's decline. Judy, suddenly regaining a sense of the enormity of what they were now doing, barked at the two younger women, "Come on, we need to get this done."

Caroline, in a jocular fury, kicked fiercely at a lump in the carpet and sent a flurry of water droplets into the air. "This fucker's not co-operating. Take that you bastard." This had Leoni laughing even louder. Caroline enjoyed hearing Leoni laughing.

Eventually they were able to wade out far enough to drop Jim into the river, where he sank. He would be discovered one day, but nobody would ever be tried for his murder. Nobody would ever miss him. Some epitaph.

On the way home, after dropping Judy off, relief and belief took over. Caroline, although soaked like the others in the car, was singing along to a tune, a tune she normally hated, one of those slushy Motown songs about falling in love and all that shit. She fancied a dance.

IN CONVERSATION

They were seated opposite each other at the kitchen table, cradling hot drinks. Leoni shook her head. "That was some night."

"You're telling me."

"I hope Judy's grateful."

"I don't think Judy does gratitude."

"The back of that car will need a thorough clean tomorrow. There'll be loads of DNA in it. I'm getting up early to do it. In fact, we can both get up early to do it."

Caroline put her hand on Leoni's. "Don't worry. The bloke's a nobody. Police aren't going to be sniffing around."

"We'll clean the car anyway."

"Yeah, you're right. We should. Who knows? We might want to borrow it again."

"When? When you kill another waste of space?"

"Possibly. There are plenty going around. And I did enjoy it."

Leoni reached behind her for the green ashtray and lit a cigarette. "What did it feel like?"

"It felt good, Lu. Really intense, like an orgasm."

"What? The killing, or just using the knife?"

"Both. I always knew I'd enjoy it. Like that pimp in Nottingham. Like I enjoyed hurting Peter. There was a buzz about both of those, and this was even better."

"Do you ever wonder what it must be like to die like that?"

"No. Course not. Why would I?"

"Just wondering."

"Never gonna spare one second of thought on how some dogshit bloke feels. Let's be honest, anybody I hurt deserves what he gets. He's either an evil dickhead or he's a stupid one. It's all the same to me."

'We're not the same, are we, Caz?'

"How do you mean?"

"I can't get the kick out of killing that you get."

"Yeah. That's because you don't like blood. Anyway, you've never actually killed anyone."

"True, but it's not just that."

"I know. That's why it'll always be me who'll be doing it."

"Why, d'you think?'

"Don't know. Perhaps we should be the same. Both had shit times growing up. Both been abused by men."

"I reckon I could kill if I had to, self-defence. I wouldn't enjoy it, though."

"Perhaps you would. You don't know until you do it."

"Why do you enjoy it?"

"I enjoy it because…I don't really know why. I think I like the power of it. Tonight, when he looked into my eyes, I just felt totally in charge, like a god watching him die. Like with that bloke at my mercy in Manchester. I know he didn't exactly die, but the fear on his face was something worth seeing, like a powerful Mahler moment."

"And Peter?"

"Yeah, Peter. He walks around with no dick, probably wishing he was dead. Oh well."

BIG INCIDENT IN
LITTLE SHEFFIELD

Some years on from the killing of Jim, Caroline is sitting on a park bench, watching the ducks on the pond that stretches out before her.

She waits. There is often waiting in this line of work.

She finds it fascinating that these birds float on water and hardly fly. They do appear to be quite heavy creatures, she thinks. She concludes that it is probably the same reason they float so well on the water, like Faye Thompson, a plump girl in her class in the primary school, who was really good at swimming too. The bullies at school would home in on her, make barbed comments and treat her like a leper. Yet Faye took it all in her stead and just kept on with her swimming. Caroline almost admired her for that.

She wonders if Faye has kept up the swimming. Did she eventually become tired and give in to the burden of her weight and, without the motivation provided by the nastiness at school, settle into the more relaxed life of a couch potato, all television and crisps, with full fat cola to wash it all down. Why did so many women have so little pride?

The twenty thousand pounds Caroline is going to collect today is going to get her much more than television and crisps. It is going to be fair recompense, handed over in return for not putting out footage of Barry Palmer in a blue dress on all fours with his tongue up her arse. Barry can carry on being the manager of a substantial building project in South Yorkshire, where his image at work will be macho and reliable, not that of somebody who can't get it up without cross-dressing and who thrives on the simulation of lesbianism. He is all performance, is Barry.

When he first proposed his unusual preference to Caroline, he had been sheepish, indicating that many before had turned him down. Caroline was hardly going to do that. A brilliant investment opportunity. The only disgusting thing, as far as Caroline was concerned, was the actual sex itself, not what its context might be.

It is five past three. Barry is late.

A woman approaches, a tall slender woman in a sheepskin jacket, with a mass of blonde hair in an oversized bob that has benefitted from some serious use of one or more hair products. She slows down. Caroline is irritated. She wants her to have gone past well before Barry turns up with the cash. Abruptly, the woman stops and turns to face her. "Are you the bitch demanding money by any chance?"

"I'm sorry." Caroline has her right hand in her jacket pocket and firmly gripping her knife's pearl handle. She considers her exit strategy. The nearest gate out of here is only a hundred yards away.

"You're the bitch who's after money. I know you are. Twenty thousand, I hear. I'm here to tell you to fuck off."

Caroline stays silent, considering her options.

"I know where you live."

She looks up at the woman, challengingly.

"Plant Street, Derby." She looks at Caroline with a hard stare. As a specialist in matters like this, Caroline recognises intent and sees no trace of bluff. "Am I right?"

Caroline keeps every part of her face still. She keeps her lips together, determined not to acknowledge the question in any way.

"I'm right. Well, you picked the wrong one this time." She turns to her right as if she is studying the long path ahead of her then turns and faces the opposite direction. Like Caroline, she wants the conversation kept private. "You have two options. You can either forget about Barry and his little quirks, or you can carry on with this little game of yours. I have to tell you something, though. If you carry on and distribute that video like you're threatening to, we will come for you."

"I don't know what you're talking about."

"My cousin's already interested. He's a bit enthusiastic, knows some other enthusiastic people too. I'll hold him off for now. Give you a chance to disappear back under your rock." She moves her face closer to Caroline, but not within biting distance. "You stay away from anybody in my family. Otherwise, we'll bury you. And I do mean that literally." Caroline can't help noticing that the woman has a hard weathered face, and up close, her skin appears as delicate as old leather.

Caroline says nothing, but inside, her steel trap of a mind is in full progress. Nothing can happen right now, but this is a new crisis, one that she hasn't had to face before. This wife of Barry's, if that's who she is, is somebody worth thinking about, it seems.

The woman is half walking away, but then turns back towards Caroline. "A word of advice. Never scam somebody whose marriage is on the rocks and whose marriage is to me. I've been doing a lot of checking up on him for a while. I want my big day in court. I intend it to be a very big day. Last thing

I want is him giving my money away to some Midlands slag. I hope I'm understood."

After a few seconds of hesitation, Caroline nods, hiding the dark thoughts that have gathered. The woman is already walking death, even if she doesn't know it. That has already been decided.

"Now fuck off. And don't come back to Sheffield, or we'll feed you to the pigs."

The older woman turns and moves away.

Caroline sits there and enjoys the darkness of this sunny day. She turns her attention back to the ducks.

* * *

Today, Leoni is exhibiting her ability as a private detective. "The cousin's Matt Shields. He runs a haulage company in Rotherham. Bit of a rough arse. Big bloke, dresses scruffy, doesn't shave. Bet he hates women."

"Sticks by his sister, apparently. Where's he live?"

"Sheffield."

"I guessed that."

"Not far from Barry and his missus."

Caroline doesn't reply straight away, but remains deep in thought.

She doesn't even look up. "They have to die."

Leoni turns her head. "What do you mean?"

Caroline's eyes widen. "It's easy, babe. We need to kill them."

"Why? We can just write off the twenty grand."

"That's already written off. We're not going to see any of that."

"So what are we going after then?"

"Nothing. We just need to remove the threat. It's too disturbing. They know where we live. They know about here."

"Does that matter, though? If we back off, I mean?"

"Of course it does. This house is a target for them. She made that pretty clear. They can act against us, either now or later, most likely when the dust has settled. I saw it in her eyes. I want to be able to sleep at night. Don't want to wake up with one of their thugs standing over me, or even that ugly bitch herself, for that matter."

Leoni laughs. "There's not much chance of that."

Caroline's eyes narrow. "That's the difference between you and me, Lu."

"How do you mean?"

"You'd have loose ends."

"Two people in Sheffield who don't like us are hardly that."

"They're exactly that. Loose ends mean we're vulnerable. We could just as well hold our necks out for our throats to be cut. I don't do vulnerable, and you know that by now. I didn't get to thirty years of age being vulnerable." Her eyes widen. "I won't be a victim. Not much chance of something threatening is way too much chance."

"What do you propose, then?"

"We need to prepare a couple of late-summer bonfires."

* * *

Four days pass following the above conversation and there is a knock at the door. Caroline goes to answer it. Leoni's brother, the ever-confident and always-resourceful Brett, follows her into the living room, carrying a large cardboard box. "I feel like Father Christmas."

"Well, you're certainly going to give a warm feeling to somebody, that's for sure," Caroline says.

Brett reaches into the box and pulls out a wine bottle with a thin rag sticking out of the end which has been wedged into hollowed cork so that the end of the rag is just above the liquid. "Let me introduce you to Mr Molotov. A regular party starter."

"You sure it'll work?"

"Of course it'll work. They'll all work. I tried a couple out this afternoon in Hawley Woods. Fucking incendiary."

Caroline and Leoni take hold of two other identical versions in the box. "What's the liquid in there?" Leoni asks.

"It's a combination of petrol and oil. Highly inflammable. The explosion will create a burst of flame and a blast of power for massive impact. A few more of these, and you could take on the army of a small country."

"OK." Caroline rolls out a map on the dining table and points like a wartime general. "I need to get to this spot when you arrive at that one. It's an old abandoned hospital and it's even deserted in the daytime, so at night it's ideal. That's for me. From there I make my way to Barry's house. From where you park up, that spot there, you'll have the same distance to cover. We need to set off from those two points at the same time at the same brisk pace."

"What if we're seen?"

"We won't be. We've checked both places. There'll be no one about and it'll be pitch black. Just you make sure you park the car next to that park, on the left side as you approach. The light is very poor there. From there it's four minutes' walk to the home of the brother, same as it is for me where my car's gonna be parked."

Brett frowns. "Are you sure you need me for this? This is murder."

"No it's not." Caroline raises her voice. "This is self-defence. These bastards will kill your sister and me if we don't kill them first. I need you to go with Leoni cause she's a crap thrower. Just target an open window. It's been very warm at nights so they're bound to have at least one window open."

Leoni turns to Brett and speaks. "I'll do the downstairs part of the operation."

"What's that?"

"The letterbox. Sealing the exit."

Brett turns to Caroline. "And are you having somebody with you?"

"No. I'm ready to do both at Barry's. That bitch is good for it. I'm going to do it all with a smile."

Brett suddenly becomes curious. "Just remind me how much you're paying for this?"

"To you? Five grand, providing we don't get caught. You make sure you do a good job with the throwing and make sure you and your sister get out straight away without any hitch. Don't hang around to watch the bonfire."

"Five grand? This is murder, you know. Carries life imprisonment. It's got to be worth more than that."

"Yeah. We can argue about the money afterwards. As I said, if we don't do it, your sister and I will be murdered, probably in the same way. These knobheads have threatened it already and they're expecting us to hide and cower. Well…" She takes hold of one of the explosive wine bottles. "This is the only cowering I do."

* * *

It's pitch black. This is a country lane, where passing cars aren't so regular a feature so street lighting is absent, leaving behind a convenient cloak of darkness for somebody with malice in mind. Wearing a black top, black trousers and a balaclava, she approaches her target. It is two fifty-seven. Ignition is due at three.

She scales the fence and is at the front door without any detection. She knows from Leoni's reconnaissance efforts 'delivering leaflets' earlier in the week that there are no motion sensors, so this might end up something close to plain sailing. She moves around the property, her bag on her shoulders and sees that an upstairs window at the side of the house is wide open. Eureka!

Totally composed, she takes the two wine bottle bombs from the bag and places them on the floor. The fuses have been soaked in petrol to take away any delay. She places another petrol-soaked rag well away from them so that there can be no mishap. She cannot afford a mishap.

Caroline looks up at the window. It is some kind of bedroom, judging by the curtains, so there will be plenty of inflammable material inside hopefully. She just has to throw with the accuracy she has displayed in practice the previous day and that morning. No problem. It's important to be confident.

First, however, she has to start the fun downstairs. This all has to be done quickly, and she is hoping the fire detectors won't be as sensitive as they might be. If she is quick, they won't do anybody inside much good anyway. The aim is for the house to be burnt to the ground. Hopefully, it will all be a black wreck within two to three hours, with a couple of charred bodies. This will be enough to guarantee her and Leoni's security and freedom.

She scans the area. Still nobody around, thank God. Not that she believes in any supreme being. Tonight she wants to be the supreme being, and this will hopefully show that.

Leaving the bottles where they are, she goes to the front door carrying a plastic spray bottle. She sprays the liquid through the letterbox and it spreads across the hallway and onto the carpeted staircase. The spray bottle is soon empty. Next, she takes the wet rag with her and pushes it through the letter box till only the end is jutting out. She takes the lighter from her pocket, one of the three she has brought for the occasion. She carefully ignites the rag and once it is clearly alight, the flames race down, lighting up the area behind the glass of the door.

She rushes around the side of the house and grabs the first of the bottles. This too is given a flame. With a heave of her shoulder and an extended arm, the bottle is tossed into the open window, where it sails through smoothly and crashes inside with an immediate blaze. She immediately throws the second bottle after it and as it enters the room there is a further massive burst of flame.

It is time to leave. She quickly scales the fence and moves quickly. There is nothing to be gained from looking back, so she doesn't. Her heart is beating like a speeding truck. She just wants away from here. She glances back and can see flames at the side of the building but little from the downstairs. She repeatedly looks back until she hurries around a corner and is out of visual range.

She will definitely need to watch the news to find out the full-time result of this.

Once in the car, she is away. For twenty minutes she drives, listening for a news report with an urgency she hasn't felt for a long time. She pulls into another country lane that leads to an area of woodland well away from houses that could pose a risk. They are to meet here, where incriminating clothes can be burnt and one of the cars is to be torched. She pulls in there and waits.

Fifteen minutes later, another pair of headlights can be seen, and the car pulls in behind hers. The unmistakable form of Leoni jumps out of the car, and runs to her. "We fucking did it. Worked a treat."

"Open window upstairs?"

"Yeah. Went clean through. He should have been a basketball player."

Brett has a look of satisfaction on his face, as if committing murder isn't the big deal he has made it out to be earlier.

"Fab. Help me get this fire going."

* * *

Leoni puts her phone back down on the table. "I've given him the five thou but he wants more."

"He can fuck off."

"He reckons he's being exploited. I actually think he's scared. Says the job he did for us was much bigger than five."

"So what's he going to do? Go to the police? I don't think so."

"Our Brett can be awkward at times."

"Well, tell him this. We'll give him another three grand. Also, tell him we'll have other work for him if he stays good on this, other well-paying jobs, so if he takes it easy, he can earn a lot of money."

"OK. That might it."

"Great." Caroline points at the TV. "The news is on."

They are in a cheap hotel in Doncaster. It seems to Caroline like a good place to be to hear the news of what's been happening in Yorkshire. Leoni has argued against it, saying that they can find out stuff just as easily online in Derby but Caroline is having none of it. "The news tonight. Two arson attacks were carried out in Sheffield last night, causing the deaths of four adults and a five-year-old girl. Kate Armitage, our reporter is at one of the scenes."

"It was in the early hours of this morning that arsonists attacked two homes in The Bradfield and Lodge Moor areas of Sheffield, setting fires both upstairs and downstairs simultaneously. The motives for the attacks aren't yet established according to police reports, but investigations are underway.

"The victims in one of the attacks, thirty-five year old Barry Fisher and his wife Sally, died in the fire at Lodge Moor alongside their daughter, five-year-old Amanda. Simultaneously, in the Bradfield attack, Matt Shields, a well-known local businessman, and his wife Patti, both perished.

"Chief-Superintendent Prescott said, 'This is obviously early days in the investigation but we intend to bring the culprits to justice for this terrible atrocity. The criminals obviously intended to murder the occupants, including this five-year-old child. We want to establish the link between these terrible callous attacks and would appreciate any member of the public coming forward with helpful information. I would urge any member of the public who has any information at all that might be useful to the investigation to contact South Yorkshire Police."

Leoni hasn't spoken. She has stayed silent, but without the satisfied expression that Caroline now wears. "We killed a child," she faintly says.

"We had no choice. It was them or us. Us every time. It has to be."

"I didn't want to kill a child. You said the child would be away at her grandmother's."

"I thought she would be. He told me she was there every Friday night. I'd made a mental note in case it came in useful."

"But a child, Caz. A little girl too. That's bad."

"Yeah, it's bad, but we had no options. No choice at all."

"Perhaps we shouldn't have done it."

Caroline becomes irritated. "Of course we should. They might have killed us or have somebody do it. The kid was collateral damage. Caught in the crossfire. Happens in wars all the time, and this was the start of a war, a war that we won."

"Collateral damage? It's a little girl."

Caroline doesn't answer. She's going back to a distant place, a time in her life when she acted decisively, but with different reasons.

"I've done it before."

"Killed someone. I know, obviously."

"No. Not him. Killed a child. I never told you."

"A young child?

"Two young children."

Leoni has a strong horrified look on her face. "What?"

"I was a child myself. They were bullying me, so I killed them."

Leoni says nothing. She stares at the images on the television set, now silent, as if looking for the answer to a difficult question.

Caroline wishes she could see into Leoni's mind, but is afraid of what those thoughts might be. "If it means anything, I might have had second thoughts if I'd known the daughter was there. I didn't know it. Really, it was an accident."

Leoni's curiosity is aroused. "How did you kill those others?"

"Pushed them under a train. I hated them. They were making my life a misery so I did something about it. Just like this, it was something that had to be done."

"I suppose that was different. You were only a child yourself. How old were you?"

Caroline tells her. She doesn't reply immediately.

"It's weird and extreme, but I can sort of cope with that. You were very young, though. How did you get away with that?"

"No witnesses. Just like tonight, hopefully."

"What we did last night though might take longer to get used to. Well for me it will. I never saw myself as a child killer."

A returning irritation now lines Caroline's face. "Don't you think that's a double standard? You're OK with adults being killed, but want to draw the line at kids. I don't think we can draw a line like that."

"A child is innocent, though. Especially a girl of five."

"I know. It was an accident, Lu. Look me in the eyes." She begins to speak slowly. "I did not mean to kill a child last night. It just had to be."

There is a long pause now, as each one of them processes event and reaction.

Leoni breaks the unpleasant silence. "OK. I suppose so. And you were right. They might have set fire to here if we hadn't."

"Exactly my thinking." Caroline touches Leoni's upper arm playfully. "Big question is, was Barry wearing male or female clothes when he drew his last breath?"

Caroline's mouth relaxes, but Leoni cannot manage even a half-smile.

VULNERABILITY

The next day, Leoni is to go with Caroline to Starbucks for lattes at 11 o'clock. This is a regular thing. What isn't so regular is that Caroline has awoken in a half-empty bed and an equally empty house, so she texts Leoni to confirm and receives no reply. She goes through with the plan anyway. When Caroline arrives, she is content to sit with her drink and look out of the window at the passing traffic. Today she has spent twenty minutes just watching the vehicles of various colours zoom past, betraying their owners' impatient lives. Oh, to have such an impatient life.

At some point she has looked at her watch and the time is now on the wrong side of eleven-thirty. Leoni isn't coming. With a gentle swell of insecurity and concern, and Caroline has rarely felt more than a gentle swell of those emotions, she senses that something is not right in the world of Caroline and Leoni. A world that a week ago was so perfect.

She checks the phone. Using 'Track my friend', she learns that Leoni is in Sheffield. Why there? She pushes her finger onto Leoni's name to contact her and waits. The phone declares that the recipient is unable to take the call, and it seems patronising, as if Caroline is insufficiently techno-savvy to work that one out. The big question is, why? There have only been two times that Leoni has been unable to take a call, and one is when that twat mauled her back in their early days. The other time was when her phone was broken. Every other time, Leoni has been reliable and contactable. This makes Caroline even more uneasy.

She sits and muses. She can go to where Leoni is but that's dangerous. She can ring her from the services on the way up, but feels that this is some kind of trouble. Why would Leoni be in Sheffield? Leoni's phone is being kept on, thereby transmitting her location, but must be set to silent. Either that, or she has cut off communication. Why would she do that?

Perhaps there is a normal reason for Leoni to be there. Can she have gone there to go shopping or meet a friend? Both are unlikely, if not very unlikely. Leoni doesn't have any old friends she would meet secretly like that. She would have said something.

There is an inescapable darkness that now fills Caroline's head. A much more likely possibility in her mind, one that hurts, is that her lover has gone to hand herself in at a police station and confess to the killing of a child. She was so weakened by this last night. She has never been as strong as Caroline is.

They have no secrets from each other. Or do they?

Caroline loves Leoni, but has never let her know how much. Everything is implicit. Is Leoni of the same mind, or has this incident, this silly accident of a child being in the wrong place at the wrong time, adulterated her feelings and created dissatisfaction? Is she in Sheffield bringing a dramatic end to their relationship? What if she has gone to the police? Is that possible? Caroline dismisses the idea, but not totally.

She begins to think. She has invested emotions into Leoni, serious emotions, but what if Leoni isn't worthy of them? All that confiding in her that she has done. What if Leoni is just another human sent to Earth to disappoint her, to let her down? Caroline suddenly feels foolish. She doesn't like feeling foolish. She decides to act. It is time to be mobile. She rushes home. As she jogs around the corner and enters their road, she scans the area, but there is nothing out of place. There is no sign of an unmarked police car or van that might be there if trouble is being unleashed. Yet, Leoni's car still isn't there either. There is just Caroline's blue Vauxhall, and when she enters the empty house, she feels like a ghost. Not a nice feeling. She packs a bag with money and her passport underneath a few items of clothing and heads out. If by some chance, Leoni has gone to the police, they won't find her that easily.

The Red Stop Café, a place she rarely goes, seems like a good place to be for the afternoon. She sits there in a state of confusion. To avoid being caught, she will need to go into hiding. There is no way she will ever give herself up to the police and she will die before that happens. If Leoni has betrayed her, that changes everything. She loves this woman, but she can't be allowed to go on living if she has turned against her. However, if Leoni is in custody now, that might be impossible. In any case, can she really kill her? To do that will be the most reluctant action, probably the only reluctant action, she has ever taken. It will be the most difficult act she has ever carried out, yet there is no alternative if there has been a betrayal.

She is into her second coffee when her phone beeps. A text. She fumbles for the phone and reads a text that says, "Hi babe. Where are you? I'm home."

Caroline rushes out.

As she enters the house, Leoni rushes into the hallway and hugs her affectionately. "I'm sorry for letting you down today. I had some thinking to do."

Caroline remains emotionless. She hasn't given up on the idea of killing her lover. It may still be necessary. "Why didn't you tell me?"

"I needed to spend some time on my own, get the dark thoughts out of my skull. I knew you wouldn't like it."

"Why Sheffield? Of all places, why Sheffield?"

"Yeah," Leoni says, sympathetically. "Wasn't intending to go there originally. Set off for Manchester but got fed up of being in the car. Traffic was bad after Chesterfield. Decided on Meadowhall instead and looked around the shops. Listen. I can see you're worried, but don't be. I'm sorted. I just had to get over what we did. I've done it now. I'm over it."

"How do you know?"

"I just know. I had to get used to the idea of it. The girl, I mean. I've sort of done that. I don't want to think about it anymore." She clasps Caroline's hand. "More importantly, I don't want it to come between us. Nobody is as important as we are."

EXPOSURE

"I've been thinking."

"Caz, you're always thinking. What this time?"

"I'm thinking we could buy somewhere nice to live."

"Isn't this nice?"

"Hardly. A house in England just doesn't do it for me."

"So where would?"

"Somewhere away from here, abroad. Somewhere safe. We've had too much good luck for too long and someday it's going to come to an end."

"True. One or two close calls."

"We've loads of money saved now, so we can afford it."

"Are you thinking retirement?"

"Perhaps." She knows that Leoni is already intrigued. "God knows how many police forces know about us. I bet we're known in half of the police stations in England."

"Yeah. We've ridden our luck."

"So it's agreed then?"

"What's agreed?"

"Spain."

"Spain? The Costa del Crime?"

"Yeah, but we won't be working. Well, not our kind of work. Something different, less stressful. Could get ourselves bar jobs or work in a shop or something for a few hours each week. Learn the language, enjoy the sun the rest of the time."

"Sounds like a fab idea."

"So you agree then? We use the money we've saved and buy ourselves a house over there. We've talked about it enough. We can do it now. It's time it happened."

"Well, when you put it that way."

"I'm glad you're with me on this, Lu. We can start preparing for it now. I just needed to know that you're cool about it."

"Yeah. OK. I'm cool about it."

"You can start using the internet tonight then."

"How do you mean?"

"Find us a good location or two and do some research into the do's and don'ts of it all. You know you're better at that kind of stuff than me."

"You won't need me, then tonight?" Leoni asks. "This will be your first time out since Sheffield. It's only been two weeks."

"It's just a first date. Just setting up another sucker."

"Well, you look like you're up for it, at any rate."

"I am. It'll be a night where I use my charm, smile sweetly and start the groundwork. Another big pay off on the way, hopefully."

"Well, it'll be the last for a while, probably, so let's go out on a high. Remind me who this one is."

"Stanley Arthur Morrison. Bank manager. Well loaded. Nice family pictures too on his profile, if you remember."

"But I've not done any search for useful info."

"I'll work without it tonight. You can find out more for me tomorrow. He's got a Bentley."

"Yeah, I remember. And you're sure you don't want me around for this?"

"I can do this one alone. He's as soft as a pussycat, I reckon. You can make a start on planning our future."

"Yeah. I'll do that. It'll be fun."

"Anyway, I'm going upstairs to get dolled up. Look like a million to make a million. You know how it works."

* * *

Having parked her car in the Great Northern Car Park, Caroline finds Manchester buzzing in the early evening. She is more or less on time, so she heads for the meeting point. This time it is the Stock Exchange, one of the classiest hotel bars she has ever been in, for sure. Fittingly, Stanley Arthur Morrison is one of the most elegantly dressed men Caroline has ever seen. She knows, of course, that the elegance is a façade, that his real intentions will be as basic and primal as every other man she has met in this line of work. She depends on it. As she sits down at the table in this five-star hotel, he signals for the waiter to come across and Caroline, displaying a full smile for impact, agrees to a Tia Maria.

"So you're JoJo. Did you find it okay getting here tonight?"

"Yes. Manchester's pretty easy once you get used to the one-way system."

"Yes, you're right. I find that so myself."

Caroline detects an accent that isn't English. She can't work out what it is. "Have you lived in England all of your life, Stanley?" she asks.

"Oh no. Not much of it at all. I have spent most of my adult life in Europe. That is where I made my money. Business and all that." He smiles sweetly, and the sweetness makes Caroline feel more confident. Experience has taught her that the sweeter the smile, the easier the sucker, and a smooth operation more likely. She wants to bleed him dry. Yet, this is a first date, so she needs to show restraint. Slowly, slowly, if she is going to catch this monkey.

Two hours later, after a conversation that Caroline has kept flowing and relaxed and hopefully suggesting plenty of potential for Stanley, Caroline feels happy that she has met her objectives. All Stanley's body language tells her that he likes her. "I knew you would be good to meet," he tells her. "That's why I contacted you."

She hopes he will be passionately wanting her after this, which she will encourage on their second date, arranged for Thursday, three days on from this. They get up to go and he kisses her on the cheek.

As she makes her way through the main door of the hotel, she has the half-smile on her face and the firm feeling that she has made another significant investment tonight towards their Spanish villa. Once Leoni does her detective work, this Stanley will be good for a lot of money, she is sure. They will find the angle, whether it is cheating on his wife, a clean reputation or just some horrendous perversion that Caroline will be willingly forced to entertain. The ends always justify the means.

She makes her way back to the Great Northern. Perhaps Leoni should have come tonight, she muses. She will be here on Thursday and play her part in how things go.

Her car is on the third floor, so she walks up the steps and pays at the machine. The floor is dimly lit. As she approaches the car, she unlocks it with the remote key fob and anticipates a dull journey home.

All goes dark.

* * *

All has stayed dark.

When Caroline opens her eyes, she is lying on her side and can see nothing. She has no idea of the time. She has no idea of how many hours have passed. The jolt that has brought her back to life informs her that she is confined in a small vibrating space, with the shape of the space and the movement leaving her in no doubt that it is the boot of a car. She is unable to feel around her, since her hands have been secured, as have her feet.

Even if she is able to break free of her bonds, she doesn't have a clue how to escape from the back of a car. For the time being, she is trapped. She has a gag in her mouth that prevents her making any sound, so if she had been the kind of woman to shout for help, which she isn't, that isn't possible. It is one of those grimace and bear it moments.

She listens. She can hear voices in the car. At least two people, by the sounds being made. The sounds of their words are not familiar to her and as she listens, she realises that they are communicating in a foreign language, one that sounds East European, like villains in a James Bond Film. Ironically, she recalls how she has always found the villains to be the most interesting characters in a Bond movie, and in several films she has actually found herself wanting the East European or Asian malcontent to win. Let them take over the world. Might make things interesting.

At this point she remembers Stanley. She remembers the date, the conversation, but most of all she recalls his accent, one just like theirs, and his explanation of time spent in Europe. She realises that he's in this car, that it's his voice she can now hear. She's been set up. She realizes that, while she thought she was manipulating Stanley, all the time he was playing her.

There is no way out.

She presumes they are taking her somewhere to kill her. They are probably armed, and what can she do anyway, with her hands and feet tied and the knife that is at the bottom of her boot totally out of reach?

She hears the voices in the car laughing, but obviously Caroline fails to get the joke. She is uncomfortable and wriggles to shake off her discomfort, but to little avail. Nobody can be comfortable in a car boot. Is that why most people discovered in the boot of a car are already dead, she wonders.

She can't feel any other objects around her, so perhaps they cleared it for this purpose. For the purpose of killing her. Why else would they go to this trouble? Why are they going to kill her?

One thing Caroline is not is afraid. If this is to be her end, then so be it. She will meet it without a shiver or a shake. She will spit in their faces as they kill her and will tell them to fuck off to hell.

To this end, she manages to eject the gag, which is little more than a cloth stuck in her mouth. It has a strange smell that makes Caroline feel slightly nauseous. Is this chloroform? That's how they got her in here.

There is no fear. She has dished out plenty of death and pain, and every time she has despised the fear and horror she has seen on faces, the desperate demeanours of those pathetic victims. She will not be that. Her last breath will be a defiant obscenity.

There's a massive question she has to ask herself. Why has Stanley set her up? Why are these East Europeans taking her away like this? She can tell from the prolonged duration of this journey, on top the time she has been unconscious, however long that has been, that they are taking her somewhere distant from where she was taken. She has never robbed an East European, hasn't killed an East European, so why are these people involved like this? They must be acting on behalf of somebody else, somebody who knows all about JoJo, and possibly about Lulu too.

Will they be after Leoni as well? They have done so much together. If only she can warn her. Then she remembers her mobile phone in the pocket of her dress. Did they take it from her when they put her in here?

She stretches her arms over and, digging deep, is relieved to be able to clasp the device and hold on carefully as she takes it out. With her hands tied like this, there is no way that she can make any kind of phone call. She wriggles some more, feeling for a dip on the edge of the boot, somewhere she can bury the phone. The phone will signal Caroline's journey and Leoni will know that something is wrong. She does not want harm to befall Leoni. She hopes that Leoni will hide, take the money and hide. If this is an East European gang, as Caroline presumes it is, Leoni won't be able to do anything against them.

Twisting and turning, she moves to the edge and, pulling up a flap, she is able to tip the phone down into a dip in the corner, presumably a sublevel where the spare wheel resides. At this point she is hoping it will be dark when they reach their destination, and that these knobheads won't be thinking about searching for a mobile phone. This will be a good indicator of how professional they actually are.

Sheffield. This is a motorway journey, she is sure. Although she can see nothing, she suddenly has the notion that they are taking her up the M1 to Sheffield. This is payback for the fires. More people may have known about Barry and the blackmail than just the bitch and her brother. This is what this is about. They are taking her to Sheffield for revenge. Barry's wife said her brother knew people. Perhaps these are them. Perhaps they are going to take her somewhere and set fire to her. Caroline trembles inwardly. They can kill her with a bullet any day of the week, but to die by fire is frightening. It will make her scream. Caroline has never been the type to scream. Dying while screaming is a far cry from dying while showing defiance. She would rather end her own life than die that way.

The journey goes on. The men are almost continuously talking, as though they are relaxed about the whole thing.

Caroline finds herself begrudgingly admiring them for this. They are creatures like her, men who operate with methods and discipline like she does. If they are professionals, they will have secured her well. She strains at her bonds and, true enough, she cannot do much owing to the tightness of the cord they have used. She has no option but to just lie there in this boot and anticipate what is going to happen to her at the other end. Will there be more people there? Will she be raped before they kill her?

She feels the car turning and speeding up at various intervals. She hears the driver sounding his horn and speculates that he is venting his fury at someone else on the road. There are no clues that it is Sheffield that they are taking her to, but it must be. Of course, she and Leoni have made other enemies, killed a few, but this has Sheffield written all over it. That scrap dealer brother is getting his revenge from beyond the grave. Caroline is convinced. Kidnappers. Does this make her a victim, a kidnapper's victim? In all her years, she has never anticipated this.

Caroline is no victim. She vows in the car that she is not going to be that. They may kill her, but she will not give them that satisfaction. No, she will maintain her swagger to the end and show class, regardless of what they intend to do. She knows that if they give her the chance, she will kill the lot of them. Of course, she also knows that she won't get the chance. That only happens in movies. These people are probably professionals, and this is an execution, something that they have probably carried out numerous times before.

She suddenly feels herself on a bumpy road. The car is now constantly jolting, and she feels herself bouncing up and down in this hell hole as the car proceeds along this part of the route. Are they near the destination? She so hopes so. Caroline is now gritting her teeth and her fists are clenched. She senses that she won't be able to put up much of a fight, not with this kind of confinement, but the attitude is there, all she has, so it is very much going to be on show in her final moments. She reminds herself how tough she has been all of her life. She promises herself that this is how she is going to end that period of time. Hers will be a death that her killers will never forget.

The car stops and she hears the engine stop too. They have parked up. She hears the car doors open and the voices move outside, those same foreign voices, the voices of men who are going to end her existence on this planet. She is ready to spit in their faces. She braces herself. It is not as if she can do much, securely bound like she is, but she can still have the attitude.

The boot above her opens and torchlight floods the small area, and she can barely open her eyes, so keeps them protectively shut even though she wants them open, for she wants to see her executioners. She wants to look each of them in the eye and wish them to hell. Maybe she won't be able to send them to hell herself, but she will be Caroline Lawrence to the bitter end.

In the end, she says nothing. She will save her energy.

Behind the men is a large house, and light from inside reveals that it is an old, dilapidated property, with old fashioned window frames and a crack in the glass of one of the windows, not the kind of place she would have chosen for her final moments.

Two of the men, both thick-set and bearded, grab her by the arms and carry her through a doorway and along a hallway. She is deposited on a rickety wooden chair in a large room. It is some kind of kitchen and dining area she guesses, with torn and stained linoleum covering that part of the room, and there is a sink on the far wall, where a dripping tap provides an eerie soundtrack. There is no dining table, however. Everything else is bare. The only things to be seen are a threadbare green carpet and boarded up windows at the end of the room.

The third man, who has just watched everything so far, obviously the leader of the operation, gestures to the two men in a loud voice. He is the one she knew as Stan the previous night. Caroline still can't understand a word, but she recognizes the impatience. At this point, a gun is pointed at her head by a bear of a man, while the other man undoes her bonds and hurriedly and efficiently ties her hands behind the chair. She can only sit there hating.

The smaller of the two men, a brute with a fierce scowl permanently fixed to his face, reties her wrists round the back of the chair. She is to be kept stationary, she realizes. The situation is totally hopeless. Stan gestures to the men to move away and he approaches to a point where he is about three feet away from her and standing above her, looking down with no expression on his face.

"Welcome to the end of your world, Miss JoJo. Somebody is coming. He is really looking forward to meeting you." He now speaks with a strong Eastern European accent, much stronger than the one he adopted in their conversation last night. "Somebody wants the satisfaction of bringing your pathetic existence to a close. We're keeping you here till he gets here. It's not going to be nice, JoJo, but you know what honour means to some people. He wants the honour of bringing out your last breath and watching you die. Can't blame him really. It was his brother after all. You know how some families feel about honour."

Whose brother? Not Barry's wife's brother, unless she had another one. Did Barry have a brother? Leoni had mentioned a sister living abroad, not a brother. Whoever it is, she is to be killed as an act of revenge.

"I'm afraid I have to leave you here for a short while. You enjoy your stay while I am gone. When I come back, I will have somebody with me who will be important to you, I think. In the meantime, Sergei and Bubka will look after you." He turns to the two men, who stand at the side of the room, leaning on the wall. He smiles as he says, "If she gives you any trouble, give her a slap. If she carries on again, shoot her in the foot." He turns to her and in a reassuring tone, says, "You can scream if you want. Nobody can hear you. There is no human being within two miles of here. We have chosen a good spot for your big finish, don't you agree?"

Caroline feels like telling him to fuck off to hell, but she says nothing. She maintains a cold silence as she thinks constantly, hoping for some kind of an opportunity, something that can get her out of this. It is a chance that she fears will not come. Rather than a show of defiance, she will die silent. She has seen films like this where the bound man or woman pleads for their life. They will have to wait a long time for that. She sees that both the men guarding her are carrying guns so, even if she wasn't bound like this, she would still have zero chance.

Stan leaves the room, and she listens as he walks down the hallway, leaving Itchy and Scratchy behind to take care of her. Well, not exactly take care of her. The fact that she is tightly bound does that. It is the guy he's fetching, the one paying them, who's going to take final care of her, and she can't stop herself wondering about the form that will take.

Will it be a bullet or a blade that will bring her last breath and end her heartbeat? She will prefer a bullet. That will be quick and it will be over without her feeling any prolonged pain or realisation. They won't do it that way. This is revenge. Whoever it is will want her to feel pain – a significant amount of pain. Is she going to be tortured? She will be good for that too. Real steel, she tells herself. She urges herself. Just let it not be fire.

At this point, she starts to move her arms, as she wants out of these bonds so that she can at least make a fight of it. It is at this moment that something like a strong electric surge lights up a bulb in her mind. In this impossible chess game, there is an available move. At this point, she considers the idea. It's a long shot but she's ready to gamble. She manoeuvres her wrists slightly behind the chair, all the while making sure that they aren't watching her doing it. These men, chatting and looking away from her. aren't as professional as she previously thought. And none of them even thought about the mobile phone left in the boot. They are next to the sink and only once in a while do they look in her direction.

Caroline carries on rubbing, till Alice's harsh gemstones start to connect truly and the sharp edges and points of the bracelet begin to make an impression on the cord that restrains her arms. She stares at her captors with contempt as she carries on rubbing. Rubbing and cutting. Rubbing and cutting. She senses that she is not making much progress but she carries on regardless. What else can she do?

Twenty minutes pass. Caroline is still rubbing slowly. It is about time now. Eventually, after what has felt like an eternity, she feels a sense of release behind her. The cords that had her secured have been broken. Alice has played her part well. It is as if she was bought back then with this moment in mind.

In an opportune moment, the brutish one leaves the room and she is left with the bear, who sports a long moustache and has the thickest eyebrows Caroline has ever seen. She makes a snap judgement. This one might just be worth a try.

She waits. The other one does not come back. She knows she needs to do something now and her mind races through different possibilities. In the end, she settles on one, something that might just give her some kind of chance of survival. She can't get up while her legs are tied together, so she has to think of something else. It's a long shot but it's worth attempting.

Caroline makes a decision. "Hey, you. What's your name?" she calls out.

The moustache smiles at her and tells her to shut up.

She apologises and then asks him again.

He tells her he is called Sergei and puts his finger to his lips.

"Sergei. I'm thirsty. Will you give me a drink?"

Sergei shakes his head. "No drink."

"Please give me a drink. I'm going to die soon, as we all know. I don't want to be thirsty when it happens."

"No drink. Shut up."

"Oh, Sergei. I know you. You're not that evil. I'll love you like a brother if you give me just one cup of water from that tap. I'll start choking otherwise."

"No drink." Caroline is studying him, seeking signs to give her hope. She notices that this time he speaks with less resistance in his voice.

"Sergei. One drink. One swallow of water and I'll kiss you. Sergei, I'll kiss you like no other woman has ever kissed you before. I'll kiss you so beautifully you will remember my kiss for the rest of your life."

"No drink." This time his words come out as little more than a whisper, but Caroline notices a tell-tale twitch at the edge of his right eye.

"Sergei, you'll want to tell your grandchildren about my kiss. It will be my kiss before dying. Can you even imagine how powerful that will be?"

Sergei stands there. Caroline wonders if the other one, the one called Bubka, is returning soon. If that happens, her chance is gone and she will have to embrace her fate. However, she does not speak.

She waits.

She hopes.

After two minutes, she watches as Sergei goes to the tap and takes a cup from a cupboard on the wall that has a door hanging off. The cup has no handle, as if that matters. Caroline's heart is beating like the engine of a Formula One car as the chequered flag rises and she is preparing herself for what might come next. She is already thinking ahead.

He approaches with the cup and pours some water into her mouth. Caroline drinks the water as though she is utterly desperate for it and smiles up at Sergei. 'Thank you. Thank you so much."

It is coming.

She prays it is coming.

She can't remind him.

She knows she doesn't have to remind him. She has seen it in his eyes. The twitch is repeated.

"I will have that kiss you promised me," he says.

Caroline is ready. Their lips come together, and the bound woman and the bear are kissing like lovers for a few seconds. He has foul breath, but not for long.

She strikes.

She bites into his bottom lip with ferocity and feels her lower and upper teeth meet each other as he screams out in agony. Half-freed from the chair, she pushes him over and is on top of him with the chair still attached to her legs. He is a strong man so she has to be quick. She flashes Alice's gemstones across his neck and she draws blood in a strong, severe horizontal cut. Immediately Sergei, panting and grunting and crying with the pain, throws her off and kicks out at her. She is temporarily in a foetal position on the ground. He stands up. He is holding his mouth, still crying out loud.

On all fours, she stares up at him with a look of concern. "Sergei. That's your carotid artery. You will die in eighteen seconds. You won't be able to stop the flow. I'm sorry."

Sergei brings his hand up to his neck and feels the blood coming out. He is consumed by the fear that his death is imminent if he doesn't act quickly. He scurries to the sink and tries to stem the flow with a tea towel that hangs next to the sink. He feels the cut. His expression changes. He has realized that the cut isn't that deep. Alice has gone nowhere near his carotid artery. Alice can't do that.

Alice has just made a bit of a mess.

Unfortunately for Sergei, Caroline is now holding the gun, dropped in the scuffle, which she now points at Sergei. In her other hand is her knife, with which she has freed her feet.

She starts walking towards Sergei. She is aware that Bubka can return at any moment to complicate things, so she has to bring this to a close.

Sergei does nothing but stare. Blood is dripping strongly from his mouth and throat, but these are the least of his problems.

She is close to him, and her stare is cold and calculating. She has done this before. This is another of those moments for her to savour later.

He waits for the bullet. "Please," he implores. Don't kill me."

The bullet never comes. Instead, Caroline sends the blade into his throat, this time totally engaging with the aforementioned artery and Sergei, with his eyes displaying drama and a final truth, falls to the ground, making sounds of agony, and he is almost instantly in the throes of death.

Caroline is standing behind the door five minutes later, when Bubka returns. She has moved Sergei's body out of sight, but leaves the messy floor as it is. Bubka sees the blood at the same time as Caroline shoots. The recoil from the weapon takes Caroline by surprise. Her arm is thrown up in the air alarmingly. However, in spite of this, it is a perfect head shot from three feet away, and the brute ends his brutish days by falling to the ground like a chopped tree, felled by the intended victim.

Two bodies. She has to carry on the thinking. This is the middle of her plight, not the end, she tells herself, a decisive moment amongst several. She has to decide on what the immediate future is to be. At this point she can just run away, make a play for freedom, and in a few hours she can be well away from here.

That is not Caroline's style. Too many loose ends.

She needs to secure her life totally and that can only happen if she sees this through till the end. There will be no fleeing the scene. At least, not yet. Hence, she drags both bodies out of the kitchen, all the time listening for a car, and dumps each of them out of sight outside, behind an old ramshackle shed at the back of the house.

She figures that when Stan comes back with her would-be killer, they will come through the front door like before, so she plans for that. She needs to firstly remove the evidence of her destructive spree. She mops the floor with an old cloth she finds underneath the sink. Both her victims have let loose a lot of the red stuff and it takes her a full nervous hour to restore the floor to how it was. An hour ago she was preparing herself for death. Now she is preparing herself for something better.

Caroline replaces the chair where it was before she took such good care of Sergei.

She waits.

While she waits, she thinks about her life. She thinks about Leoni. What she does now will ensure that Leoni and she will be in no danger. That will have passed. She knows she has to think like a predator. Whereas, with Sergei, it was a case of lunge and strike, with a pretty similar approach to the killing of Bubka, for Stan and his important friend she is going to take a slightly different tack.

There are going to be at least two of them, and there may be more than that. She reminds herself that it's not too late for her to just run and take her chances, since she does have a gun and a knife now. Even if they catch up with her, she will have a fighting chance. More likely, she can keep out of sight till the darkness falls, then make for the nearest town, wherever that is.

Wherever that is. She has no idea of where she is, so where exactly will she be running to? Once again, she convinces herself that remaining is the right strategy. She will stay here and embrace her fate. Mahler's Fifth Symphony is playing in her head, filling her with resolve, and she finds herself feeling ready to do what must be done.

Two hours pass. Caroline finds herself growing increasingly excited.

It begins as a faint hum. Then it becomes a stronger, continuous sound.

It is a car, probably the same car that brought her here.

Caroline steels herself. Every nerve ending in her body has become charged with a serious voltage.

Car doors slam. Probably three car doors. A door opens and eventually closes, signalling their entrance, just as the door to this room opens.

Stan comes in. Following behind are two Asian men in smart suits. All are grim-faced. He looks around and shows obvious displeasure. "Where are they?" he asks Caroline. "Where are Sergei and Bubka?"

"I think they went to Costa," Caroline says. She now knows the source of the planned revenge. Kaleel. That's the only Asian connection to her and it had ended very badly. His brother or whoever this is must have known about the blackmail, either before or after he had taken his life.

Stan's demeanour has totally altered. In his world this is unthinkable. Sergei and Bubka should be still here taking care of the job in hand, for which they are being handsomely paid. He cannot fathom how either of them, never mind both of them, can leave their cargo unguarded like this. This has never happened and does not happen. He picks up his phone and presses some numbers. There is no response, so he puts the phone away. He is clearly uncomfortable, sensing that something is wrong, and Caroline silently congratulates herself on being more professional than they are. The batteries of both Sergei's and Bubka's mobiles are in a dustbin outside.

"So you're JoJo." The older of the two Asian men, both in smart dark blue suits, approaches. He has the same grim, non-nonsense expression on his face that she is growing used to. "I'm Shah, Kaleel's brother. Do you remember Kaleel?" The way he says his brother's name shows suppressed anger and Caroline knows that another time this would have been very bad for her. She anticipates that he has torture and a slow death in his mind.

There will be no slow death today. There will be no burning alive.

Caroline brings the gun round from her rear and this time she has a tighter grip on the handle and the trigger. The first finger of the right hand is about to repay kindness. She pulls the trigger and fires three bullets in sequence, then moves off the chair and back towards the boarded up window. Stan can only look at her with horror and shock etched on his face and that expression is unchanged as a dead pool forms under his shirt. He totters like the precarious tower in a game of Jenga and tumbles onto his knees as his eyes can only stare in disbelief.

Caroline feels like a gunfighter in a cowboy film. This is 'High Noon.' She will show 'True Grit'. The adrenaline is magnificent. If she survives, she will replay this many times in her mind.

She instantly turns her attention to the other men in the room, since Stan is virtually dead. Shah has moved back in trepidation, but is still inside the room. She pulls the trigger again twice. One of the bullets misses, hitting the wall, whilst another fortunately reaches its intended destination. The Asian man next to the cousin, with a newly-formed red spot on his forehead, is dead before he even starts his fall to the floor.

Shah, already retreating, now senses that there is going to be no survival for him if he stays in this room. He is too late. Another shot rings out and catches him in the shoulder, whilst another bullet fired immediately after misses and makes a hole in the wall as he exits the room .

At this point, he is being pursued. Caroline launches herself forward after the man who wants her dead. He will have to go on wanting her dead for a little longer.

If he escapes, he will be one massive loose end. There can be none.

He reaches the end of the hallway, but he is fat and slow, while she is following close behind, equally determined, but more athletic. He finds himself outside and runs towards the car, desperate to make a getaway.

Caroline reaches the outside door. Such a getaway will mean that Caroline will be forever looking behind her, forever suspicious, forever with a sense of vulnerability. What happened tonight can happen again.

No chance.

As he struggles to get the car door open, she shoots again and hits him again, this time in the leg. He lets out a cry. She knows she has him now. He has fallen into a seated position on the ground and is now leaning against the wheel arch of the BMW. Caroline has grown tired of shooting. This man has two bullets in him that probably aren't fatal, but death is coming anyway. She grabs hold of the body of the gun, gripping it tightly. She walks slowly towards this man, like a tiger who is stalking and waiting for the best moment to strike. Suddenly, she is standing over him. He is looking up at her, his face pleading. His voice, so assured a few minutes ago, has now become a whine. "Don't kill me. Kaleel is dead from shame. My mother died of a broken heart. I was angry and upset. Don't shoot me. I'll pay money."

Caroline gives her customary half-smile. She grits her teeth and brings the butt of the weapon crashing down onto his skull. He is immediately unconscious from the blow, but she has more to do. She rains blow after blow as she unleashes all of the tension that has built up since that awakening in the car boot. She carries on striking till the inner contents of his head start to be exposed and only pauses when she is absolutely certain that his life is in the past tense. Caroline's anger is still present, however, and several unnecessary blows are testament to that.

What next? Not the car. It is essential that she leaves no evidence of her presence at this house so she knows she must head for the woods and somehow keep herself unseen for as long as possible. She has the gun, which, after wiping it thoroughly with her sleeve, she places in Shah's right hand. This will confuse the police, perhaps buy her some time.

From the BMW's boot, Caroline retrieves her phone. She won't make a call from here. That would be stupid. She needs to be utterly disconnected from the scene of these terrible bloody deaths, these terrible bloody deaths that have given her immense satisfaction. Now she knows how James Bond feels. She takes one last look at the chair on which she has had her worst fears, her most inspired thinking and her greatest victory.

Caroline starts walking. The crisis might not be totally over, not until she has secured her freedom by having changed out of these clothes, dumped them or burned them, and followed it all up with a wash in some kind of bathroom. She must not be arrested any time soon, since the police would be able to establish that she had recently fired a gun. The threat to her life has passed, however. She will continue to exist.

* * *

Twelve hours later, after a restless night comprising plenty of stealthy walking and a small amount of difficult sleep, she finds herself at a small town called Porter Bridge. She knows she doesn't look good after a night of roughing it, so she checks for her credit card in the little pocket of her dress and heads for the local pharmacy. There, she selects a few items: a tube of foundation, some mascara and a cheap lipstick. They don't have much here, but these will suffice. They have to. She is also able to acquire a pair of dark sunglasses. She presumes that the carnage at the house will not yet have been discovered. Perhaps it won't be known for several days, since it is such a remote place they chose for her execution.

Beginning to relax, Caroline makes her way to the railway station, which is well signposted. She turns a corner and an old stone building serves as the ticket office and waiting room. The station is only small, a two-platform affair, but at least there is a man there behind an old-fashioned counter with a glass window, happy to sell her the train ticket she desires. She is able to board a train to Derby and when she arrives there, she decides it is a good time to contact Leoni.

"Hi, babe."

Leoni has shock and desperation in her voice. "Caz! Where the fuck have you been?"

"I've had some trouble. It's sorted."

"Trouble? What kind of trouble?"

"The murderous kind. I'll tell you all about it when I see you. Listen. I need to you to do something."

"Of course. I'm so glad to hear your voice. I was worried. Not slept all night. I've rung you loads of times."

"I didn't have my phone, babe."

"You've got me confused now."

"I'll explain, but not now. Now listen. There's a chance the police are going to come after us. If not the police, somebody worse. I've sorted out some knobheads but I don't know if that's the end of it."

"How? Who?"

"I'll tell you later. It's not important now."

"OK. So what do you want me to do?"

"Pack two cases. Put them in the car and grab our passports. All the money there is too. We're going abroad till the heat's off."

"Where to? Spain?"

"Yeah, like we planned. Spend some time on the Costa Del Crime. It'll be good for us."

"Where will I meet you?"

"Meet me at East Midlands Airport. We'll get the next plane to the Spanish coast.'

"Right. I'll get to it. How much danger we in? Out of ten?"

"About eight." Actually, she has no idea, but this will add to Leoni's urgency. "Don't forget the swimming gear."

Caroline hangs up. She presses another button or two and waits for a second call to be answered. "Hi Judy. It's me. Got some news for you. I'm going away."

"What?"

"I'm going away. Away from England."

"Away where? Why?"

"Don't worry about that. Now listen, I'll be away for a while, so I'll be sending you some money to help you through, but you won't be seeing or hearing from me for some time."

"So what's this then? A payoff to ease your conscience?"

"Of course. I'm totally horrible, aren't I, Mother of the Year? Bottom line is this, Judy. Look after the money I'm sending you. Spend it carefully. And stay away from dodgy men. They don't suit you."

"So won't you be in touch at all?"

"No, so I won't be around to sort out anybody who uses you as a punchbag, so be careful."

"For how long?"

"A year. Could be longer."

"Will you write?"

"No. You won't hear from me at all, apart from somebody I know dropping some money off for you from time to time. If any police come knocking, say nothing. In fact, you won't know anything anyway. Any Asian or East European guys come poking noses in asking for my whereabouts, either scream or ring the police. In fact, don't answer your door for a few weeks."

"What? What kind of trouble have you got yourself into exactly?"

"Never mind. I'm going away, so the trouble should go with me."

"Where will you be?"

"I said, didn't I? Aren't you listening? I'm not telling you where I'm going. I'm just getting away from some shit. I'll be seeing you. Bye, Judy."

IN CONVERSATION

Two tanned, glamorous-looking women, both wearing Ray bans, are sitting outside a bar looking out at the azure glory of the Mediterranean, whose waves lap the shore quietly, each gentle movement of the tide having its own individual beauty. The sound of an acoustic guitar is emanating from a speaker somewhere.

"It doesn't get much better than this," the brunette says, the taller of the two women, a woman who is looking out to sea and taking in the full panorama of the horizon.

"It's never been as good as this."

"It's just been a fabulous time we've had here. The food, the shopping, the drinks by the pool."

"One massive holiday."

"Make up for all those we missed out on when we were younger."

Both women laugh then one becomes serious. "It has to end, though."

The blonde woman turns to face her. "I know that. And you know I know that. Doesn't stop the feeling that we're turning our backs on something great."

"We've been through all this. It's fab, of course it is, but it's just not us. This whole situation is not us. You've said so yourself." Caroline finishes her drink and signals for a waiter standing at the bar to bring two more.

"I know. And I'm with you on this. I'm just thinking out loud. Deep down, I know what we have to do." Leoni looks around. "It's paradise but we need more."

"It's been twelve months of rest and pleasure, Lu. Hitting the bars and restaurants and chilling out the rest of the time has been good for this past year, but it's not really us. Not in the long term. You're not happy with it. That wretched bar work. Whenever you've had a few drinks you've been more vocal about this than me. We're not going to be a permanent fixture here. In a few years, we could come back. For now, we need to be scheming and doing things. That means England."

"Just as long as the heat's off."

"It appears it is. Can't have been much heat anyway, since nobody bothered Judy at all."

"So when we going back then?"

"Give it a month. I'm sure we can wear this place out once and for all in that time."

"What will we be doing in England?"

"Dunno. Perhaps we could set up some kind of business."

"What kind of business."

"Dunno. Got six months to think of one."

"Won't you miss it though? Here?"

"I'll miss it. Of course I'll miss it. It's just that we're meant to be in England, bobbing and weaving. We both grew up risky, with trouble around us, next to us, inside us even. This is just too fucking easy. We've not had a single difficulty since we came here all those months ago. Hardest thing here has been to avoid getting sunburnt."

"Not for me. Biggest challenge for me…the cockroaches."

"Well, we can have that challenge at home, but it will be the human cockroaches, and we do have a few ideas about how to deal with them."

EPILOGUE I:
JUDY IN DECLINE

One month becomes three months, which continues to grow. A year later, after all of the stuttering hesitation, Caroline and Leoni are back in England at East Midlands Airport, this time in a hectic and noisy Arrivals area standing next to the conveyor belt that will soon deliver the contents of their life overseas. "After dropping the stuff off at the house, I'm going to pop and see Judy."

"Have you missed her?"

"No. Not really. It's not like I owe her anything. I'm still angry at her most of the time. To be honest, I don't quite know exactly how I feel where she's concerned. Useless mother and a useless woman, but I wouldn't be alive without her."

"It's probably all subconscious," Leoni says. "Therapy?"

Caroline just shrugs her shoulders. "Dunno. Confirmation more like?"

"Confirmation of what?"

"Dunno. Just sounds better than therapy."

A few hours later, when Leoni enters, Caroline is sitting at the dining table looking through an Argos catalogue in a silent house, with five cigarette stubs in an ashtray that was empty and clean an hour ago. "Judy's in hospital."

Taking off her coat, Leoni makes a tutting noise. "What is it this time? Drunk?"

"Not exactly. She went walkabout in the middle of the night. Apparently she's done it a few times. Had a fall. Got a fractured hip."

"What now?"

"She can't go back there. She's a danger to herself."

"What do you propose? Euthanasia?"

Caroline shakes her head.

"You aren't telling me you have a sense of loyalty to her."

"I think I do. No idea why, but I do."

"Solution then?"

"We use some of our money to get her a place in a home."

Leoni frowns. Both her parents are mercifully gone from this Earth. "That's a lot of money, paying for her to live in a home."

"Well, it's only a small proportion of what we have, and we're going to make lots more. Wait till we hit London next week."

"Well, sweet, you know I'll support whatever you decide. I just don't think she's worth it."

"There's a place in Chesterfield. Sunny Vale it's called. Has a nice ring to it. I'm going up there tomorrow to have a look. Fancy coming with me?"

"Why not? What else would I be doing?"

EPILOGUE II:
REVELATION

Three months later, back from an eventful period in London, Caroline gets out of the car and, with some red flowers in her hand, makes her way to the entrance. She rings a bell on the wall next to the door, attached to which is a sign saying, 'Don't allow residents to leave with you' and a woman comes to the door with a welcoming smile on her face. Ahead of her, she can see a common room full of ageing women gathered around a television set. Two of them stare at her as she makes her way to the lift.

Caroline doesn't like lifts. She trembles as she gets in, but knows she must conquer this fear. Once on the second floor, she passes a row of numbered rooms all with their doors open. In one, a tall slender woman looks out of a window; in another, a man sits at a table with a pint of beer, watching TV, looking totally at peace with himself. She reaches number thirty-eight, knocks then goes in.

For an hour she sits across from her mother and looks out of the window. She won't be in a place like this ever, she tells herself. She knows that Judy's battle for a life, one that has incorporated a thousand bad decisions and some awful flaws, will be over soon, courtesy of early onset Alzheimer's. With that, Caroline's reluctant daughter role will be over too.

"Life's not so bad. The sun is nice. Don't you think so?"

"Yes. I suppose so."

"When am I going home?"

"Judy, this is your home now. You're in this lovely place."

"You have to let me go home. I have the shopping to do."

"This is your home. You don't have to do shopping anymore. And you have your Neil Diamond photos." She points up at the wall, behind the television set. "And the television. Your lovely meals are cooked for you too."

"You're mean, making me stay here."

"No, I'm not. I know you're safe here."

"She wouldn't keep me here."

Caroline looks around, amused. There is no one else in the room.

"She?"

"The other one."

"Which other one?"

"The one like you, the one I sold."

"What do you mean?" Another demented fantasy?

" I sold her to that nice couple. Well, she was nice. He was a twat."

Caroline is sitting up. "What are you on about, Judy?"

"The police were interested. They wanted to know about the other one. Your twin, she would be. I bet she looks like you too."

"Why are you saying this? Stop it."

Judy looks into her eyes. "It's true. That's why I'm saying it. She would be nicer to me than you are."

"The couple. Who were they?"

"They were from Mansfield." She stops. "Or was it Nottingham? He was called George and she was called Ruby, or was it something else?"

Caroline is bewildered but decides to play along. "How much did they pay you, this George and Ruby?"

"Thirty thousand pounds. Fifteen when she was born. Some more later. That was when we moved."

"Why didn't they adopt me too?"

"I don't know. I can't remember."

Caroline is sitting there, not saying another word. "I'm coming to see you again tomorrow. We can talk again."

Twenty-four hours later, Caroline is back at the home and the same story is retold. This version has the same key details but with the added details of how some couple wanting a baby had been in a hurry to leave.

On a third consecutive visit, Judy doesn't want to talk about it. She acts as if she has never said anything. "It's a long time ago. I can't remember that far back."

The frustration hurts. Caroline wants to know more.

When she visits the following weekend, the story is repeated. "The woman was called Lillian. I never saw them again. They didn't know about you. You came after they went." Doubt is falling away. Caroline feels like strangling somebody. If not this mother of hers, perhaps somebody else with a neck that she can grab hold of and vent her frustration on. "I had to keep the money somewhere safe," Judy adds.

If this story is true, and it is still very much an if, this gives a whole new meaning to Caroline's life. That terrible childhood she had could have been a different one. Could this tale of Judy's be true? Could she possibly be a woman who has been cheated out of everything from the very moment of her birth?

She comes to the home several times that week and on a couple of those days, dementia permitting, she gets to hear a partly coherent version of her mother's story several times. Her acceptance grows. Every time she is told the details, it hurts. Every time, she wants to know more. She needs to know everything.

The bottom line is this. If a rich couple adopted her twin, then there will be money, money that really she is entitled to have a share of. After all, it could have been her they'd adopted, not this other baby, whoever she is. The things she has done, getting the money should be more than possible.

Deep down inside, something else simmers. She may have something and somebody new to focus on. There may be a woman walking around somewhere who actually cheated her out of a better life. While she was saddled with poverty and the most miserable of childhoods, the other one would have had a silver spoon life. That other one will not have endured the misery that she has had to tolerate, but will have had the comfort and security that Caroline has always longed for.

Caroline will see about that. She will see what she can do.

* * *

Within a couple of weeks, Leoni comes up with the goods, as usual. "There's a George and Lillian Stewart in Mansfield, apparently. They're loaded. He paints."

"What do you men, he paints?"

"He's a portrait artist. He has portraits hanging in art galleries all over England. She's a housewife. Must be boring, that."

"What about…"

"They have a daughter called Laura. She's married now and lives in Sheffield. Sheffield? What about that? Same age as you. I found her on the net." Leoni looks at her with a caring expression as she presses the left-hand button of the mouse. She pauses, before turning the laptop so that Caroline can see the screen. "Get ready for a shock."

Caroline feels herself shudder. She sees a picture of herself with a big smile on her face, holding up a glass of champagne. She reads the picture and perceives a happy life, plenty of luxury, a pleasant childhood, a lovely bedroom. She is able to imagine a hundred positive details, all missing from the years of her existence.

"She's your double, isn't she? Except for the big smile, that is. Looks like your mother was telling you the truth."

"I knew she was. Do you know where in Sheffield? It's a big place."

Leoni hands her a piece of paper. "That's the address. Sheffield, of all places. When are we going?"

"Not you. Just me. This is something I have to do."

THE STORY CONTINUES IN...

BENEATH THE

BLOOD

MOON

Death is coming.

The question is, for whom?

DARREN WILLS

Matador

For exclusive discounts on Matador titles,
sign up to our occasional newsletter at
troubador.co.uk/bookshop

CPSIA information can be obtained
at www.ICGtesting.com
Printed in the USA
BVHW070400280321
603587BV00004B/1025

9 781800 462168